ABSCONDED

J. ARENS

BIG TOWN PUBLISHING

Copyright © 2025 by J. Arens

Cover Art by Salient Books

www.salientbooks.shop

Edited by: E. Paige Spear

CollaborativePassages.org

First edition 2025

ISBN: 979-8-9893041-7-2 (Hardcover)

ISBN: 979-8-9893041-8-9 (Softcover)

ISBN: 979-8-9893041-9-6 (Ebook)

Published by: Big Town Publishing

districtdetectives.com

CONTENTS

To The Unlikely Friends
Let's be honest. They're the best friends we never went looking for.

CHAPTER 1

THE ONE WITH THE SEA CAMEL

I t all started in 1897.

Just as the year turned, she was christened Sea Camel. Nearly 170 feet, sporting a 30-foot beam, she wasn't much to look at, with her white-washed timber above the water level, simple painted name on her stern and a bare-nothing crew, but she was strong and had a purpose.

Before The Great War, she was tasked with pushing large schooners out of the bay and into the open water for their travel to England or further along the coast, destined for the bigger cities. Once the war started, the Camel had double duty. When she wasn't moving transport ships back and forth in The Harbor, she was hauling troops from Bay City to Big Town and back.

After The Great War was over, the little tugboat was decommissioned. She was old, leaky, and needed more repairs than she was worth. A terrible man with a short temper bought her at an auction, using the Camel to haul scrap parts, almost sinking her more than a few times with the over-weighing.

More than once, the Camel hauled newer ships with fewer miles and easier lives back into The Harbor and to the scrappers.

Eventually, the Sea Camel was brought to the scrappers' dry dock where she had brought so many before her. But she wasn't even given a rest there. Yet again, she was press-ganged into service, tugging and shoving around scrap ships between one dry dock line or another. Or pulling scrap barges out of the slips and to the main part of The Harbor, guiding them out to the deep waters of the sea before heading back for another run.

By now, she spewed deep black smoke. Her travel had to be slow, her screws barely turned fast enough to stave off the list to port that had started so long ago that no one cared, nor bothered to figure out why. Oil spill slicked out after her, trailing like a rainbow puddle wherever she chugged. And chug she did, shuddering at times, creaking, groaning. Her deck was splintered and unswabbed. Water seeped through the cracks in and between the deck boards, creating nearly a steady drizzle below deck. Algae made traversing from end to end a dangerous and slippery task. When her motor was running, it knocked terribly and was always one strong rock away from a few hours of work to re-patch it before it up and running again. Somewhere over the last decade, it had lost a piston, contributing to the oil slick problem.

Thankfully, the Camel's servitude finally came to a close when she sprung another leak while weathering one last winter storm that squalled across The Harbor. That alone would not have retired her, had it not been for the main beam cracking between two extra-large swells.

The gate creaked and clanked for a moment before slowly starting to screech-groan its way open. A wiry dock worker pushed the gate open a little further and leaned against the support pole before nodding once in a big way and gesturing the dark red Desoto through the opening in the gate. He watched the car roll through, ducking his head slightly to see who was in the car.

Three people in the car.

One large man driving the car, ignoring the dockworker, completely focused on the task of threading the Desoto through the gap between the gate and the far support pole. A thin, red-headed man with a dangerous glint in his eye glared at the dockworker for a moment. The look pointed and extremely clear.

Mind your own business.

The third figure was on the far side of the car, and didn't look up from the paper that was spread open between his hands, reading while the car rolled along.

The dock worker looked away from the interior of the car and looked back in the direction of the road that led up to the gate he was holding up with his shoulder. He didn't need any trouble. His boss had sent him up to open the gate for a red Desoto <u>only,</u> and no one else.

The road was how it always was-pavement cracked and unloved for decades. Emptier than a church on a Monday morning. It had been easy to see the car coming, and he didn't need to worry about checking to make sure it was the <u>right</u> red Desoto.

It was the <u>only</u> one.

Once the Desoto was completely through the gate, it puttered toward the rest of the dry dock. With a small heave, the dockworker started to pull the gate shut, using all his weight to pull it back to rest against the side support pole. He looked after the Desoto as he picked up the chains to lock the gate up. It wasn't often that the scrap yard got visitors. No one wanted to come there.

"I don't want to waste much time here. If he doesn't have what he says he does, we're leaving right away." Two-Timer closed the newspaper that he had been reading and folded it on its main fold, while dropping it into his lap. He rested his forearms over it and folded his hands over his knees, the sleeves of his coat mostly obscuring the bold headline about the tragic death of Alan Wainwright's wife and her brother in a hail of bullets in front of Wainwright Detective Agency. "I don't have the patience for time wasters. I want to get this little project up and running as quickly as possible."

The large man behind the wheel glanced back over his shoulder and nodded once.

"Ya really gonna go through with this then?" the dangerous-looking red-headed man next to Two-Timer wondered, his lilting Irish accent confirming that the red hair was no accident.

Two-Timer glanced over at him shrewdly and nodded once, a wicked smirk pulling at the corner of his mouth. "The way I see it, Seamus, it's time that I started up my own little operation or two. Joey has his hands full with the <u>gundog,</u>" he spat the word like it tasted terrible to utter out loud, "and his pet is basically running the family for him while he's...otherwise distracted. Where does that leave me?"

"Out in th' cold it sounds like." Seamus shrugged and adjusted the driving cap on his head. A dull glint from something metallic winked between the edge of the bill and the material in the dull sunlight filtering through the clouds.

Two-Timer tapped the side of his nose. "Which means, I think that it's time that I start my own business venture." He glanced around and then shook his head bitterly. "Seeing as it appears that I won't be inheriting the family after all."

Seamus grunted and nodded. "You know we're with you."

Two-Timer looked at him and smiled tightly. "You'll be well rewarded for this." He glanced up at the driver and smiled at him too.

The driver half glanced over his shoulder at him and tipped his chin once. "Where we goin'?" he wondered, his voice a deep baritone.

Two-Timer half gestured toward a building that was just off to the right of the direction that they were rolling. "Main office."

The driver glanced at him and then the direction that he was pointing before slightly adjusting the wheel and guiding the Desoto toward the building that Two-Timer pointed out. Once they were close to the building, he stopped the car and turned off the motor. "I'll stay here?" he wondered, setting his hand on the large gun that was sitting on the front seat next to him.

Two-Timer glanced at the movement and set the paper next to his leg on the seat between him and Seamus. "I would appreciate that."

Seamus pushed the door open and stepped out of the car. He flipped the collar of his coat up. He looked around the dock as he buttoned it against the wind. One more glance, and he pushed his hands into his pockets. "Seems all quiet here, Boss." Seamus pivoted to look across the roof at Two-Timer.

Two-Timer looked at him and nodded once. "Thank you Seamus." He pivoted and walked toward the door that was set blandly in the middle of the lack-luster building that looked like it hadn't been updated or well-taken care of in decades.

Seamus trailed after Two-Timer by a few yards, looking around skeptically. Almost like he thought that a shadow was going to jump out to snatch at his boss.

The driver adjusted how he was sitting behind the wheel and looked around in a lazy way. His job was the easiest. He draped his arm on his door and rested his fingers against his steering wheel. He set his hand on the butt of the gun next to him and looked over the dock, the movement loose and languid.

Two-Timer trotted up the three shallow steps to the nondescript building and pulled the door open. He didn't stop to check if Seamus followed and walked into the building like he owned it.

Seamus sped up a couple of steps and caught the door. He slipped through the opening between the door and the frame and fell into step behind Two-Timer two steps or so, his hands still in his pockets.

Two-Timer walked down the hallway past two doors and knocked on the last door. He waited, controlled and patient, looking at the door expectantly.

The door swung open and a middle-aged man stood in it. He looked like he drank too much and cared little for what happened beyond the neck of his bottle. "'Sssabout time," he mused, waved his hand and stepped back into the office.

Two-Timer's nose wrinkled for barely a half second before he glanced at Seamus. "I'll be right in here. Stay out here."

Seamus slowed to a stop and nodded. "Sure Boss."

Two-Timer walked into the room without looking back at him again.

Seamus leaned against the wall next to the door and watched the hallway that led out to the door.

Two-Timer looked around the room and let the distaste show for a moment. It was filthy, not that there was much to be surprised about, since the outside of the building was so well taken care of. He looked around and frowned again. "So. I hear you found something that I've been looking for, Kneller?"

Kneller shuffled over to a desk that looked like it should have been put out of its misery years ago. He leaned on the edge and picked up a small flask. He took a large pull from it and nodded. "I got just the thing for you. Old trawler was just brought in. A little rough around the edges, but I think she'll do nicely for what you're looking for. Fresh coat of paint-" he paused to take another swig from the flask.

"And what?" Two-Timer used the break to half interrupt. "I go out fishing to my heart's content with a couple of my friends?" he wondered dryly. "I don't want a dingy that smells like dead fish."

"Hey-hey-hey!" Kneller protested, holding his hands out in a small protesting gesture, the top of his flask clanking softly against the body of the flask. "This is no small lifeboat!" he shook his head and took another sip. "This is a nice one. She's still floating close to center, too! I'm telling you, you can just give her a quick clean and she can do whatever you need."

Two-Timer's left eyebrow dropped down slightly and his lips pursed together tightly. "I see."

Kneller sipped again. "You want to see her?"

Two-Timer looked like he regretted where he was for a moment before finally nodding. "Yes. I suppose I would. If it's in that good of condition-"

"I doubt that you'd ever get noticed when you're running about in this ole girl. She's not going to win any beauty pageants, but it'll do you good."

Two-Timer walked toward the door and paused when he made it nearly the entire way there. "If you're not going to come with me, the least you could do is tell me where to find this boat that I'm spending so much money on?"

Kneller waved a hand and stood up and off the desk. He kept the flask in his hand solidly and scuffed toward the door. "All right, all right. I'm coming."

Two-Timer watched his movement and looked at him skeptically. "I can see that," he ground.

Kneller opened the door and shuffled down the hall toward the front door. He didn't look at Seamus as he passed him and took another pull from his flask.

Seamus, leaning against the wall with his entire back while he waited, dropped his right foot off the wall and pushed his shoulders up and off it, coming to stand straight up. He looked at Two-Timer and then glanced over to watch Kneller walk.

Two-Timer half shook his head, rolling his eyes. He walked after Kneller, trying to rein in his frustration.

Seamus fell into step behind Two-Timer, back a step or two from him. He pushed his hands back into his jacket pockets as he walked.

Two-Timer brushed out of the front door and paused for a moment to wait a beat for Kneller to start down the steps. Once he was down the steps himself, he looked over at the Desoto and made a small waving motion with his hand, pointing with one finger in the direction that they were walking.

The Desoto started and idled after them.

Kneller shuffled along with Two-Timer, sipping from his flask as he walked.

Seamus half wandered along, clearly long bored with the pace they were walking at. He looked around the yard as he walked, not really looking for danger, but keeping an eye out for trouble, nonetheless.

Two-Timer didn't look where he was walking. His attention was completely taken up with the skeletons of the ships that they were walking past.

Nearly every single one received the same amount of scrutiny and attention.

Barely any.

There was something specific that Two-Timer was looking for, and he had yet to see it in any of the hulks of abandoned metal so far.

Kneller walked a little further and stopped in front of the boat that they were there to see.

Two-Timer nearly walked past him, his eyes already dismissing the tired-out hull already. He walked a few more steps before he realized that Seamus was the only one walking with him. After a small, exasperated sigh, he pivoted and looked back at Kneller. "What's wrong?" he wondered, allowing the irritation to creep into his words.

"This is the one I was telling you about." Kneller shrugged, ignoring or completely missing the tone that had been used. He used the flask to gesture to the one in front of him.

Two-Timer looked around for a moment, unsure what he was talking about. "Beg pardon?" he demanded.

"I think he's talkin' about the hunk of junk." Seamus gestured in a scoffing way to the hull in front of them.

"It's not junk!" Kneller defended.

"We're in a junkyard," Seamus pointed out. "It is."

Two-Timer shook his head. "Absolutely not. It's too far gone."

Kneller looked between Two-Timer and the boat and back. "Too far gone!?" he protested. "It doesn't even leak!"

"It's burned to a crisp," Two-Timer snapped.

Kneller shrugged.

Two-Timer shook his head. "No. We keep looking."

"This is the best I got."

"On the upside, it doesn't smell like fish," Seamus piped up with a smirk. He pushed his hands into his pockets and looked over the ship with a condescending smirk.

Kneller shook his head slightly. "It doesn't."

"It has a nice bonfire smell instead. We move on." Two-Timer pivoted and started the way he had been going again.

Kneller didn't react for a moment. He looked at Two-Timer and made a few protesting noises while he rushed after him a few steps. The fastest that he had moved to date. "No-no. Wait. I can't just let you walk around like you own the place!" he protested.

Two-Timer waved off his concern and continued to walk through the options that were left around them. "You need to calm yourself," he chastised.

Kneller looked put out for a moment and took another sip from his flask and huffed. "My boss-"

"Is being paid well to look the other way," Two-Timer pointed out, not even bothering to look back at Kneller as he talked.

Seamus chuckled quietly and shuffled along at a lazy pace.

Kneller looked like he wanted to protest but clamped his mouth shut.

Two-Timer stopped and tilted his head for a moment. He looked at the hull that was in front of him critically for a moment.

"Boss?"

Two-Timer pointed in front of him and looked at Kneller. "This one."

Kneller cut his sip off sharply and looked at the boat that Two-Timer was pointing at. He scoffed a little. "You're joking."

Two-Timer looked at him for a moment too long and then glanced at Seamus before refocusing on Kneller. "Does it look like anyone is laughing?" he wondered, his eyebrow tipping.

Kneller swallowed tightly and looked over his shoulder a little to glance at Seamus in a half nervous way. "N-no?"

"You're not sure?" Two-Timer asked again, tilting his head.

Kneller pursed his lips and cleared his throat again. "I don't think...you don't want that one." he half pointed toward the ship in front of the three of them.

"Don't tell me what I want." Two-Timer looked at him blandly. "How much."

"That old lump of junk is slated to be cut up in less than eight hours! My boss will notice!"

"Then run the paperwork like it has. I want no records anyway."

"What are the welders supposed to cut up tomorrow morning?"

"You know what that sounds like, Seamus?" Two-Timer looked at him.

Seamus tilted his chin and smirked. "Not your problem, Boss."

Two-Timer nodded once. "That's exactly it."

Kneller looked at the ship and then Two-Timer again. "You want me to fudge the paperwork?"

Two-Timer shrugged and half shook his head. "Honestly, I don't much care how you do it."

Kneller took a nervous sip of his flask and cleared his throat tightly. "Right."

Two-Timer snapped his fingers without looking away from the hull that was in front of him.

Seamus reached into the inner chest pocket of his jacket. He pulled out an envelope. "He wants you to take this," he explained without preamble.

Kneller started a little and looked at the envelope for a moment before slowly taking it like it might bite him.

"Inside is all that you need for the boat. And some instructions." Two-Timer looked at him slowly. "I expect them to be followed to the letter. If not-"

Kneller half leaned forward for a moment, waiting for the rest of the sentence. "And then?" he wondered, looking at him half expectantly.

Two-Timer looked at him for a moment and his eyebrows moved slightly. "Well then, I send Seamus back."

"How ya doin'?" Seamus smiled tightly. "That'd be me then."

Kneller turned to look at Seamus slowly, his look baleful and half uncomfortable.

"And you don't want me to be comin' back," Seamus assured, his smile bright as he pushed his hands into the pockets of his pants. He rocked up onto his toes and dropped back down flat-footed in an easy movement.

Kneller did a small, anxious double take and cleared his throat. "Right. To the letter." he nodded.

Two-Timer looked at him and smiled a little. "Wonderful." he pivoted and started to walk toward the Desoto quickly.

Seamus smiled at Kneller wolfishly for a moment before following after Two-Timer at a leisurely pace.

"Oh." Two-Timer stopped and turned to look at Kneller again. "One more thing."

Kneller looked like he was ready to panic but nodded. "What is it?"

"What's her name?" Two-Timer pointed to the tired out hull he had just bought.

Kneller cleared his throat. "Sea Camel."

Two-Timer wrinkled his nose a little and shook his head. "Oh, no. That will do no good." He turned and walked to the Desoto.

"Aces." Olli's voice broke the silence in the office, the tone half confused and shocked.

Dallas didn't look up from what he was doing. "What is it?" he wondered, typing awkwardly on the typewriter in front of him on his desktop. His fingers pecking away quickly, despite the fact that he was only using the first finger on each hand.

Olli looked over the desk and splayed out her hands slightly and half turned her head to the left while she looked over the top of her desk, wide-eyed. "This is a strange feeling."

Dallas stopped pecking at the typewriter and looked over at her with an exaggerated head bob of attention. "What's that?"

"I'm done."

"Done?" Dallas repeated, skeptically. His eyebrow tilted as he reached over, picking up his coffee mug without looking. He sipped what was left in the mug and made a small, disgusted face.

It was cold.

Olli looked over at him, her eyes wide, before she tilted her head down toward her desk. "I'm done." Her hands spread over the empty top of the work surface in front of her. "For the first time since I started here...I don't have any paperwork."

Dallas paused with his mug halfway to his mouth again. He stopped and frowned at the mug, not knowing why it was that he was trying to drink it again. He set the mug down and looked at her skeptically. "You're done?"

Olli nodded, not glancing at him, still not looking at him, her focus completely zeroed in on the desktop in front of her. "I'm done."

"There's not any in the drawers?" Dallas looked at her shrewdly.

Olli shook her head. "I did those too."

Dallas leaned forward and balanced his elbows on the front edge of his desk. "None under the back edge of the desk."

Olli shook her head, finally looking at him for the first time.

Dallas held up a finger and shook it a couple of times. "Floor behind your chair."

Olli looked over at him. She rested her palms against the front edge of the desk and shoved sharply against it.

The chair rolled back easily and bumped against the wall with a soft 'thung' noise.

"And it's all filed?" Dallas looked at her and tilted his head skeptically.

Olli gestured toward her desk and the floor between her and it, the gesture a dramatic answer to the question.

Dallas sat up and leaned back against the back of his chair. "You're done," he announced, looking at her in surprise.

Olli laughed in a confused and skeptical way before walk-scooting her chair to the near edge of the desk. She sat where she was for a moment, looking completely lost. "What about you?"

Dallas pulled the sheet of paper from the typewriter and set it into the folder that was next to him. "Done now." He set the folder into the small wire-sided box designated for files being sent to a different section of WDA.

The silence stretched for a few more seconds.

Olli picked up a pencil that was laying out of place and set it into the cup set on the left top corner of her desk slowly, the motion like she was worried that someone would hear it. She dragged her hand back and set it, palm down like the other hand, on the desk in front of her for a moment. "Very quietly," she instructed. "Very slowly. Get up and go before someone notices."

Dallas stood up in the same measured way that Olli did, watching the door like he was expecting someone to walk through it at any moment and ruin their chance to have an early afternoon off.

Olli tip-toed slightly and slipped around the far edge of her desk before whisper-stepping across the floor toward the hall tree set up to the left of the office door.

Dallas slunk-trotted after her.

Olli grabbed his fedora and offered it to him while she picked up her jacket with her left hand. She shook her jacket open and swung it around her shoulders.

Dallas took his hat and dropped it on his head with the same hand as he reached for his jacket with the other. He didn't bother to put it on, but took a large step to open the door of the office, just fast enough that Olli could walk through it without slowing down. "Quietly now," he advised, falling into step behind her, swinging around the door and pulling it closed after him.

Olli clicked the switch, turning off the lights before she was completely out the door. She pulled her hand back sharply so her knuckles wouldn't hit against the door frame and sneak-trotted a few steps before walking along at a brisk, heel-to-toe walk that carried her along at a sweepingly fast pace. Her heeled, knee high, laced-up, black leather motorcycle boots making barely a whisper of noise.

Dallas carefully trotted after her and caught up after a few hurried steps. "Let's head to the back door. If they don't see us—"

"They can't stop us with a fresh case," Olli finished as she started to trot down the first set of stairs.

Dallas nodded once and touched his nose. "Out the back door, through the alley, across the street, and straight to the Corner Diner for lunch."

Olli nodded and smiled. "That sounds like a great idea to me."

Exactly five steps across the landing of the second floor, and the detectives were quickly trotting down the last flight between them and the freedom of an entire afternoon to themselves. Dallas on one side of the railing that ran down the middle of the stairs, Olli half-skipping down the stairs on the right side.

Olli glanced at the main part of the lobby before half shoving Dallas' shoulder toward the back door. "Hurry, hurry," she whispered.

Dallas herded her toward the rear door. He reached for the door handle. "Almost there," he half-whispered as he opened the door.

Olli skittered through the door. She pursed her lips together in a nervous way. "What are you going to do with your free afternoon?" she wondered, trotting down the outside steps sideways so she could look back at him easier.

Dallas shook his head a little and shrugged, glancing at the steps to gauge where his feet were. Unlike Olli, he hadn't grown up in the Wainwright Detective Agency. Certainly didn't grow up sneaking out of the building. "Probably tryin' to convince you that you shouldn't go into The District on your afternoon off."

Olli looked back at him and smirked. "I wasn't going to The District this afternoon."

Dallas looked at her, and an eyebrow jumped slightly. "Aren't you?"

Olli shook her head. "No. _Aces_. You act like I would lie about something like that!"

Dallas tilted his head slightly, and his other eyebrow jumped a little to match its mate.

"All right! All right! If you _must_ know..." Olli held up her hands. "I was thinking I would see if Birdie was free this afternoon and if she wanted to go shopping."

Chapter 2

The One With the Shopping Surprise

Dallas stopped short. "Wait."

Olli walked a few more steps and then looked back at him. "For...?" she wondered.

"Who are you? The Olivia Wainwright that I know thinks shopping is mundane and...foolish." Dallas pointed at her and scoffed. "She told me herself a while ago."

"I did not. When was that?!" Olli protested, her voice jumping an octave and cracking. She turned and walked toward the street, brushing her hair over her shoulder as she walked.

Dallas chuckled and walked after her. "You were sittin' on the window seat, we were havin' lunch while we waited for Tanner to break us out...remember?"

Olli looked thoughtful for a moment. "I vaguely remember that..."

"I asked you what you did in your free time. When you didn't answer right away, I asked if you went shoppin'. You laughed at me."

Olli looked up at him for a moment and then bobbed her head. "I didn't lie to you."

Dallas looked at her and tilted an eyebrow. "No?"

Olli shook her head. "No. I don't like to go shopping <u>often</u>. Usually I don't go at all."

Dallas nodded slowly, processing the information. "I see."

"In fact, the last time that I went shopping was almost eight months ago," Olli mentioned in an informative tone.

Dallas chuckled and made a thoughtful noise. "All right. I believe you."

Olli pushed her hands into her pockets and swung the flaps of her coat in a shrugging sort of motion. "It's just not my style. I don't need a lot. And it's not like I need fancy things."

Dallas looked at her and bobbed his head. "You really are one of a kind, Olli."

"Part of my stunning charm." Olli smirked.

The detectives stood patiently as part of the small crowd, waiting for the lights to change so they could walk across the street. Once the direction of the intersection changed, the crowd started to move.

Dallas offered his elbow to her as he stepped forward.

Olli glanced at him and smiled softly. She pulled her nearest hand out of the pocket and slipped it through his elbow, just as she stepped off the curb.

From there, it was only half a block between them and their favorite—usually dinner—stop. Clarence's Corner Diner had been the place to decompress from a rough day or case since they had become partners. They had their favorite booth, the same one that they had been sitting in when they were shot at during their first case.

It was the same booth that Dallas had first crossed paths with Anderson Paul, the reporter that he had the displeasure of dealing with alone while Olli had been sitting in Cross Bay's plush prison.

The detectives walked up to the door together, Dallas pausing half a step to open the front door.

Olli walked into the diner and straight to her usual bench. The inside edge of the third booth in. She paused and unzipped her jacket while smiling at the lunch crowd that had already gathered.

Dallas appeared behind her and gently helped her pull out of her jacket. Once she was free, he lightly tossed the jacket into the far corner of his side of the booth. He dropped his jacket on top of hers a moment later before he sat down onto the bench himself. Dallas lightly pulled the fedora off his head and set it loosely on top of the menu stand.

They wouldn't be needing it, anyway.

Olli scooted a little deeper into the booth and smiled at him. "Thanks."

Dallas half shrugged and scoffed quietly. "Sure, Olli."

Clarence, the man with deep black hair, greying at the temples, bustled out of the swinging door that led to the kitchen. He had a large plate full of food in each hand. As he walked, he muttered to himself under his breath like he was frustrated at something that was going on.

Probably a customer, as the lunch rush had just started to wander in off the street. Maybe something in the kitchen that was broken.

Either way, the sour look on his face instantly lifted when he saw the two people sitting in the third booth from the front door. He grinned and walked to a table with two portly men at it. Clarence nearly dropped the plates in front of them and smiled in a forced sort of way before pivoting and almost running to the table that he wanted to be at.

"My <u>friends</u>!" he gushed, holding his hands out wide enough to set one on each of their nearest shoulders. "How are you?! Are you hungry? Of course you are! Why else would be here?" he laughed and shook them a little in a friendly way. He chuckled and half turned, letting go of Olli's shoulder and looking back at the large stainless-steel hood that was over the range just behind the bar top counter. "Unless it was to admire the shine I have put on your wonderful mark that you added to my restaurant?!" His free hand gestured back to the large dent that dinged deeply into the hood, nearly a direct line from the booth to the range.

Olli looked at the large dent and cleared her throat. "Why won't you let us have that fixed?" she wondered.

Clarence clicked his tongue a couple of times like he was disappointed in her. "Never. That is a badge that I wear with honor!"

Dallas shook his head. "Well. At least let us apologize for it?"

Clarence scoffed. "My friends. You are hungry! Let me make you something. You must be starving." He turned and bustled away, back to the swinging door, and burst through on his trip back to the kitchen.

Olli watched him go and looked across the table to Dallas. "I just don't understand why he's so enamored with that."

Dallas shook his head. "I spent a lot of time here while you were away." He rested his arms on the table and looked at the large scuff mark on the hood. "Honestly, Olli, the more that I think about it, the more I'm convinced that it's a status symbol for him."

Olli looked where he was for a moment and then made a thoughtful noise. "Seems an odd way to go about it, but all right."

Dallas shrugged.

Olli looked out the window and made a thoughtful noise. "It's a beautiful day."

Dallas smiled and nodded. "It's nice to finally see the sun again."

The sun had decided to come out earlier that morning, which had led to a slew of gripes from Olli about being cooped up in their office when it was <u>such</u> a nice day outside. Dallas had to begrudgingly downplay and talk her out of it, despite the total agreement he had to what she had carried on about.

The clouds had broken apart not soon after the sun came out, which made Olli more distracted for a bit.

But, somehow, the both of them got through the distraction long enough to get all their paperwork done. And for the first time, they were both completely caught up.

"It looks like it's going to be a good day for you to go shoppin'." Dallas smiled at her.

Olli looked away from watching out the window and glanced at him before snorting quietly. "That is important." She smirked. "Otherwise my bags might get wet."

Dallas laughed and shook his head. "What am I goin' to do without that razor sharp wit all afternoon?"

Olli shrugged. "What <u>are</u> you going to do?"

Dallas looked thoughtful for a moment. "Maybe take a walk toward the park. See what there is to see over there."

Olli nodded slowly and made a thoughtful noise. "The park."

"There's a chess game that goes on during the day. I'd like to see if I can sit in."

Olli's eyebrows jumped, and she folded her hands on the table. "You play <u>chess</u>?"

"Is that so far out of the realm of possibility for you?"

Olli stared at him for a moment and then nodded. "Honestly? Yes."

"Why?" Dallas wondered, tilting his head.

Olli's eyes roved for a moment before she shrugged. "I don't know! Maybe it's just too...mundane?"

"<u>Mundane?!</u>" Dallas scoffed. "What did you <u>think</u> I did when I'm not out with you?"

"Maybe finding a place to meet a pretty girl or two? Go on dates? Honestly, Dallas, I hadn't really thought about it." Olli shrugged and sipped from the water glass that was placed in front of her at one point.

It wasn't a complete lie, but it wasn't the full truth, either. She had managed to get past her initial crush on Dallas a few months before, though there were still some lingering feelings that went beyond what she considered normal for a partnership. Not that she would ever admit to them. She did her best not to think about Dallas' personal life when they weren't together.

Dallas tilted his head and scoffed quietly. "Olli," he chided. "You know that you're the only girl for me."

Olli shook her head and sat back against the booth when Clarence walked past to set two plates with meatloaf and mashed potatoes down in front of them. "Dallas, please." She looked at the plate in front of her and smiled brightly. "Clarence, this looks amazing!"

Clarence smiled and knocked on the table brightly. "Eat up. It's the dinner special and I don't want to sell out before dinner."

"You didn't have to do that, Clarence," Dallas protested.

"You come to me. You say that you need lunch. Is this not lunch?" Clarence protested, pointing to the plates and looking at them.

Olli smiled and dipped her head. "Thank you, Clarence."

Clarence nodded after one more stern look split between the two. "Now. Eat. You eat." He bustled off to greet customers that came through the door and gestured for them to sit at the counter facing the large stovetop under the hood that he refused to replace.

Olli looked at the meatloaf in front of her and shrugged. "Might as well before it gets cold."

Dallas grunted. "It would be a shame to waste."

They ate at a normal pace, not really talking, pausing for a couple of small conversations with people who passed by their booth.

Clarence stopped by once or twice to check on them and made sure to take their plates as soon as they were finished eating.

Olli finished the last of her water and smiled at Dallas. "Mind if I take off?"

Dallas laughed softly and shook his head. "No. No, not at all. Go on. Go have fun shoppin'."

Olli smiled at him brilliantly and nodded. "Thank you."

Dallas chuckled and reached over to grab her jacket. "Here." He stood up out of the booth and opened the jacket for her. "Go on. Don't want to be late."

Olli smirked and slipped first one arm and then the other into her jacket sleeves. She shrugged into the shoulders and smiled at him. "Thanks. I'll see you at the office?"

Dallas nodded. "Tomorrow mornin' bright and early."

Olli smiled. "But not too early or bright."

Dallas laughed. "Sure."

Olli giggled and zipped up her jacket before heading for the front door. As she walked toward the front door, Olli pulled her hair free of her collar. "I'll see you around, Clarence!" she called over the noise of the conversations swirling at the counter.

Clarence turned from the grill and held up a metal spatula in a small wave. "Goodbye my friend! Come back soon!"

Olli grinned and pushed the front door open with her shoulder, hip and arm at the same time. "You know I will." She waved, including Dallas in the movement, and stepped out the door.

Dallas slipped out of his side of the booth and picked up his jacket. He swung the jacket around him while sliding his arms into the sleeves. A quick reach, and he scooped up his hat. Dallas kept the brim in his hand and walked to the counter. "What do I owe you, Clarence?"

Clarence half glanced over at him in the middle of flipping a patty. "No-no. I put it on your tab."

Dallas narrowed his eyes slightly. "Clarence. My tab must be runnin' a little rich at this point," he tried to rationalize.

Clarence fussed with the grill for a moment before glancing toward Dallas. He did a small double take. "My friend!" he protested, gesturing at him with the large metal spatula in his hand. "What are you still doing here? It is a nice day. Go. Be free! I put it on you tab."

Dallas leaned on the countertop for a moment longer. "Clarence."

"You go!" Clarence ordered, waving the spatula at him in a half threatening gesture. "Go."

Dallas scoffed slightly and stood up. "Thank you, Clarence." He started toward the door. "Listen. Next time I see you, I'm payin' that tab off."

Clarence scoffed. He waved his free hand at him in a dismissive gesture. "Ah! Go on! Go!"

"I'm serious, Clarence."

"Hey, Clarence!" one of the men at the counter piped up. "Why do I have to pay every time I'm here?"

Clarence pivoted toward him. "You say to me that you want to have a tab?" he gestured around with his hand and spatula. "And yet every time you come here you barely have enough for the lunch that I give you!" he held his hands toward the man that was protesting before swinging his arms around. "You pay." He turned to the grill and started cooking again.

"What's so special about him?!" another voice protested.

"He pays!" Clarence snapped, pointing the spatula at the newest to protest.

"How do you know if you won't let him?!"

"Ay? Are you coming into my diner and telling me whose money is good?!" Clarence scolded.

Dallas chuckled quietly and leaned against the door with his weight enough to jangle the little bell over the top corner of the door. "Thanks for lunch, Clarence. I'll see you later!"

Clarence waved the top edge of the spatula slightly. "Goodbye, my friend!"

Dallas dropped his hat onto his head with a smile and stepped out of the door and onto the sidewalk, letting the door close behind him. He looked up at the sky for a moment before deciding to walk to the park.

It was a <u>beautiful</u> day.

"Pull over here, please?" Olli wondered, sliding forward on the back seat and leaning her hand on the backrest of the front seat.

The man behind the wheel of the hack glanced back at her. "Sure thing."

Olli smiled at him and looked at the sidewalk where he was pulling over. She was a little early, but she was hoping that Birdie would arrive soon. When the hack rolled to a stop, Olli pulled a couple of bills from her inside pocket. "Here you go." She held them over the seat and smiled. "Thank you."

Olli smiled brightly. "Thank you. I really appreciate the lift." She slid across the back seat to the door closest to the curb and pushed the door open. She stepped out and up onto the sidewalk. Once she closed the door, Olli knocked on the roof of the hack. A simple step up and back, and Olli was standing on the sidewalk a step and a little more. She slid her hands into the pockets of her jacket and looked down the sidewalk to her left. Olli rocked on her toes a little and glanced to her right. She didn't see Birdie yet, so she would have to find a way to entertain herself while she waited.

Olli meandered along the sidewalk. Her pace wasn't in any hurry to get to the end of the block. Birdie would be there soon, and she didn't want to be too far down the way. As she walked, Olli slid her hands into the pockets of her jacket. Her progress slowed for a moment while she held the door for a young mother—probably the same age she was—and her three little children. Olli smiled and waved at the children as they walked past, leaning her shoulder against the front edge of the door and holding it open with her weight.

"Olive!" a bright, chipper voice called down the sidewalk.

Olli looked up and smiled brightly. She stood up off the front edge of the door and waved to the kids before adjusting to wave at the platinum blonde that was flouncing toward her on the sidewalk. "Hiya there, Gloria!" she called back.

Gloria's bright-red painted lips pulled up in a bright smile. "You're here!" She rushed forward a couple of steps, her bright platinum blonde curls bouncing with each step.

Olli shrugged and giggled a little. "Of course I am. You promised me a day of shopping!" she smiled and hugged Gloria when she got close enough. "Look at <u>you</u>!"

Gloria giggled brightly and spun. "I just got it last week! Isn't it <u>fine</u>!?" she smoothed her hands over her light-blue, drop waist, satin dress.

Olli bobbed her head and made a noise of agreement. "It's quite a dress, Bird."

Gloria looked at her and clicked her tongue. "You shouldn't call me that out here."

Olli looked at her and bit her lips together. "I'm so sorry. I slipped."

Gloria clicked her tongue and waved her hands a little. "No need to worry about it. I doubt that anyone heard you. It was one time. Now. Why are you wearing <u>pants</u>?!" she held her hands out toward Olli's legs. "We need to get you a new dress!"

Olli looked at her for a moment and pursed her lips. "I don't need a new dress, Glor—"

Gloria clicked her tongue a few times. "But what about that charming fella ya got?"

Olli looked at her blandly. "Aces, Gloria. Don't be ridiculous. He's my partner."

Gloria smiled at her brightly and tapped her nose. "Whatever you want to say, Olive."

Olli rolled her eyes. "Come on. Where do you want to start?" She pivoted toward the street lined with the most shops and looked down it expectantly.

"Tielmen's?" Gloria offered.

Olli nodded. "Sure. A little rich for my blood. But—"—she smiled at her brightly— "—I'll come with you and help you find something pretty."

"Too rich for your blood!" Gloria tittered and hugged Olli's nearest arm. "That doesn't even make sense! You have money."

Olli looked at her sideways and scoffed. "Sure. But come on. Not the kind of money that a canary has! Especially not the most popular one in the city."

Gloria preened a little and fluffed her curls a little. "Aw. You are so sweet. But I don't know about all that."

Olli shrugged and walked with her to the corner. She watched the traffic in front of her for a moment. "You ate lunch?"

Gloria nodded. "I did." she looked at Olli and smirked. "What about you, Olive?"

Olli half glanced at her. "Yeah, I did. What's that smirk?"

Gloria tilted her head and smiled at her and bit her lip a little. "So?"

Olli glanced at the traffic again and started them both across the intersection purposefully. "So, what?" She glanced in Gloria's direction.

"Was he there?" Gloria prodded, trotting a couple of steps and looking at Olli a little more squarely.

Olli tilted her head. "Who?"

Gloria looked at her and lightly smacked Olli's arm. "Olive! Listen to you."

Olli clicked her tongue and stepped up over the curb on the other side of the street at the same time as Gloria. "I know a lot of 'hes'. You're going to have to be more specific."

Gloria shot her a look of exasperated patience, sighing like Olli was trying to be difficult, and then half shook her head. "Your partner!"

Olli half shrugged and bobbed her head. "Sure. Sure, he was there. Aces, Glore...what would it matter if my partner was there while I was eating lunch? Of course he was. We snuck out of the office together. And it was lunchtime."

Gloria shook her head and rolled her eyes. "I will never understand how it is that you don't see how incredibly yummy he is."

Something sparked in Olli, flaring up angrily and slightly defensive. She started to take a breath and then swallowed it before she could actually act on it. "Oh, come on."

"Me?! You come on!"

"Aces, Glore!"

"Don't you 'aces Glore' me! You spend hours and hours a day with him!" Gloria waved one hand in front of her face. "I don't know how you focus."

"I don't know how you sing in an illegal bar...looks like both of us have some things that we need to just go along with." Olli paused at the correct door and opened it for Gloria.

Gloria looked at her and clicked her tongue. "I make more money that way."

Olli started to take a breath and then bobbed her head. "Well...sure. But you could switch over now."

Gloria flounced into the store. "And give this life up? Olive, honestly."

Olli rolled her eyes and stepped into the store. "I feel wrong just stepping into this store..." she muttered.

Gloria must not have heard her, she pivoted and smiled brightly in Olli's direction.

Olli smiled back at her tightly and wandered over slowly.

This shop was one of the most expensive and exclusive shops in Big Town. The dresses in this shop commanded such high prices they bordered on ridiculous.

Olli did have a couple of dresses from the racks, but it was only a couple. Most of her clothes she picked up from shops that were the same size but weren't nearly in the same price bracket. She usually did her best to save as much money as possible for people who needed it. Hack drivers and Clarence. The man who sold fruit during the summer on the side of Cicero.

The people who needed the money.

Olli wandered slowly through the store, looking back at Gloria from time to time as she moved through the racks. "Find anything, Glore?"

Gloria hung up another hanger and shrugged a little. "I found a couple. I'm going to go try them on." She hugged a couple of options to her ribs for a moment. She gasped and looked at Olli sharply. "Olive!"

Olli jerked and looked at her sharply. "Aces. What?" she tilted her head.

"We should go dancing tonight!"

Olli rested her hands on the shelf that was closest to her. "Dancing?" she repeated.

"Yes! Dancing. We'll get you a new dress and me a new dress and then we'll go hit a couple of clubs and dance the night away!" Gloria grinned at her brightly and nodded.

Olli started to take a breath. "What's wrong—"

"Olive," Gloria tutted. "You can't wear pants to go dancing!"

"—with the dresses that I already have?" Olli finished like she hadn't been interrupted, a small smirk on her face.

Gloria looked at her for a moment and pouted. "What's wrong with the dres-" she shook her head and blinked a couple of times in a confused sort of way. "What's that supposed to mean?!" she laughed in a carefree sort of way.

"I don't have to buy them. I have them already." Olli shrugged.

"But...Olive?" Gloria protested. "New dress."

Olli huffed softly and shook her head. "I don't need a new dress."

"How are you going to get a boy?" Gloria protested.

"Aces..." Olli stood up and looked out the window of the shop. "I don't—" her voice trailed off for a moment and her head slid to the left a little. She looked out the windows.

"Olive?" Gloria wondered, stepping back toward her. Her platinum curls bouncing to the side sharply as she tilted her head.

Olli took a couple of steps to the left and leaned a little to look out the windows a little further. "What were you saying?" she shook her head a little, seeming to shake off whatever it was that was bothering her and smiled at Gloria expectantly.

Gloria narrowed her eyes a little and tilted her head. She shook her finger at Olli, her whole face darkening a little. "No-no. I know that look. Something...you noticed something, didn't you. Olive, no working!" she scolded. "We're shopping."

Olli held up her hands. "No working. I promise. Just...thought that I saw something."

"No! No seeing something." Gloria shook her head, her tone scolding. "We are shopping."

Olli waved her hands a little and smiled apologetically. "You're right. I'm here to spend time with you."

Gloria smiled and nodded once. "That's better. Come on. We're going to have so much fun today!"

Olli laughed softly and shooed her toward the dressing room. "Go try them on! I want to see them!"

Gloria clapped her hands and trotted on her toes a few steps toward the dressing room. "They're so pretty!"

Olli watched her and laughed quietly. "Make sure you show me!" She waited until the door on the dressing room was closed before looking out the window critically. She could have sworn that she saw the same Auburn sedan rolling down the road outside of the shop for the second time.

It wouldn't have caught her attention if it wasn't for the fact that the car had gone by twice. The same direction.

Olli frowned a little and gnawed on the inside left corner of her bottom lip for a moment. Maybe they were just looking for parking somewhere nearby.

Maybe Gloria was right.

Maybe it was time to stop looking for trouble in the middle of broad daylight in the best part of town, and focus on helping her friend find the new dress that she was set on having.

Olli shifted her shoulders a little and made herself look away from the windows. She started to peruse the rack that was in front of her, shifting dresses one hanger at a time from right to left while she waited for Gloria to step out of the dressing room in her first choice.

Still, there was something nagging at the back of her thoughts. Something that she didn't want to acknowledge. Something that skipped its way right past a minor worry and straight to the point that it made the hair on the back of her neck stand up a little.

"What do you think of this one, Olive?" Gloria wondered, stepping out of the dressing room with a loud, strapless red dress that hugged every curve, the stitching slowly fluting around Gloria's ribs. The skirt was tight, almost to her knees, before it loosened up to a small tulip flare that would swing wildly with every step. She waited for a moment before ducking her head a little. "Olive?" she tried again, tilting her head. After a couple more seconds of waiting for something to happen, she kicked her right foot out to the side and tilted her head. Her hands snapped to her hips, and she frowned. One perfectly manicured eyebrow dipped a little.

It dipped further.

She stamped the heel of her t-strap black shoe against the tile of the floor and raised her eyebrows. "Olive, you promised!" she whined. "No working, remember?"

Olli shook her head and blinked a few times before looking over at Gloria. "Sorry, Bir—Gloria." She smiled tightly and waved her hand a little. "Sorry. What is it?" she wondered. "Aces," she whispered to herself under her breath.

Gloria made an exasperated noise and snapped her fingers. "Olive? My dress?" She spun around in a small circle, the skirt flaring wildly as she pivoted on the toes of her shoes.

Olli watched her and smiled brightly. "It's a looker, Glore."

"Should I get it?" Gloria looked at her and tilted her head. She quaffed her curls and looked at Olli expectantly.

Olli shrugged. "It's the first dress. What if you like the next one better?" she wondered, pushing her hands into the pockets of her leather jacket and half shrugging.

Gloria looked at her for a moment, like she hadn't considered the possibility, and turned to look at the dressing room. "I'm going to say this is the one that I want to take, but I should try on the others just to make sure."

Olli smiled and nodded. "All right. I'll be right here." she looked around. "Or somewhere close."

CHAPTER 3

THE ONE WITH THE PROMISE

"No working." Gloria pointed at her and raised an eyebrow.

Olli held up her hands and giggled. "Go on! I want to see what else you found!"

Gloria clapped her hands. "Go find a dress too!"

Olli nodded. "Promise." She smiled.

Gloria smiled and clapped her hands. "Yay! This is going to be so much fun!" She pivoted and trotted toward the dressing room on the toes of her shoes again.

Olli shook her head and looked over the racks. She shifted the hangers from right to left, but her heart really wasn't in it. She glanced up at the windows that faced the front street. Olli watched the traffic for a moment and waited to see if the car she had seen before would drive past again. Three more hangers and Olli was starting to think that she was getting paranoid.

She started to look down at the next piece of clothing that she was going to bypass when she thought she caught a glimpse of the same color that she had seen before. Olli stepped a couple of steps to her left and shifted the hangers from left to right as she looked out the window. She dipped her chin a little and tilted an eyebrow.

"Can I help you find something?"

Olli looked over at the sales clerk, that wasn't much older than her, and cleared her throat. "Oh. No. Thank you."

"You have a...very interesting style," The clerk mused, tilting an eyebrow.

"Function over fashion." Olli shrugged. "I think your time would be better spent with the two that just walked through the door. I'm just waiting for a friend."

The clerk looked over at the doorway and nodded. "I like it, though. It works for you. Those wrinkles might need a good iron."

Olli looked down at her bottom of her pants and frowned a little as the clerk walked away. "I don't know about all that," she muttered to herself. She looked down at her pants. The wrinkles were more like deep creases from the bottom of her knees to the large hems that brushed the top of her black boots. Olli frowned a little and bobbed her head. "She's not wrong," Olli mused to herself. She shrugged and shook her head.

There was nothing that she could do at this point, and there was always a chance that a case could sneak up on her.

Olli made it to the end of the rack of short dresses and had just turned to look at the rack that was behind her when the not-so-fine feeling of the hair on the back of her neck starting to stand up returned. She shifted a little to her right, so the reflection in the large mirror a few yards away was showing the road behind her. She watched for a couple of seconds before slowly taking a breath. Another large breath to pull herself back together, and Olli was starting to sort through the dresses in front of her again, only glancing up at the mirror from time-to-time.

Just to make sure.

"Checking on whether or not that clunky leather jacket goes with your blouse?" Gloria wondered, standing right next to Olli, looking at her shrewdly.

Olli side-eyed her for a moment, glanced at the mirror and then held up a blue dress with a bias-cut diamond that covered the middle of the front and back of the dress. "Think this will brighten up the blue in my eyes?" she wondered, holding it upright under her chin.

Gloria looked at her for a moment and then looked at the mirror. "Olive, what is it with you and mirrors?" she wondered, tilting an eyebrow.

"I'm confused, does that mean yes...ooooooorrr?" Olli half shook her head and tilted it slightly. She hefted the dress and looked at Gloria pointedly. "Glore? The dress?"

Gloria looked at her and then over the dress critically. "No. It's the wrong color blue. Takes all the color right out of your cheeks. Even the blush isn't helping."

"I'm not wearing any," Olli protested.

"You're no—..." Gloria shook her head. "Well. That explains everything."

Olli wrinkled her nose and blinked a couple of times. "Aces, Bir—Glore. You really know how to hurt a girl." She set the dress hanger back on the rack. "You choose something."

Gloria didn't seem to notice the slip-up and frowned a little as she looked over the rack in front of them. "No. I don't think that there's any in here for you. We need something a little more fun if we're going dancing tonight and there's nothing in your style here. Let's go down the block. Lemme just buy this dress, and we can go."

Olli pulled her head back a little and blinked a couple of times as Gloria pivoted and walked toward the front counter with a little sashay of her hips as she walked. After a minute of standing on the same spot that she had been, Olli started to shake her head, ignoring the sting of the unintentional poke at her appearance.

She forgot about it completely when she saw the Auburn again.

"Aces." Olli stepped forward and walked through a couple racks to get a better look out the window that allowed for a little more view down the street. "There's a perfectly good spot right there," she mused to herself.

That decided it. She wasn't going to ignore the prickly feeling on the back of her neck anymore. She stood up and walked pointedly across the store. "This way, Glore."

Gloria looked at her, confused and off balanced when Olli grabbed her arm. "Olive—" she protested, resisting long enough to grab the bag that was offered to her, before almost having to run after her a few steps to catch up. "Where are we going?!" she pulled on her arm a little, trying to claim it back.

Olli tightened her grip around Gloria's arm just over her elbow. "Aces, will you keep up? We're going out the back door if you must know." Olli glanced back at her and tilted her head toward the back of the building. She nearly dragged Gloria around the last part of the final rack and made a beeline to the back door.

Gloria made a couple of protesting, whining noises and pulled a face as they moved along. "Olive-! Olive, you're going to bruise my arm!" she protested.

Olli ignored her. She pushed the thumb press down and threw her weight against the door, barely slowing down as she motored them both through the door.

Sunshine bathed the parking lot that had been set up behind the buildings of the block.

For Olli, it felt like she stepped out of a thunderstorm and into a ray of calm, beautiful weather. She relaxed visibly and let go of Gloria's arm. "Shall we go this way?" she wondered, pointing toward their right.

Gloria looked at her for a moment, like she had grown a second head. "What in the world are you talking about, Olive?!"

"Shopping?" Olli wondered, shrugging slightly and smiling at her brightly.

Gloria clicked her tongue. "You can't just act like you didn't just drag me out of the store like you thought we were being followed."

Olli looked at her for a moment and bobbed her head. "Honestly, Glore, I'm not sure, but I don't want to be right."

"You promised me that you wouldn't be working."

Olli looked at her and frowned a little before walking the direction that she had pointed. "It's not something that I can just switch off, Glore. Something's bothering me. I'm not sure what it is, but I just would rather be proven wrong."

"You're too skeptical of everything, Olive," Gloria sighed, walking briskly to catch up with her before hooking her elbow into Olli's. "You always see the rain clouds and never the rainbows."

Olli smirked and half shook her head as they walked. "It's something that I'm good at, Gloria. There's a reason that I'm so successful."

"Because you're paranoid?" Gloria offered.

"Aces, Gloria!" Olli stared at her for a moment. "I'm not paranoid."

"You seem like you are. You stare out the window and drag me out the back door like I'm some rag doll to just be pulled along."

Olli looked chastised for a moment and bobbed her head a little. "You're right. I'm sorry. I should have just told you that I've seen the same car five times while we were in the store while you were trying on dresses."

Gloria scoffed and shook her head. "Olive. There's no way it was the same car." She clicked her tongue and walked the two of them toward the other side of the parking lot and the next store.

Olli tilted an eyebrow. "How could you know? You didn't see it."

Gloria shrugged and giggled quietly. "Because, silly goose, who would drive in front of the same store five times without parking?!"

"Unless they were looking for someone..." Olli muttered to herself, trying not to get irritated.

It really wasn't Gloria's fault that she didn't see the car, since she was in and out of the dressing room and had no interest in watching cars outside the window.

Gloria didn't seem to notice the words that Olli had muttered, she just continued to talk about the best way to get the most fun possible out of the dance that they were going to.

Olli listened to her as intently as she could while walking to the back door of the next shop. She didn't feel like anyone was watching anymore, so maybe it was time to relax and have fun. She started to laugh with Gloria and actually began to pay attention to the dresses on the rack.

A few hours later, Olli and Gloria tumbled out of the latest store that they had been in, multiple bags in hand, laughing at something that had tickled their fancy.

"I'm starved!" Gloria complained. "Can we find something to eat?"

Olli looked at her and nodded. "Aces! I think that sounds like a great plan. Where?" Olli looked at her and tilted her head.

Gloria made a thoughtful noise and then pointed toward the higher end of town. "Let's see if there's something uptown that calls to us?"

Olli nodded and smiled. "Sure. Sounds good."

Gloria tugged at her arm and pulled Olli along toward the upper side of town. "Come on, Olive. Let's find a real swingin' joint and meet some new people!"

Olli rolled her eyes. "I don't want to meet new people, Glore!" she protested. "I like the people that I know!"

Gloria tutted and shook her head at Olli. "Honestly, Olive, if it wasn't for the fact that you have the job that you do, I would accuse you of being a homebody! You should meet new people! You only have two friends!"

Olli spluttered for a minute before stopping short. "_Two_?!"

"Me and Monte," Gloria informed stoutly.

"And Dallas would be...?" Olli floated the question, her tone heavy with half confusion.

"Oh, Dear Star," Gloria scoffed, "He is _so_ much more than a friend." she flounced forward a few steps before stopping and looking back at Olli. "Olive? Coming?"

Olli was standing where she had been left, staring at Gloria like she was completely insane. "Aces...what is that supposed to mean?"

"He's your partner, right? Isn't that what you're always harping on about?"

Olli's shoulders dropped a little and her head followed them with a sharp tilt to the left. "Oh sure. Right." She shook herself and started toward Gloria and uptown in general. "Coming."

Gloria looked at her and one perfectly shaped eyebrow rose a few inches. "What was that?"

"I'm not in love with him, Glore. I work with him. Every. Day. He's saved my life a few times. That's all." She smirked. "Now stop prying, and tell me about these folks you call—" Olli held up two fingers from each hand—"'new people'."

Gloria giggled and hooked her arm through Olli's again, her demeanor suddenly bright and upbeat. She waved her free hand a few times and then reached for the pillbox hat that she had bought at the last store.

Olli did her best to listen to her. She laughed when it was appropriate, for the most part. There were even times when she was able to interject questions or statements.

It wasn't until two blocks later when the hair on the back of Olli's neck stood up again.

They were back on the main sidewalk, and had been for almost six blocks. Which meant that Olli could use her favorite trick to see if they were being followed.

Store windows.

As they walked, Olli subtly glanced at the windows to her left. She didn't see anything out of the ordinary the first couple of windows.

She saw the Auburn in the fourth window. She pursed her lips for a moment.

It was probably a few years old, not surprising in this financial climate. Large front fender swells, conical chrome headlights and the sliver leaning lady with her swept back, wing-like arms on the hood giving it away instantly. The inclined chrome radiator and the front bumper built like crossbow limbs made it a sure thing. Convertible top and that strange mustard tan color material that caught her eye the first time. It was rolling slowly in the same direction that they were walking.

Not that it was strange that a car would be rolling slow this close to downtown, with so many shops around...

Olli couldn't get past the feeling that stood her hair on end. She didn't know how, but something was off. She glanced back at the next window and stared for a moment too long.

"Olive, what are you looking at?" Gloria wondered.

Olli turned to look at her and shrugged. "That cute little number right there?" she pointed to a bright yellow striped dress. "Don't you think that would look amazing on you?"

Gloria stopped to look at the dress for a moment. She made a delighted noise and darted toward the door. "Come on, Olive! I want it for my next set!"

Olli giggled and then turned to face the street. She looked at the car squarely and raised an eyebrow. A couple more seconds and she tossed her head. Once she had done it, she turned to walk into the shop.

Hopefully, the motion would slow down whatever it was that was going on. Usually, looking at the problem head-on was enough to deter most things from happening.

Olli wandered around the store for a moment, waiting while Gloria and the shop clerk chatted about the patterns and colors. She pondered about all the different reasons that the Auburn would have been following them.

Maybe it was someone who had just happened to be in all the same places that <u>they</u> had been for the last few hours, and it was nothing more than a strange crossing of paths. It wasn't something that was completely out of the stretch of possibilities. Big Town was only just so big, after all. And there was only one good section of town to shop in if one had any taste or money.

Olli wasn't the best at math, but she was sure that there had to be some overlap there. The odds couldn't have been that out of control to dictate that something like this could happen, eventually.

But there was that nagging feeling. The hair standing up on the back of her neck.

Olli shook her head a little to herself. No. Something was going on.

Maybe it was someone who tracked down the sultry singer from The Phoenix and started to get a little too attached?

Olli discounted that almost as soon as the thought popped up into her head.

Say what you would about him, but Razor was <u>incredibly</u> protective of the woman in his life that he considered to be under his care. He often went to great lengths to make sure that they were kept as safe as possible. Odd behavior for the head of the largest moonshine moving crime family in Big Town, and probably the surrounding area, but it was part of what made Razor...Razor.

Olli glanced over at the dressing room when Gloria twirled out of the dressing room and grinned. "Don't you just look like the prettiest bird that ever took flight!?" she crowed, clapping her hands.

Gloria giggled brightly and spun to the right and then to the left. "I love this. I can't wait to wear it at my next show."

Olli nodded. "You're going to knock their socks off. Those boys won't know what hit them."

"You should get one too!" Gloria gushed. "Don't you shake your head at me, Olive! With your body?! You'd look amazing!"

Olli pursed her lips. "Glore...where would I even wear something like that?"

"My club?" Gloria offered almost instantly and smiled. "It's been ages since you've come to see me sing."

"I can't come to you club, Glore," Olli protested, her voice jumping up an octave and her head sticking out a couple of inches before pulling back.

"Why <u>not</u>?" Gloria pouted. "There's great dancing and new people to meet?"

"And booze, drugs and bookmaking," Olli pointed out, her tone dry while she did so.

Gloria tilted her head. "You wouldn't come while you were <u>working</u>, Silly Goose."

Olli blinked. "And the fact that they all know me there?"

"I'll make sure that Eddie gets you some coffee or ice water or whatever you want, Olive," Gloria assured with a small swing of her perfectly manicured hand.

Olli's mouth popped open slightly before she snapped it back shut again. "Aces...that is...not even close to remotely the point that I was trying to make with that."

"If they know who you are and that you're coming, I doubt that they'll do any of those things while you're there."

Olli's eyebrow dipped. "If I try on the dress and promise to go dancing with you a couple of weekends will you drop it?"

Gloria clapped her hands together and squealed brightly. "Yes!"

Olli dipped her head and looked at the store clerk that had clearly no idea what to do with the conversation that she had walked up on. "Afternoon. Could you check to see if you have that in a sixteen please?" she gestured toward the dress that Gloria was wearing.

The store clerk bobbed her head and turned to walk away.

Olli mumbled a small, mostly meant sentiment of gratitude and risked a glance out the door while Gloria was back in the changing room getting back into the dress that she wore when she walked in.

The Auburn was nowhere to be seen.

Olli slowly let out a breath, and the tension out of her shoulders at the same time. Maybe the stern look was all it took to move the driver along and it would be a harmless evening from now on in.

Gloria didn't seem to notice the change in Olli when she stepped out of the dressing room, decked out in the dress that Olli had pointed out to get them into the store and off the sidewalk.

Olli gushed and laughed with her, feeling completely at ease. She took Gloria's nearest hand and spun her a little.

"We need to get a dress for <u>you</u>!" Gloria insisted, doing her best to sweep Olli along with her.

Olli nodded slowly. "All right. If you find me one worth wear-" she laughed a little when Gloria's little excited squeal cut her off.

Gloria trotted away from her and over to the rack with mid-length dresses and started sliding hangers along the rack critically.

Olli let her have her fun and suggested dresses over Gloria's shoulder.

Gloria giggled and shook her head. "I want something <u>pretty</u>, Olive."

Olli shook her head and took the dresses that Gloria handed her. She happened to glance out the window when she walked toward the dressing room. She paused with her hand on the door of the dressing room and looked out the window.

There was that Auburn. Parked across the road in one of the angled parking spots. It looked like it was empty.

Olli stepped into the dressing room and closed the door. She frowned and hung up the dresses.

Maybe they had just parked to go into the restaurant across the road. Or the department store a couple of doors down.

Olli shrugged out of her jacket and did her best to put the Auburn out of her mind. The first thought that popped up into her head was to wonder if Dallas was having a good time.

She scoffed a little.

Dallas playing chess. Who would have ever thought...

Dallas shifted in his chair and looked at the board in front of him. It was the fourth game of the afternoon. He sat patiently while he waited for the man across from him to decide what move to make. Dallas had boxed him rather well, and it would take some skill to get out of it without losing some major pieces. He looked up at the sky to the west of the park and clocked where the sun was. It would be dark in not quite an hour. He smiled at the man across from him and nodded in a friendly way. While he waited, Olli crossed his mind again.

He wondered if Olli was having a good time shopping.

Olli shopping. Seemed so incredibly out of character from the girl that he had grown to love so dearly. The girl with the tall black motorcycle boots, dark grey pants that she tucked into those boots so long and often that every pair that she owned must have been permanently wrinkled from the knees down. The girl with the leather jacket and the ability to throw a punch that any man would be proud of...

Dallas could hardly picture her standing in a room full of racks hung with the dresses of the newest fashion. It was <u>so</u> far from the dark, dusty tunnels that she preferred.

He chuckled just thinking about it. He hoped that she was having a good time.

Olli looked at Gloria and smoothed the fabric over her torso. "You're <u>sure</u> about this, Glore?" she wondered.

Gloria nodded. "It's <u>perfect</u> for you. Your color and great for dancing!"

Olli looked at the deep yellow dress she had on. It was down to just above her knees, bias cut in a diamond over her ribs. A small shift of her hips and the skirt swung wildly. She smiled a little.

It was a beautiful dress. The dress, the shoes and the fur stole that was around her shoulders loosely at a jaunty angle. "You're sure it's not too much?"

Gloria scoffed and shook her head. "Let's go dancing! You look perfect!" she shoved Olli's shoulder a little and shook her head. "Good gracious. It's like you don't want to go dancing with me!"

Olli looked down at herself one more time and then nodded. "Let's go dancing."

Gloria grinned and pointed at Olli while she looked at the store clerk. "She'll take the whole thing."

The clerk nodded and clicked away toward the desk.

Olli turned toward to step off the small podium that she had been standing on, but froze.

The Auburn.

There it was again. Parked across the road, just a couple of parking spots down.

Olli's eyes flinched and she tilted her head a little. This was the fourth parking spot that she had seen it in throughout the day.

In the same number of stores.

Olli put her hands on her hips and narrowed her eyes a little more. Now she was fully suspicious. There was no way that this was accidental or unintentional anymore.

"Olive? Where's your jacket? I need your wallet." Gloria's voice interrupted.

Olli blinked a couple of times and looked at her. "Dressing room on the hook."

Gloria spun and walked toward the dressing room. She paused and looked at Olli closely. "Olive...you're not working..."

Olli turned her head away from the window, her eyes the last to tear away from it. "No."

Gloria smiled brightly, satisfied that her denial was enough. She walked into the dressing room for a couple of minutes before coming back out, with Olli's wallet in her hands, opening it as she walked. "Here. This should be enough to cover everything." She pulled out a wad of bills.

Olli's eyes flared. She stepped off the podium and snatched the bills away from Gloria. "Aces, Glore! That's my slush fund for the entire <u>month</u>." She snatched the bills away and shook her head for a moment. "It is <u>not</u> that much." She looked at the clerk and raised an eyebrow. "How much is it, <u>really</u>?"

The clerk giggled and offered a receipt. "This is the total."

Olli glanced at the receipt and then shot Gloria an exasperated look before peeling off only a couple of bills and offering them to the clerk.

Gloria half shrugged and flipped her hair. "I wasn't going to give her <u>all</u> of it. I'm not <u>that</u> bad at math."

Olli blinked at her a couple of times before smiling at the clerk and offering her hand for the change that was extended to her.

Gloria tittered and shrugged. "See. All better."

Olli clicked her tongue and handed her wallet over. "Put this back in my jacket, will you?"

Gloria took the wallet. "I think I should put this in my purse, actually. Since we're going—" Gloria's voice jumped up to a sing-song tone, "daaaaannnnnccccing."

Olli nodded and bobbed her head. "Right. Dancing. What about the clothes that we were wearing?"

"I can arrange for the clothes to be shipped to whatever address you'd like them to be?" the clerk offered, tilting her head.

"Yes!" Gloria spoke up, throwing her hands up and then clapping brightly. "Yes! Can I arrange that right now?" she walked toward the counter chatting with the clerk.

Olli watched them walk away and leaned slightly to look out the window toward where the Auburn was parked.

It wasn't there anymore.

Olli frowned a little and took a step off the podium. She walked over to the window and shifted a few spring coats while looking over the street.

Just when she thought that the hair on the back of her neck should be smoothed down, everything was on end.

All of her alerts were flashing.

Something was <u>definitely</u> wrong.

Olli looked across the store, trying to find where Gloria was. As soon as she spotted Gloria, she wandered toward the counter where Gloria was standing. She did her best not to move like she was trying to rush that direction, trying not to make it too obvious that she was heading straight for Gloria.

Gloria looked at her and smiled brightly. "Olive! Let's go?"

Olli nodded. "Is there a back door to this place?" she wondered, leaning her torso and elbows on the counter and pointing in the general direction of the back of the building.

"Uhm...su-sure?" the clerk looked a little confused and half turned to glance at the back of the building. "B-but we don't usually let customers use it."

"Why do we have to go—<u>no</u>. We don't need the back door. We'll be going out the front door, like <u>normal</u> customers." Gloria looked at Olli pointedly. "She's just paranoid."

Olli smiled brightly and picked up Gloria's purse. She fished out her wallet and set a couple of bills down on the counter. "For you." She smiled at the clerk. "Come on, Gloria. Don't want to miss out on the dancing." She caught Gloria's elbow and started them both toward the back door.

Gloria tried to slow her down while doing her best to tug her arm out of Olli's grip. "Olive! We don't have to go out the back door! Why can't we just go out the <u>front door</u>?!" she pointed in the general direction of the front of the building while she half trotted down the short flight of stairs that was leading them toward the back door.

"Aces, Glore. Would it cost you <u>so</u> much to trust me enough to just <u>go with me</u>?" Olli glanced back at her and stepped off the last step. She power-walked toward the door that was right in front of them.

Gloria stopped short, managing to pull Olli to a stop with her. "No. Not until you tell me what is going on. You told me that you weren't going to work today. You <u>promised</u>."

Olli took one more step and then turned to face her. "All right. Fine." She took a step toward Gloria and lowered her voice. "A car has been following us all day, and it's making me nervous."

Gloria narrowed her eyes a little and stamped her foot. "How do you <u>know</u>?" She tilted an eyebrow.

CHAPTER 4

THE ONE WITH THE NATURAL ABILITY

"How do you know what key you want to start a song in?" Olli tossed her hands a little and tilted her head. "How do you know where to walk and flirt as you go through your set?"

Gloria looked like the thought had never crossed her mind. "I...I don't, really."

"It's natural. It's something that you don't have to think about. And it's not something that you could explain, right?"

Gloria nodded slowly. "And this...is one of your detective gut moments?" she clarified in a bemused tone.

Olli nodded. "This is just one of those times when you're just going to have to trust me."

Gloria pursed her lips for a moment before she nodded. "Yeah. All right. Let's go to through the back door."

Olli smiled at her and nodded once. "Thank you." She pivoted and walked to the back door.

Gloria walked after her and huffed.

Olli glanced back at her, and shrugged. "Just let me do this." She smiled at her once before slowly opening the back door and looked over the small alley that was in front of them suddenly. "All right. It's empty. Let's go." She pushed the door open the rest of the way and stepped out.

Gloria walked through the door, waiting half a beat so that Olli could close the door and hooked her arm through her elbow. "We're never going to get a hack from here."

Olli shrugged a little. "You're not allergic to walking a little while, are you?"

Gloria shook her head and quaffed her curls. "No. Is that your plan?"

"I figured we'd walk until we got to a busy street."

Gloria looked at her and frowned a little. "You know how we could have caught a hack?"

"Do _not_ say walk out the front door," Olli warned. "You know why we're back here."

Gloria huffed and shook her head. "All right, All right! But if I wear the heels off these shoes, you're buying me new ones."

Olli laughed and rolled her eyes. "Aces, Glore, we're not walking to Bay City! You're being dramatic."

Gloria half stuck her tongue out at her before she nodded. "Down this alley, and then where are we?"

Olli thought for a moment. "We're going to be on Seventh. We can walk half a block down and then we'll be on Archer. From there, we can catch a hack."

Gloria looked like she was trying to pull up a mental map before she nodded. "Perfect. Let's do that."

Olli nodded and walked with her down the alley.

Once they were out of the alley and down the block toward the corner of Archer, Gloria tugged on Olli's arm. "Can we not walk so fast? I'm getting winded. My makeup will start to run."

Olli almost instantly dropped her speed. "Sorry."

"Do you always walk this fast?"

Olli shrugged. "I guess I never really thought about it."

"You're going to walk right away from that boy if you keep walking that fast." Gloria giggled, smirking at her.

Olli rolled her eyes. "Aces, Glore," she half-whispered. "Can you just let it go?"

Gloria giggled and shook her head. "It's just a little harmless fun."

Olli stopped when they reached the corner of Archer and shook her head. "Maybe for you it is."

Gloria didn't seem to notice the comment. She stepped forward a couple steps and tossed a hand up in the air.

A bright-yellow hack with a black-and-white checkered stripe down the middle of the doors slowed and started to pull toward the curb, blinker on and the light on the top flicking off as it came to a stop.

Olli glanced at the hack before double checking that the Auburn wasn't around them, hovering to keep pace with them yet again.

"Coming, Olive?" Gloria wondered, one foot in the back door of the hack, her hands on the door waiting while she looked at Olli.

Olli blinked and looked toward her. "I'm coming." She walked toward the back door, content that the Auburn wasn't around.

Gloria smiled and slid into the back seat of the hack, scooting over far enough for Olli to fit. "Let's go dancing!"

Olli smiled at her and dropped into the seat next to her before closing the back door. "Where to?" she wondered, looking at Gloria, knowing full well that she would know the place to go.

Gloria grinned at her brightly and leaned forward toward the front seat eagerly. "Corner of Cicero and Tenth?"

"You got it, Doll." The cabbie leaned forward and flipped on the meter. "You two going out on the town?" he wondered, his tone and smirk in the rearview mirror wolfish.

Gloria smiled brightly and nodded. "We haven't gone dancing together in forever. We both have the night off! We're going to paint the town red."

Olli nudged Gloria pointedly with her elbow and her eyebrows went up.

Gloria looked at her, completely confused, a little bit of irritation flashing across her face. "Lighten up, Olive."

Olli frowned and shook her head a little.

"So this painting the town red...I don't suppose that you need some assistance?"

Gloria tittered and shook her head. "I guess if you want to come along..."

"Gloria, <u>no</u>!" Olli snapped. She scoffed a little when the silence in the hack went a little too long. "You promised me a girl's night. If I'm not allowed to work, then you can't pick up a <u>date</u>!"

Gloria looked at her for a moment and then frowned a little. "All right...<u>fine</u>." She shrugged and looked out the window, conversation completely forgotten.

Olli looked at the cabbie in the mirror and waited for him to blink. She narrowed her eyes and wrinkled her upper lip at him.

He looked forward again and shook his head a little.

It was a couple of minutes later when the hack pulled up to the curb and the cabbie looked back at them. "We're here."

Gloria started to dig into her purse. "How much do we owe you?"

"Ten cents."

Olli scoffed. "The meter says fifty-three cents." She looked at him blandly. After a quick glance at Gloria, Olli offered the cabbie some change and one eyebrow went up.

The cabbie took the change and nodded once. "Thank you."

"Thanks for the ride." Olli smiled and swung the door open. She stepped out of the hack after checking to make sure that there was space in traffic and smoothed her light yellow fishtail skirt.

Gloria closed her purse quickly and opened her door. She stepped out and looked around for Olli. "Ready to go dancing, Olive?"

Olli smiled a little and nodded. "I think so."

"You only think so?" Gloria pouted. "But _dancing_, Olive."

"Fine. I'm excited. Are you happy now?" Olli smiled at her and walked with her toward the short line that had formed outside a building.

Gloria nodded and slipped her arm through Olli's nearest elbow. "We're going to have so much fun!"

Despite the fact that Olli wasn't convinced at the fun that was to be had, once they were in the building, the band that just finished warming up did sound lively.

Olli waited for Gloria to check the new coat she had just bought and looked over the club with a small smile. Maybe it wouldn't be so bad to dance for a little while. Dee was always harping on her to go out on the town a little more.

She would be so proud.

Gloria walked back from the coat check and smiled at her brightly. "Are you ready to dance?" she swung her shoulders and pivoted her hips a little. A bright, happy smile on her face.

Olli nodded and gestured to the main part of the dance hall. "I'm ready for this if you are."

Gloria giggled and trot-stepped toward the middle of the room excitedly.

Olli walked in after her, not in a brisk hurry to dance. She figured she would spend most of her time watching Gloria dance. She was perfectly content to watch. Dancing wasn't exactly her strong suit.

Which worked out, since she was rarely asked out onto the dance floor.

Olli walked over to a tall, small table with only a set of chairs with it. She scooted onto the chair that faced the door. After a small shift to the right. She looked to her left at the dance floor.

A small scoff escaped her.

Gloria had already managed to find herself a partner and was dancing with him, a large smile on her face.

Olli looked around the room. She didn't know what she was looking for, but the habit ran deep and she couldn't keep from checking to see what there was to see.

No one seemed to be watching Gloria more than the next person. But Olli still couldn't shake the feeling that something was...off.

The Auburn following them around for most of the day really made the hair stand up on the back of her neck. Even now, she couldn't shake it.

It was almost the exact same feeling that she had just before she met Dallas. Something was going to happen. She just wasn't sure _when_.

Gloria was just left of dead center on the dance floor. Her smile wild and easy. She swung herself around her latest partner and shimmied her hips a little bit with a wide grin.

Olli shook her head. Gloria could be such a ham when it came to impressing the boys. She sipped on the South Side drink that she had requested from a bustling waitress. It wasn't a strong drink—the Volstead Act saw to that. But the tart flavors of lime juice, mint and blueberry mixed with something else tart and sharp—there to do it's best to mimic Capone's favorite drink. Olli swirled the shallow, wide-mouthed, long-stemmed glass and took another small sip.

Gloria trotted back to the table and hopped up onto her seat. "What are you drinking?"

"A South Side." Olli shrugged.

Gloria shuddered a little and wrinkled her nose. "Without gin?"

Olli tilted her head. "They're not allowed to sell an <u>actual</u> South Side here. There's a law against it."

Gloria huffed a little and pouted. "Still."

"And even if it <u>had</u> gin you wouldn't like it," Olli pointed out, her tone laughing.

Gloria nodded and smoothed her skirt a little. She hooked one knee over the other and set her elbows on the table. "Did you order me anything?"

Olli shook her head and swirled her glass carefully between her fingers on the deep red coaster she had been given. "No. I was too busy dancing."

Gloria sat up a little sharper and tilted her head. "Were you really, Olive?!"

Olli laughed and shook her head. "<u>Aces</u>, Glore. No. I wasn't sure what you wanted. So, I asked them to bring you a water to start.

Gloria looked at the waitress with a smile when her sweating glass of water was dropped off in the bustle. "That's fine. I wouldn't trust you to order a drink, anyway. It would be too sour."

Olli scoffed. "I figured you wouldn't like anything they're serving here. No gin." She smirked.

Gloria clicked her tongue and adjusted her glass and coaster on the table in front of her. "Have you been out on the floor yet?"

Olli shook her head. "No."

Gloria pouted. "Why not, Olive?"

Olli shot her a dull look and tilted her head pointedly. "You know why, Glore. No one ever notices me with you around to steal the spotlight."

"Don't be ridiculous. There's not a spot in the world that would miss the chance to shine on you. If only you'd give it the chance."

Olli stared at her for a moment before smiling softly. "You're a good friend, Glore."

"Of course I am, Olive." Gloria beamed at her.

Olli rolled her eyes in a smirky way and sipped her drink again.

"What do you think of this place?"

"The Moderne?" Olli looked around and smiled. "It's nice."

The tables were spaced out every four feet or so, allowing the feeling of privacy despite the hustle of the rest of the club. They all had deep-red sheer tableclothes draped over them. Everything from the flatware to the flower vase holding a single light-pink carnation was a tasteful version of the Art Deco movement.

Bright brass shone all over the room. A merry nine-piece band was occupying the stage that was directly to their right. Piano, two trombones, a small drum kit, two trumpets, French horn, saxophone, and a clarinet. It was a wonderful mix of music that they played. Two bright, blue-white beams shone down on them from the lights attached to the second level. Cigarette smoke danced around the edges of the light and took the sharp edge off everything.

Not so hazy that one couldn't see what was happening, but enough to give the air a soft, clouded look.

"I think it's pretty swingin'." Gloria smirked. "And you know what else?"

Olli made an interested noise around the mouthful of her drink she had just swallowed. "What's that?"

"You're actually in the front of the house for once in your life."

Olli scoffed and laughed softly while shaking her head. "You can't expect me to wander my way through the front door of The Blinking Lights?!"

"Why not?" Gloria pouted. "You never hear me sing."

"I'd love to hear you sing, dolly," a man, not much older than them mused, suddenly appearing next to Gloria's right arm. He draped his left arm across the backrest of Gloria's chair and rested his right on the table, effectively blocking Olli from the conversation.

Gloria preened and smiled at him brightly.

Olli sipped her drink and watched them, completely unsurprised at the way that she had been so casually dismissed from the table. She didn't blame Gloria, or the fellow talking to her. Gloria was a sight to behold.

Platinum hair shining in the light, bold, oxblood red lip stain making her teeth only appear more white and perfect. Add in the perfect amount of an icy blue eye shadow—usual in the sea of pinks and purples more popularly favored—an aggressive swipe of pure black eyeliner, with a small supporting swipe under perfect, baby blue eyes, and perfectly applied fake lashes. And a single beauty mark that looked surprisingly real on perfectly smooth, alabaster skin.

It honestly was no wonder that no one noticed Olli.

At least, not to <u>her</u>.

Gloria tittered a little and batted her eyelashes that the man that had suddenly claimed her entire field of vision. "Would you?"

"Yeah, dolly." He smirked at her and looked her over, his gaze something along the lines of a dog finding an unattended bone.

Gloria giggled a little and brushed at her bangs over her right eye.

Olli shook her head a little and fought the urge to roll her eyes. She sipped her drink and looked over the dance floor again. She briefly wondered if she should wander away for a bit to give the two of them the privacy that they apparently desired. Maybe if she slipped far enough away, she could duck outside and get back to doing what she did best.

But she had promised to spend the night out on the town with Gloria, and she wasn't about to go back on it.

"…I'd love to dance, but my girlfriend has been sitting here all night babysitting my drink and this table while I've been out dancing and that just doesn't seem fair," Gloria's pouty, flirty tone cut into Olli's thoughts of escape.

Olli blinked and looked across the table at her. She leaned the top half of her body so she could see past their sudden guest's head. She flared her eyes and tilted her head a little, her eyebrow jumping after a second. "I don't need to dance. And I'm really good at guarding things."

Gloria focused on her and shook her head slightly. "But, Olive, you promised to dance with me tonight."

"I'd rather you dance with me, dolly." The man shifted a little to pull Gloria's attention back to him.

Gloria preened and smiled at him brightly. "In a minute. Ok, honey?" She patted his arm without really looking at him.

Olli half rolled her eyes. "All right. Fine. Someone asks me to dance and I will. But don't miss out on a dance on my account. Go. Dance with the man. He's clearly not going to go away until you do."

"Your friend has a point."

Gloria looked between them. Her eyes shifted back to Olli, before she nodded and her large, flirty smile was back again. "All right. I'd love to dance." She offered her hand and pivoted in the seat of her chair for an easier escape.

Olli waggled her fingers and smiled as the two of them walked away. She swirled her glass a little more and sipped it.

The waitress swung past again, a small smile on her face. She set an identical glass, with the same color liquid in it.

Olli looked at the drink and then the waitress. Her eyebrow dipped. "Oh. Thank you. I didn't order this, though."

"It's from the dreamy blond man over at the bar." The waitress half nodded toward the bar, a small smile on her face.

Olli blinked a little and smirked. The waitress clearly thought that he was something to look at. She pivoted a little in her seat and looked over her shoulder at the bar. "Him? Aces, really?"

He was about Dallas' height, dirty blonde hair, just enough hair on his jaw to look like he had neglected to shave that morning. An uncharacteristic choice. He wore a light-tan vest and matching pants. A deep-chocolate pinstripe cut across the set at a forty-five degree angle. His shirt was a deep-wine red. Bright silver tie, perfect Windsor knot. Little red polka dots marched down the tie in neat rows.

Olli's eyebrow dipped at the bright platinum cuff links. Why was someone with that level of money in a place like this? There were clubs a few blocks over that catered to the ritzy playboy type. This was not one of those places. She looked at the waitress and smiled a little. "Thank you." Olli pivoted slightly and hefted the new glass in the general direction of the man at the bar that the waitress had indicated sent the drink. A small, tight smile crossed her face.

His smile, in sharp contrast, was bright. He waved a little and lounged against the bar.

Olli smiled tightly again before pivoting back to face the table in front of her. She rested her arms on the near edge and slowly worked on finishing the last little bit of her first drink as she tracked Gloria on the dance floor. After a few minutes of ignoring the newest glass on the table, Olli finally caved and picked it up. She took a small sip of the drink and looked at the bright colors of the dresses on the dance floor. She started to relax a little more and smiled a little easier.

A few more sips and Olli started to feel a little warm. She shifted in her seat and relaxed a little. Olli blinked slowly. Her head was starting to feel heavy.

Olli snapped her eyes open and blinked sharply. She looked around and tried to find Gloria. Once the platinum blonde bob was discovered, Olli relaxed into herself. She didn't know how long her eyes had been closed, but the song had changed.

Olli sipped her drink again. The feeling of having a nice, weighted blanket dropped on her shoulders and swirled around her tightly. She wasn't sure why she felt like she was floating, but she was sure that it was wrong. Olli looked at her glass and sniffed at it carefully.

It didn't smell suspicious.

Olli shrugged to herself a little and took another sip. The warm blanket feeling swirled around her shoulders again.

Gloria was still out on the floor, dancing her heart out, laughing and generally having a good time.

Olli tried to set her elbow on the edge of the table and missed. She caught herself a half second too late when her elbow scrape-bounced off the edge and nearly hit her thigh. Her eyebrows knit together a little and she looked at her glass.

Something was very wrong.

"May I have a dance?" a male voice wondered.

Olli looked up, feeling like she was trying to move it through a heavy fog. "What?" she wondered, her voice sounding like it was from a different person.

"This dance? May I?" he smiled at her and offered a hand to her.

Olli blinked a couple of times and shook her head. "Not really a dancer. I'm just waiting for my friend."

Something was horribly wrong. Her thoughts weren't meshing together very well. She felt like she was floating in a fog and exhausted at the same time. Colors were starting to blur together and the music, which had sounded so good just a few minutes ago, was incongruous and clanged against her eardrums.

Olli blinked a couple of times and rubbed her temple a little. Her head felt heavy and fuzzy at the same time.

"What do you mean? Are you saying that you don't dance?" the voice asked again.

Olli purposefully looked up at him and shook her head. "I'd rather not. But thank you." She was not a fan of the way that her head felt now that she had shook it. Before she realized it was happening, Olli leaned a little too far and tipped out of the side edge of the chair.

The man stepped forward and caught her, just as she would have stumbled completely. "Whoa there. Here. Let me help you." He scooped his arm around her ribs and hefted her up to keep her on her feet.

"I'm all right," Olli protested, not believing herself.

"I'm sure you are." He skirted the dance floor, mostly dragging her as they walked.

Olli tried to stand up and pull herself away from him. The whole room spun and tilted a bit. She stumbled and had little choice but to lean on her newfound escort.

"Easy there. Don't forget to pick your feet up."

Olli looked at him for a moment and tried to process what his face looked like. She had lost sight of Gloria. It made her nervous suddenly. "Where are we going?" she mumbled, hoping that her words came out more clear than she heard them.

"Juss relass," the garbled, convoluted voice assured.

Olli blinked a couple of times and tried to force her eyes to open. She licked her lips and stumbled a couple of steps.

Her human crutch bore her up a little more and talked in a soothing tone. His voice never wavering from the quiet volume.

Olli crashed down in a jumbled heap somewhere dark and far enough away from the music that it was almost quiet. She stretched and groaned a little. It seemed like no matter what she did, she couldn't clear her head. Every movement that she made felt like it was through a thick sludge. Olli picked up one of her hands and scrubbed her face with it, trying to get the blood moving again.

Nothing was helping.

Was it getting darker? Olli couldn't tell, but now exhaustion was starting to overtake her. It was hard to remember the last time that she was this tired. Olli didn't have the energy to stop the yawn that escaped her.

Maybe she could close her eyes for just a couple of minutes...

"Hey!"

Olli blinked, her eyes not fully opening, and started a little bit. Her head was pounding. She picked her head up slightly. It felt like she was trying to move it through sludge. She had felt this feeling before. The colors that swirled around her weren't quite as bad as the time that she had woken up in Cross Bay's holding room.

Olli swallowed hard, trying to get past the feeling of her tongue. It felt two sizes too big. It felt like cotton had been shoved into her mouth and down her throat. She coughed a little and smacked her tongue and licked her lips a bit, trying to get the feeling to go away.

How?

<u>Who</u> drugged her?

It didn't make any sense. She didn't remember drinking anything that was out of the ordinary.

But now that she thought about it, she couldn't remember much of last night either.

Olli looked down at herself and groan-sighed. "Aces...a <u>skirt</u>?!" she protested, mostly out loud. "Not <u>again</u>!"

"Hey!"

Olli started involuntarily at the voice that cut through the soft buzzing that hummed in her ears. She grunted and picked up her head a little, squinting against the light that hit her eyes.

When did it become light out?

"You have to get up."

Olli winced and looked toward the sound, resisting the urge to close her eyes, lay back down and sleep again. "Wha?" she wondered, her voice scratchy in her throat.

A blurry figure of a man hovered near the edge of wherever she was.

"Where am I?" Olli grumbled, trying to pick herself up. Her hands flailed around a little and found two edges that seemed solid. She tried to pull herself up and flared her eyes a bit when the world spun and her head throbbed.

"Where you shouldn't be. Get out of my club. Go be drunk somewhere else. Home perhaps."

Olli blinked a couple of times and forced herself to swallow. "Drunk? Who's drunk?"

"You."

"I'm not...<u>drunk</u>." Olli tried to pull herself up again and made it up to one elbow. "I was <u>drugged</u>."

"I don't care if you think that you're the queen. Time for you to go."

Olli muscled herself up a little further and half glared, half squinted in the general direction of the hazy-man-figure. "That's not going to happen."

"I don't know why you think that you have a choice."

"Where's my friend?" Olli re-directed.

"Doesn't matter to me." the man-figure stepped toward her.

Olli gritted her teeth and willed her left foot up. By sheer will-power alone, she managed to connect her foot to the figure and shoved him back a few steps. "Aces." she managed to get herself sitting upright, finally realizing she was in a booth against the wall of the building. Olli looked around for a moment and then finally managed to focus on the man that was in front of her.

"What do you think you're doing?!" he demanded. "Throw the drunk broad out of here."

Olli held up a hand and shook her head a little. "I have a better idea."

"You'll be leaving all on your own. Great."

"Or you could call the police." Olli shrugged, blinking a little hard, trying to clear the cobwebs out of her brain.

"Why would I do that?"

"Because someone drugged me in your club and my friend is gone."

"Sure your friend didn't just leave you behind?"

Olli shook her head. "She would never do that. She may be a bit of a flake sometimes, but she wouldn't leave without telling me."

The man put his hands on his hips. "She wants me to call the cops. Let's call the cops." He walked toward the front of the building. "Don't go anywhere!" he called back over his shoulder. "Don't let her leave!" the next order was tossed to the three other men that were standing in the room.

Olli closed her eyes for a second and tried to ignore the ringing that echoed through her head. She blinked a couple of times and rested her head on the first two fingers of her right hand, using her elbow on the table to prop herself up.

The phone rang.

Dallas cleared the top of the second flight of stairs and started toward the office. As he walked, he started to run the zipper on his jacket down.

The phone rang again.

Dallas' eyebrows knit together. That sounded like the phone in their office. He sped up a little more, wondering where Olli was. It was about the time of the day when she should have been in.

Maybe he just beat her by a couple of minutes.

Dallas trotted a couple of steps and brushed through the door of the office at the same moment that the phone rang for the third time. He walked up to Olli's desk and scooped up the phone. "District Detective Office."

"Oh good. You're in."

Chapter 5

THE ONE WITH THE PRE-ARREST CALL

Dallas blinked and pushed his left arm out in a sharp gesture to get his sleeve back a few inches so he could see the face of his wristwatch. "I get to work this time just about every day. I don't usually get a phone call to celebrate it..."

There was a tired sigh. "*It's too early for this. Where's your partner?*"

Dallas looked around the office and shrugged. "I'm not sure."

"*I am. I'm looking at her right now.*"

Dallas stiffened. "Who is this?" he demanded, suddenly suspicious.

"*Mack.*"

Dallas searched his memory. "As in <u>Harrison</u>?" he wondered, leaning heavily on the name.

"*That's the one.*"

"Olli's with you?" Dallas wondered, looking back at the door of the office half over his shoulder. He tilted the receiver down past his jaw and tipped his head slightly. He brought it back up to his mouth. "Are you <u>sure</u>?"

"*Hey. Listen. She's over her demanding that you come down here. She won't go home. Keeps carrying on about being drugged again? All I know is I'm about two minutes away from arresting her.*"

Dallas pinched the bridge of his nose and closed his eyes for a second before he blinked them back open. "What? Where are you exactly?"

"*Know the dance hall near tenth?*"

Dallas thought for a moment. "Sure. Sure, I'll be right there."

"*You've got ten minutes. Then I'm arresting her.*"

"I just said I'll be right there. You don't need to do that man. ...nothing good is goin' to come from it." Dallas hung up the phone, deciding to ignore whatever it was that the detective on the other end of the line said.

Dallas zipped his coat back up and walked out of the office. He trotted down the steps and tried to figure out why Olli was at a dance hall still. And why it was that Olli was only a few minutes away from being arrested. "It's too early in the mornin' for this," he muttered to himself as he rushed down the first flight of stairs.

"*Dallas? I thought that I heard your voice. Have you left already?*" Dee's voice popped up in his ear as he was about halfway down the next flight.

34

Dallas stepped off the last flight and sighed quietly. "Good morin', Miss Dee. Yes. I was in the office, but I got a phone call. And apparently Olli's already out causin' trouble."

"*Already?*" Dee sounded skeptical. "*It's a little early…isn't it?*"

Dallas snorted and half shook his head. He stepped aside so a couple of detectives that had just entered the building could get clear of the door. He smiled and dipped his chin a little and stepped into the right revolving door. "That's exactly what I said."

"*Where are you off to?*"

"A dance hall off Tenth. I'll brin' her back with me."

"*A dance hall…They're not even open at this time of the day.*"

Dallas nodded and trotted down the front steps to the sidewalk. "My thoughts exactly." He walked to the edge of the curb and looked over traffic, waiting for a hack.

The first one he saw. He tossed his hand up and whistled sharply. He tossed his hands a little and watched the hack drive past.

At this rate, he was going to have to go straight to the police station.

Two more tries later and the third hack rolled to a stop at the edge of the curb.

Dallas pulled the back door open and dropped in. "Thanks for stoppin'."

A cowboy hat pivoted and a friendly smirk flashed from under it. "It's nigh on my job t' pick ya up."

Dallas chuckled. "Mornin', Monte."

Monte touched the brim of his hat. "Where t'?"

"The dance hall on Tenth?"

Monte blinked a couple of times and turned to look at him. "Come agin?"

Dallas nodded and grunted. "I'm off to meet up with Olli before she gets arrested."

Monte stared at him for a second, arm resting on the top of the backrest of his seat. "Beg pardon?"

Dallas shrugged and pulled his fedora off. "That's what I thought. But Mack Harrison is there and bothered to call me to warn me."

Monte turned forward. He merged into traffic quickly. "Why would she git arrested?"

Dallas relaxed against the seat and shook his head a little. "You would know better than me. What <u>is</u> their beef?"

Monte chuckled and shrugged a little. He glanced at Dallas in the mirror. "Hones'ly. It was before my time. Those two have been goin' a' it since they were children, from what I understand."

Dallas looked a little unconvinced and shook his head. "Well. Apparently, they're in the exact same place."

Monte grunted. He drove through the next intersection and turned left at the first alley.

Dallas sat quietly and rotated his hat in his hand as Monte drove him toward the dance hall. "What in the world is goin' on…"

"I want her out of here! I called you to make her <u>leave!</u>"

"Sir. She'll be leaving in just a couple of minutes—"

"I'm not leaving just because you're talking for me, Mackenzie," Olli interrupted, stepping into the conversation and folding her arms.

"Don't make arrest you."

"I'd like to see you try." Olli stared at him. "I'm not leaving until someone tells me where Gloria is."

"Gloria?! You're still friends with her?"

Olli looked at him and tilted her head. "<u>Aces</u>. What is <u>that</u> supposed to mean?!"

"You know what she does."

"And I know what <u>you</u> do..." Olli shrugged and tilted her head a little. "Good thing I don't make my friends based on how they make their money."

"Hey, Boss? There's a detective here that says you called him? Says he's from WDA."

"Yeah, let him in." Mack waved his hand in a thoughtless gesture, while still half glaring at Olli.

"You called my <u>dad</u>?!" Olli's voice leapt two octaves and nearly cracked.

Mack put his hands on his hips and glowered at her. "Maybe I should if you keep being so belligerent."

Olli narrowed her eyes. "You think <u>this</u> is me being belligerent?"

"Mornin', everyone," Dallas wished, stepping through the doorway and looked between them. "I see that you two are gettin' along like a couple of clams."

Olli looked at Dallas and seemed to relax incrementally. "Mack is just a <u>peach</u>."

"Hey. I called your partner, didn't I?" Mack snapped.

Olli glowered at him. "You could just look for Gloria like I asked you to...or believe that I've been drugged..."

"You've really got to stop. The man said you were passed out drunk—"

Olli stared at him for a moment and looked at Dallas. She took a hard, frustrated breath and her eyebrows went up slightly.

Dallas pulled his fedora off and cleared his throat. "Maybe before I take sides, someone could tell me fully what went on?"

"I woke up here this morning—"

"She assaulted the man over there that owns the place."

"He tried to grab me after I told him to call the cops." Olli shrugged and looked at him blandly.

"Maybe that's because you were being an annoying broad!"

Dallas held up his hand and half stepped between them, facing Olli. He looked at her and tilted his head a little, imploring her with a look to stand-down.

Olli took a breath and then closed her mouth. She clamped her lips together and folded her arms.

"See? Even your <u>partner</u> thinks—"

Dallas pivoted and looked at Mack, his expression hard. "Do you mind entirely? Someone around here has to be an adult. I don't know what history the two of you have and frankly I'm—"—Dallas shook his head a little and shrugged—"<u>really</u> not all that interested."

Mack sized him up for a moment and pursed his lips a little. "So, you're taking her side then."

"I am her partner." Dallas shrugged. "But I didn't say that either."

Olli wrinkled her nose and made a protesting noise behind his back.

"<u>However</u>," Dallas continued, ignoring the noise that Olli made, his voice stern and pointed so no argument would be made, "if you use that same tone and call her somethin' like that, you and I might have a problem. And I might just step out of her way and see if the stories about the fights in school were true."

Olli smirked and scoffed a little. The next moment she rubbed her forehead a little, her left eye closed, and sighed quietly.

Mack slowly relaxed. "Fine."

Dallas nodded once slowly and stepped out from between them. "All right. Olli—"

"I was in the booth over there."

"Good. Go stand over there and I'll meet you there in a minute." Dallas gestured toward the booth.

Olli looked the direction he pointed and walked back toward the booth that she woke up in.

"I don't understand how you can work with her," Mack grumbled.

"For one, I'm not stupid enough to think that I'm smarter than her," Dallas mused, turning to look at him. "Why don't you tell me what's goin' on?"

Mack shifted like he was irritated at being questioned and adjusted his hands on his hips. "All right fine. You know I really don't have to tell you. I can just make her leave."

"You're not worried about the friend that's missin'?" Dallas tilted his head.

"Why would I be. It's Gloria."

Dallas waited for a moment, expecting some sort of explanation. "You're goin' to have to fill me in. I'm not from here like you."

"Maybe you should just let me tell it so that you can get out of here like you want to," Olli called from across the room.

"You'd just love that wouldn't you!"

Dallas whistled sharply, the sound echoing sharply across the dance hall. "All right." He turned to look at Mack. "Do you want to just hand this off? I may be new here, but in the last few months, we've bumped into you a half dozen times and you two do not get along. Why not wash your hands of it?"

Mack looked at him for a moment and then shrugged. "Yeah. Sure. Sounds good to me. The less time I have to spend with her the better."

"Oh, thank goodness! And here I was, worrying that you thought that the feeling wasn't mutual!" Olli snapped.

"Olli!" Dallas looked over at her harshly. "You're not helpin' or being very professional either. Let it go."

Olli huffed slightly and leaned against the edge of the booth.

"I'm good to take off?" Mack jerked his thumb toward the door.

Dallas nodded. "Yeah. I'll talk to everyone here. You go ahead."

"Good luck with that, man." Mack waved his hand a little and looked at Olli pointedly before walking toward the door. He snapped his fingers at the two cops that were floating nearby.

Dallas watched the three of them walk out the door and turned to the man that was sitting at the far edge of the room. "Sir?" he walked toward him. "Can you tell me what happened here?"

"I already told the other officer that just left."

Dallas sat on the nearest stool at the bar and rested his elbows on the bar top. "I understand that. But I'm going to be takin' over this case—"

"Case?!" he scoffed. "There's no case! She won't leave and dared me to call the cops."

"It's been mentioned." Dallas nodded.

"You know, she kicked me right here." He poked his chest between his ribs. "I'll probably have a bruise!"

"And I'm very sorry about that. Her fight or flight tends to lean a bit more towards fight in scary situations." Dallas pivoted to look at Olli for a moment and frowned a little. "She said that you tried to grab her?"

"She wouldn't leave. Dumb broad."

"That's Olivia Wainwright. Daughter of Alan Wainwright? She's the District Detective. The words 'dumb' and 'broad' will not be used to describe her for the rest of our conversation, do I make myself clear?" Dallas nodded once when the man nodded. "Good. What's your name?"

"Royce."

Dallas nodded slowly. He waited for a moment, hoping for more information and then nodded once. "All right. Royce. Why don't you tell me what happened? Last night, this morning...anythin' and everythin' that you can think of."

Royce shrugged and shook his head. "Not much to tell for last night. It was busy. I didn't see your friend last night. If I had, I would have tossed her out for drinking." Royce rubbed a glass and held it up to the light from the windows to check for fingerprints.

Dallas watched him for a moment. "Quite a thing to say from a man who's acting like a barkeep right in front of me..."

Royce looked at him, unamused. "There's a Prohibition going on, Friend."

Dallas nodded. "I know." He looked over Royce and tapped his fingers on the bar top. "So. What do you serve to your guests then? Since there's a Prohibition goin' on and everythin'?"

Royce shrugged. "Patrons order drinks, I make them but without any alcohol."

Dallas nodded slowly. "You're the only one makin' these drinks?"

Royce wiped the newest glass in his hands. "If that girl got that drunk here, it's not because of a drink that got made at this bar."

"So you're sayin' that someone walked into this dance hall with their own drink?"

"It's a busy place, and people will do what they want. I'm not their father."

Dallas tilted his head and nodded slowly. "So you really have no idea what happened to Olli."

"She got drunk. And then accused <u>me</u> of drugging her!"

Dallas nodded slowly. "Did you see her at all last night? She has a very bright dress on. Did you see anyone near her?"

Royce looked at him for a moment like he thought that Dallas was insane. "It was wall to wall. I didn't go looking for girls."

Dallas grunted. "All right. Just a couple more questions and then you can get back to not bein' a bartender."

Royce nodded and sighed like he was irritated at the thought but couldn't stop it anyway.

"What time did you get here this mornin'?"

"About three hours ago."

"And when did you call the police?" Dallas watched him closely.

"About an hour ago now?"

"You're not sure?"

"I didn't check the clock the second before I called."

"And you were here for almost two hours before you noticed Olli?" Dallas wondered, tilting his head slightly as he asked the question.

Royce looked at him for a moment and frowned. "I wasn't exactly looking for random people sleeping off a drunk night in my booths."

Dallas held up a hand slightly. "I mean no offense. Just tryin' to understand what happened."

Royce shrugged a little and then bobbed his head. "I left last night around two-thirty. Back here again at around nine. We don't open until five, but I had some paperwork to do and I didn't want to be disturbed." Royce looked at Dallas like he blamed him for everything but was resigned that there was nothing that he could do about it.

Dallas pursed his lips and nodded a little. "How did you notice that she was here?"

"She made a little noise. I happened to be near her and heard something like a sigh. I thought it was strange since I was the only one in the building."

Dallas nodded slowly and then looked at the two men that were sitting at a table, playing cards. "What about them? When did they get here?"

"About the time that I found the girl."

"Who are they?"

"My bouncers."

"Do they always show up for work five hours early?"

"I let them if they want to. I have them help me move things. Or keep unwelcome people out while I'm here."

Dallas grunted and nodded. "All right. I won't take any more of your time." He stood up and started to the booth that Olli was leaning against.

"Just get her out of here soon, will you?"

Dallas turned to look at him for a moment before nodding. "Sure." Once he was across the dance floor, Dallas leaned his hip against the opposite side of the booth that Olli was up against. "Seems like I can't leave you alone for longer than a couple of hours..."

Olli looked at him blandly for a moment and snorted. "Apparently not."

"What happened? Why are you in a dress?" Dallas used his fedora to gesture to her. "Why is it the second that you have a dress on things start goin' weird."

Olli tossed her hands and shrugged. "This is why I don't wear dresses often."

"What happened?"

"Gloria's gone and it's my fault." Olli picked at her right thumb nail and gnawed on the inside left bottom corner of her lower lip.

"Who's gone and why would that be your fault?" Dallas tilted his head.

"Gloria." Olli sighed and glanced toward the front of the building like she was checking to see if there was anyone listening to them.

"I thought that you were goin' out with Miss Birdie?"

"I did." Olli nodded. "Her real name is Gloria."

Dallas looked a little confused for a moment while he processed the fact that The Phoenix's main singer had an actual name. "Her name..."

"Gloria isn't that great of a stage name. Some guy sometime said that she sang like a bird, and it stuck." Olli shrugged. Plus, it means that she can live in the normal part of town and not be arrested."

"But _you_ know it. Shouldn't _you_ arrest her? Isn't that our job?" Dallas clarified, looking Olli over for any physical injury.

Olli looked insulted for a moment. "I don't because she tells me anything that I want to know when I ask. That's worth way more to me than if I booked her for what she does." She shrugged. "I'm not even sure what we would arrest her for."

Dallas thought for a moment and bobbed his head. "Sure. Fair." He looked at her for a moment and shifted the brim of his hat back and forth in his hands for a moment. "So. Want to tell me what happened?"

"She can tell you what happened outside, right?!" Royce called across the room.

Olli looked over at him and then looked at Dallas. "Aces, the man is really bent out of shape about me being in this building." She leaned forward a little. "It's almost like he's hiding something."

Dallas looked at her like he was wondering the same thing. "One step at a time, right?"

Olli nodded. "I guess we can get out of here for now. Come back later if we need to."

Dallas grunted and gestured for her to go ahead of him as they walked away from the booth. "Were you sitting at that booth last night?"

Olli shook her head. "That table over there." She pointed to the tall table that she remembered sitting at.

Dallas stopped and looked at the table. "You were over there?"

Olli nodded. "Yes."

"How did you get over there?"

Olli took a breath and thought for a moment. "There...there was a guy."

Dallas looked at her slowly. He stared at her for a second like he didn't know who she was. "There was a what?"

"It's not like I came out cruising for a date!" Olli looked at him with her nose wrinkled. "Aces." She waved her hand and started toward the door. "He just popped up at the table. Bought me a drink."

Dallas pivoted to watch her. He held up a hand and cleared his throat. "Wait-wait-wait." He trotted a couple of steps to catch up to her. "Someone bought you a drink."

Olli stopped short and looked at him. "I was drinking South Sides—fake ones—obviously." She waved her hand a little. "And it was like the third or fourth one a girl dropped it off and told me someone at the bar bought it for me."

"And you just...drank it?!" Dallas looked at her, his eyes flared, hands swung out and head tilted sharply. "Olli, you just...drank it?!"

Olli froze and looked at him. "Aces!" She tossed her hands and covered her face. "Oh, I'm such an idiot!"

"Did you see who sent it over? How much of it did you drink?"

Olli shook her head and walked a few steps before groaning and shaking her head again. "I basically finished it!"

Dallas rushed a few steps to catch up with her. He grabbed her arm and pulled her to a stop and held up a hand. "You drank a drink that someone sent over without even thinking about it. Are you all right?"

Olli looked at him for a moment and then shrugged. "My head is still buzzing. But yeah, I'm all right. I'm more worried about the fact that Gloria's missing."

"Are you sure that she's missing?" Dallas pushed the door open for her and paused a beat for her to go ahead of him.

Olli stepped through the door and looked back at him. "Yeah. She wouldn't have left without trying to find me."

"Fox…" Dallas walked a couple of steps, pressing his fedora onto his head, and offered his arm. "But…be fair now. The man who runs the place didn't realize that you were there until almost two hours after he showed up."

"So you think that she wandered around the hall once and then gave up and walked out?!" Olli protested, spinning to look at him.

Dallas held up his hands a little. "Hold on. I just…I'm just askin'."

"I know that she seems like the sort of person that isn't the least bit real. But she's…" Olli fumed for a minute and pivoted to walk toward the hack that was sitting on the curb.

Dallas rushed after her. "Wait for me!"

Olli pulled the front passenger door open and smiled. "Monte. You know where Gloria lives right?"

"Mornin', Oliver. You look like a proper girl!"

Olli half rolled her eyes and sighed as she nodded, her eyes fluttering closed. "Yeah. I know. Gloria wanted to go dancing and she insisted that I wear a dress—" Olli stood up and looked back at the building sharply. "Aces!" she looked at Dallas wildly. "My clothes!"

"The clothes you were wearing yesterday?" Dallas looked at her and his eyebrow dipped.

"Yes! I bought this on the way…I don't remember where I left my clothes…"

"All right. Let's go make sure that Gloria's all right, and then we can double-back and look for your clothes. Maybe Gloria has them?"

Olli took a breath, physically calming herself down, and half-ducked her head to see Monte. "Same question."

"Do I know where Gloria lives?" Monte offered, smiling at her a little.

Olli nodded. "Yes."

Monte shook his head. "Sorry, Oliver."

Olli looked at him, shock crossing her face. "You don't?"

Monte looked at her for a moment. "I don' know where everyone lives."

Dallas walked up to the hack and scoffed a little as he leaned on the hack. "You're jokin' right?"

Monte looked between the two of them. "I don'!"

Olli made a small, surprised noise before looking back at the dance hall.

"What is it?" Dallas wondered.

Olli shrugged and took a breath. "That jacket is really special to me. I don't want to lose it."

"If you do, we can get you another one," Dallas offered.

Olli shook her head. "Not like that one. That one I've had since…well, since I was in school."

"You bought that when you were in school?"

Olli glanced at the him and then stepped into the hack. "Yeah…bought."

Dallas scoffed and stepped forward to the hack. "Would you like me to go look for it and you can go check to see if Gloria is in her place?"

Olli nodded and pulled the door closed after her. "Thank you."

Dallas waved a hand slightly and nodded. "Go on. I'll go lookin' for it."

"It's in a paper bag. Honestly, I don't care about the other clothes. I just want the jacket."

Dallas nodded. "Store logo?"

Olli shook her head. "It's plain."

"Did it come into the club with you?"

"Checked it with the coat check."

Dallas pivoted and walked back toward the dance hall. I'll find it. Go see if you can find Gloria."

Olli leaned out of the car slightly for a moment and nodded. "All right." She pulled herself back into the hack and shifted in the seat to look at Monte. "All right. You don't know where Birdie lives…guess that means that I have to give you directions." She smirked at him.

Monte snorted and nodded once. "You do. Where we goin', Oliver?"

"The apartment building on Glendern."

Monte thought for a moment and then started the hack. "Glendern. She lives in a better part of town than you do."

Olli grunted. "Don't remind me."

Monte pulled away from the curb. "Glendern. You've go' it."

Olli shifted a little in her seat and adjusted the skirt of her dress.

Monte glanced at traffic and then back at her. "A dress, huh?"

"Gloria insisted that we go dancing, and I wasn't allowed to wear pants and boots." Olli looked at him and tilted her head a little when he laughed. "Aces. It's not that big of a deal! I've worn a dress a couple of times."

"Sure. But...no' a whole lo'."

Olli rolled her eyes. "I can't wear it for work. I'd get into a lot of trouble."

"I know. It's jis' nice t' see you wear one."

Olli looked down at herself and bobbed her head a little. "Thanks, Monte."

Monte looked over at her. He reached over and shook her shoulder a little. "Hey. You feelin' all righ'?"

Olli blinked a couple of times and half shrugged. "I'll be all right."

"Yore lookin' a lil green around th' gills there, Oliver." Monte glanced at her and frowned a little. "Are ya sure ya wan' t' go find Birdie?"

"She's on the third floor. I can make it there, check to see and then sit down. If I look as bad as you say, Dallas won't let me do anything else."

Monte nodded slowly and took the next corner carefully. "Glendern and then the office."

Olli nodded and smiled a little. She scooted down in the seat a little further and rested her head on the top of the backrest. She let her eyes close, content that Monte would bring her to where she needed to get without any further watch or request.

Monte looked at her and frowned a little. He drove through traffic quietly, making sure to keep the movements gentle and soft. He made one more turn and carefully rolled to a stop in front of the biggest apartment building on the block and turned off the motor.

Olli blinked her eyes and squinted. "Are we there already?"

Monte looked over at her and smiled slightly. "Wha' number?"

Olli looked at him, half out of sorts. "Hm?"

"Third floor. Wha' number?"

CHAPTER 6

THE ONE WITH THE APARTMENT

"I can go."

Monte scoffed a little. He picked up his hat and set it on her head. "No. You stay righ' there."

Olli looked like she wanted to protest before she nodded a little. She swallowed a little and shifted a little lower in the seat. "Thanks, Monte," she mumbled, pulling the hat down a little lower.

Monte reached over and shook her shoulder again, gently. "Oliver? Th' number?"

"Twelve. Third floor."

Monte nodded once. "Don' le' anyone walk off with th' hack." He opened his door and stepped out in one smooth motion. He gently closed it behind him.

Olli snorted a little and rolled her eyes under the hat. She sunk down a little lower in the seat and took a small careful breath, trying to ignore the nausea that washed over her.

She hated the feeling of waking up from a drugging.

Monte breezed into the building and started up the wide-swept steps that curled up the outside right-hand edge of the main lobby to the second floor. He quickly made the first landing and followed the curve of the stairs up to the next floor. He marveled at the fact that the singer lived in a building like this.

Only a few blocks away from the large Victorian house that Olli's grandfather had built for his family, this building was on just as grand of a scale as the house that Olli slept at every night.

And the fact that a speakeasy singer could afford to live here was beyond him.

Maybe he was in the wrong business.

Monte walked down the hall after he reached the third-floor landing. He looked at the gold-plated numbers next to the doors and stopped at the door with a large gilded twelve next to it. He knocked on the door and leaned his head slightly to listen to any movement from the other side of the door.

Nothing.

Monte frowned a little and knocked against the door again, his knock a little sharper and more demanding. "Miss Gloria?" he wondered as he knocked again.

There still wasn't any noise from the other side of the door.

Monte frowned and reached down to try the knob, for no other reason than curiosity.

The door swung open just a couple of inches the moment that his fingers touched the doorknob. The strike plate was broken in toward the apartment.

Monte looked at the strike plate and then at the door itself. "Oh, oh," he mumbled to himself. He used his elbow to nudge the door open. "Miss Gloria?" he wondered again, half leaning around the front edge of the door.

The little bit of the room visible from where Monte stood looked like a tornado had flown through it.

Monte blew a breath out and looked around for a second. He carefully pulled the door back closed. He spun and power-walked to the stairs and charged down them quickly.

"Oliver."

Olli started and half groaned. "Aces."

"Oliver, you're goin' t' wan' t' see this."

Olli opened her right eye and pushed the hat up on her head a little so she could see him a little better. "See what?"

"Come on. Call Dallas." Monte pulled the door open and offered her a hand.

Olli looked at his hand balefully for a second before taking it and standing up and out of the car. "All right. I'm coming."

Monte closed the door and walked her to the building. He opened the lobby door for her.

Olli walked in and looked at the stairs for a moment. "Why are we calling Dallas?"

"You all righ'?" Monte wondered. "You'll see."

Olli looked at him and swept the hat off her head. She shoved it toward him. "Here. I don't need this."

Monte took the hat and set it back on his head. He shook his head and walked to the stairs with her.

Olli started up the staircase. One hand firmly on the railing as she took each step.

Monte matched his pace to hers and walked with her slowly. He didn't complain.

It took a few more minutes than the first time to make it to the third floor.

Olli walked up to the door with the gilded twelve and looked at Monte. "I don't see any reason to call—"

Monte nudged the door open a few feet.

"—Dallas..." Olli's voice trailed off as she watched the door swing freely. She stepped into the doorway and looked through it. "<u>Aces</u>..."

Monte grunted.

"Yeah. We need to call Dallas."

Monte nodded once and picked up the collar of his shirt to get it closer to his mouth. "Miss Dee, can you git Dallas down here?"

Olli stepped past the threshold and walked into the apartment, looking around her carefully. She walked into the main part of the apartment and looked over the general chaos of the room. "What did you get yourself <u>into</u>, Gloria?" she wondered, half shaking her head.

Dallas stepped out of the hack. "Thanks. I appreciate it." He ducked his head a little and smiled at the man driving in the front seat. After elbowing the back door closed, Dallas stepped onto the sidewalk. He adjusted the black leather jacket that was hung over his left arm. His eyes ran over the front of the building, and he whistled, mostly to himself.

A <u>singer</u> lived here. This building was in better shape and more high class than the boarding house that he lived in. He walked to the main door of the building and pulled it open.

If he hadn't been so worried about the fact that Dee said Monte had called and that he was needed here right away, the lobby would have given him pause.

It was grand, looked only just a couple of years old too.

Dallas trotted up the first flight of stairs quickly. He switched the jacket to his right arm. The next two flights went up quickly. "Olli?" he called, looking down the hallway.

Monte stepped out into the hallway and raised his hand in a short wave. "Down here."

Dallas nodded and walked toward him quickly. "What's goin' on?" he wondered, looking at Monte skeptically. "Why were you the one to call me in?"

"I called cause I'm th' one with Miss Dee's ear righ' now." Monte shrugged. He glanced at the jacket and smiled. "You found it!"

Dallas nodded. "I did. Dumped in an alley almost two blocks away."

Monte tilted his head a little. "Tha's a ways away...sure it's hers?" he gestured Dallas toward the open doorway. "This way."

Dallas reached past the zipper and felt around inside the jacket for a moment. He pulled out the well-loved wallet and flipped it open.

Monte glanced at the badge and ID and smiled a little. "I see. Quite a powerful level of detective work there."

Dallas snorted and stepped into through the open doorway. "Fox? I've got your..." his voice trailed off as he looked around the room that he was suddenly in. "What in the world?"

Olli was perched on the far-most front edge of the daybed styled couch that ran along one edge of the living room. Still looking a bit pale, but otherwise put together.

A far cry from the disorganization of the room around her.

Dallas' eyes took in the broken, upside down chair and the rest of the cushions of the couch flung across the room.

There were a few pictures that had dropped to the floor. The single picture on the wall still was leaning at a hard angle. There were a few knickknacks that looked like they had been thrown across the room. There was a hole in the plaster not far from the couch.

"What...happened."

Olli looked at him. "I'm guessing you believe that someone absconded with Gloria now?"

Dallas glanced around the room again. "I believed you before."

Olli looked at him dully. "Did you."

"I wanted to be sure, Olli. <u>Now</u> I am." Dallas looked down the hallway that was just to the right of the couch that Olli was sitting on. "Does the rest of the place look like this?"

Olli shook her head. "No. The bedroom doesn't look much different than her bedroom usually looks."

"She means it's such a mess tha' you couldn't tell if it was <u>actually</u> a mess," Monte piped up.

Dallas looked back at him and then faced Olli again.

Olli shrugged and bobbed her head. "He's not wrong."

Dallas grunted. "All right. I think we need to put this on <u>you</u>." He pulled the jacket up off his arm and opened it for her. "And then we're goin' to figure out when this started, and how we're goin' to fix it."

Olli looked at the jacket and cracked a small smile. "I can't believe you found it."

"We got the jacket back. We'll get Gloria back too." He turned and looked around the room for a moment. "Know anyone that would do somethin' like this?"

Monte stood up a little straighter and tilted his head. "What are you askin' me?"

"Do you know anyone that would do somethin' like this to Gloria?" Dallas repeated.

Monte tilted his head and clicked his tongue. "I don' run in tha' circle. How am I supposed t' know?"

Dallas looked at him with disbelief. "Come again? You don't expect us to believe that after you just finished runnin' 'shine for Razor?"

"Monte doesn't get involved. He drives."

Monte tapped his nose and pointed at Olli quietly.

Dallas looked at Olli and then at Monte. "You've got to be kiddin' me."

"I never go' involved." Monte shook his head. "It didn' concern me. I pick th' produc' up. Drop it off where it needs t' go."

"What about when you weren't drivin'?" Dallas protested.

"Remember when I said tha' I did th' lon' hauls?" Monte shrugged. "If I was around, I was tryin' t' catch up on sleep."

Dallas sighed and nodded. "Yeah, I remember you saying that..." He put his hands on his hips for a moment. Dallas looked around the room one more time while pushing his hat up higher onto his head. "What about you?" he looked at Olli.

Olli took a long breath and half shook her head. "I've been sitting here since we called you, trying to figure out how I could have possibly thought that drinking while we were at that dance club..." her voice trailed off and she shook her head again. "There was an Auburn following us all afternoon. Gloria kept demanding that I stop letting work interfere with the fun we were having. She wanted to dress shop." Olli rubbed her face for a moment. "She wanted to have a fun day with her girlfriend, and all I could focus on was that car. I begged her to let us do something else, tried to get her to go home—or to let us go through alleys and take hacks—She was having none of it and I caved." Olli looked at him and sighed, her lips pursed tight. "Aces. I let this happen."

Dallas let her ramble for a bit and then shook his head. He walked over and sat-leaned against the arm of the couch. Dallas pulled his hat off his head and looked at her for a moment. "It's not your fault. You know that."

Olli looked at him for a moment and frowned a little. "It is. And I know that you're just trying to make me feel better about the fact that I went against my instincts..."

Dallas held up a hand. "Olli, Olli stop." He looked are her and dipped his head a little. "Fox. You know very well that you did nothin' wron'."

"And yet my best friend is still missing."

"I'm <u>righ'</u> here," Monte mused, a small smirk on his face.

Olli looked over at him and tried to glare at him but ended up fuming for a moment.

Dallas looked over at Monte and shook his head dryly. "Monte," he admonished.

Monte shrugged a little. "Jus' tryin' to ligh'en th' mood."

"It's all right, Dallas. He's just trying to make me feel better for letting my friend get taken. Just like you are."

Dallas grunted. "You know...they clearly thought that you were a threat."

Olli smirked, and her head shook a little. "Aces...I thought of that. Once...once my head stopped hurting enough for me to process what was going on."

Dallas smiled at her. "So. The man that drugged you. Did you know him?"

Olli shook her head. "No. Haven't seen him before."

"Think you could work with Miss Dee and make up a sketch?"

Olli shrugged. "Maybe...maybe."

"Yore lookin' a little green, Oliver. Maybe you should lay down?" Monte wondered, tilting his head slightly, his voice filling with concern.

Olli frowned a little and rubbed her face again. "You're probably right."

Dallas nodded. "Monte will bring you home, and I'll go to the office and see what kind of things that I can cook up at the office. Don't come in until you feel better."

"I should come to the office, too."

"Fox. No." Dallas shook his head. "You look like you feel terrible."

"I do feel terrible." Olli pushed up off her knees and stood up with a soft grunt. "But Gloria's been gone for at least eight hours. The longer we wait, the worse it's going to be. Did you talk to the bartender? Had he seen her?"

Dallas stood up and held his hands out around her without touching her, trying to make sure that he was prepared if she swayed too far and fell.

Olli blinked a couple of times and shook her head. "Aces..." she carefully swallowed. "Did you talk to the bartender about her?"

"He didn't see anything, Fox. And was rather upset that I asked the same question that the cops had asked."

Olli pursed her lips and frowned. "Mackenzie asked if he noticed Gloria leaving with someone?"

Dallas shrugged a little. "Honestly, I'm not entirely sure that he asked about her. He seemed to think it was so out of the realm of possibility that you two are still friends."

Olli rolled her eyes. "Mack always was an A-class idiot."

Dallas scoffed quietly. He turned to look at Monte. "Well. Olli''s not hurtin' too bad. We can stop worryin' now. She's still crackin' jokes."

Olli looked at him dully.

Dallas swung his hat for a moment, half awkwardly. "All right. I think we need to take you to the hospital—"

"Hospital?!" Olli's voice cracked slightly. "Aces! No. I'm all right."

Dallas plunked his hat on his head and shook it slightly. "No. You're lookin' really green, Fox."

Olli folded her arms. "No. I want to go home then."

Dallas looked at Monte. "You heard the lady. Time for her to go home."

Monte touched the brim of his hat and stepped around the half-shattered coffee table and offered his hand to her. "Come on, Oliver."

Olli looked between the two of them and took his hand. "All right. Aces. All right. I will go home until lunch. And then I'm coming in and we're going to figure out where Gloria is."

Dallas scooped her jacket out from under his arm and draped it around Olli's shoulders. "All right. Let's just start with you gettin' you home for now."

Olli smiled a little and gripped Monte's arm with one hand and the jacket with the other. "All right. But...get started without me?"

Dallas smiled. "Of course I will, Fox. I've got a lot of questions to ask and a lot of ground to cover. I'll catch you up the next time that I see you."

Olli looked at him, trying to make sure that he was telling her the truth. "You promise."

"Of course I do." Dallas nodded.

Olli smiled a little, and half leaned against Monte in a moment of unsteadiness.

"All righ' time for you t' ge' home," Monte announced, hooking his arm around her ribs, under her jacket. "Dallas. I'll be back for you in about ten minutes."

Dallas nodded once. "I'll still be right here."

Monte smiled a little and started to guide Olli toward the front door of the apartment.

Olli walked with him, her pace slow but strong. "I'll see you this afternoon, Dallas."

"Of course you will, Fox. And I'll have a full report ready."

Olli looked back at him and smiled a little. She walked down the hallway with Monte and looked up at him. "Monte-"

"If yore abou' t' ask me if I can brin' you somewhere other than yore house..." Monte looked at her sternly. "I'll drive you straigh' t' th' hospital and you can tell all them wha' happened."

Olli clamped her mouth shut and shook her head a little. "I wasn't going to."

Monte looked at her closely, clearly not ready to believe her, but nodded once. "Good. Yore allowed t' have a mornin' off here and there.

"I just spent half a year away from work," Olli complained.

"Tha' doesn' coun'." Monte shook his head.

Olli looked up at him and frowned a little. She started down the flight of stairs, keeping her pace slow and controlled.

Monte matched her pace and didn't complain at the amount of time that it took to get down to the main lobby. He guided her out of the front door and straight to the back passenger door of the hack. "You go ahead and lay down. I'll ge' you home before you can fall asleep."

Olli dropped into the seat heavily. She nodded slightly, her face a bit more pale. "Ok." She scooted into the hack a little further before laying across the seat and using her jacket as a pillow.

Monte gently closed the door and walked to the front door on the driver's side and softly settled in under the steering wheel.

Dallas watched them go and looked around the room. He couldn't believe how destroyed it was.

It didn't make any sense. Why would someone, very nearly, turn the whole room upside down? Especially since it was just <u>this</u> room.

Was there something that was in this room?

Or <u>not</u>?

Did Gloria tell someone that she had something that she really didn't? It wouldn't be the first time that someone had lied to impress someone that wasn't their friend.

But what could a singer at a speakeasy possibly have lied about having that someone would do <u>this</u> to her apartment?

Dallas set his hands on his hips and walked to the far end of the room. He spun and looked at the room from the new angle. After standing where he was for a few more minutes, Dallas pushed up on the underside of the brim of his hat.

Maybe he was trying to bite off more than he could chew, asking the questions about the room. Maybe they should try to figure out what it was about the singer that made someone want to take her.

"Why would I want to take a girl that <u>sings</u> at a speakeasy?"

The room didn't respond.

Dallas was reminded how terrible it was to have to work alone. No one to bounce ideas off of. He sighed quietly to himself and looked around a little more.

"Dallas?"

"I'm still here," Dallas looked over at the general direction of the door.

Monte walked into his line of sight and smiled once. "She's restin'. I don' think she's goin' t' stay there lon'."

Dallas grunted and looked over at him and pursed his lips tightly. "Sometimes I hate that about her."

Monte grunted and half shrugged. "She's a Wainwright."

Dallas looked at him and adjusted his hat a little. "Are you sayin' that she inherited the insane need to constantly be workin'?"

Monte picked up a chair that was upended and sat on it. "Her granddad built that agency. I can' imagine tha' was an easy task."

Dallas watched him and bobbed his head. "That's true."

"I think...I think tha' she works so hard cause...well..." Monte pulled his hat off his head.

"Because she's a woman in a man's world?" Dallas offered.

Monte nodded and spun his hat in his hand a little. "Yore the firs' one tha' she's me' who gives her an actual chance."

"You aside," Dallas pointed out, shifting a couple of pillows that were on the floor with his right toes.

Monte nodded once. "True. I don' coun'."

"Of course you do. You've been her friend almost as long as Birdie has." Dallas froze and thought for a moment. "Did you know that she had an actual name?"

Monte shook his head. "I didn' even know tha' Th' Phoenix had a singer."

Dallas stared at him for a moment. "You're jokin'."

Monte shook his head again and looked at him seriously.

"How could you not know?" Dallas tilted his head and moved a couple other things with his foot.

"I was ou' drivin' all th' time." Monte glanced over at him.

"All the time?"

"And I don' drink."

"You've never actually been in the club?" Dallas looked at him in a half-disbelieving way.

Monte scoffed. "Sure. Bu' no' when it was open."

"Birdie wasn't around when it was closed?"

Monte shook his head. "It usually was jist me an' th' boss."

Dallas sighed and looked around the room again. It didn't make a whole lot of sense that Monte had never seen the singer, but he couldn't argue with it either. "So you have no idea why...this happened?"

Monte shook his head and shrugged a little. "Oliver would be the one to know..."

"And she doesn't."

Monte shook his head.

Dallas stood where he was a moment longer and then pivoted to look at him. "Let's go. It's not doin' me any good standin' here staring at somethin' that I don't know what I'm lookin' at."

Monte stood up and plunked his hat on his head. "Back t' th' office?"

Dallas looked over at him. "Good. Yeah. I think so."

Monte started toward the door. "Unless there's somewhere you want t' go t' ask questions."

Dallas followed him and shook his head. "No. I've asked everyone anything that I could ask."

Monte shrugged and stepped through the doorway.

Dallas pulled the door closed and fussed with it to get it to stay closed. "We're goin' to have to get that fixed..." he mumbled.

Monte glanced back at the door and nodded. "I'll stop at th' office a minute."

Dallas shook his head. "I can do it too. You don't need to go out of your way."

Monte grunted softly. "Jist th' driver?"

"I would never." Dallas shook his head. "Olli would be more insulted than you would."

Monte scoffed and shook his head as he trotted down the stairs next to Dallas.

"Think she's all right?" Dallas wondered when they were about halfway down the second flight of stairs.

Monte frowned a little and bobbed his head. "I sure hope so."

Dallas grunted softly and looked around the building as they made it to the lobby. "Does it surprise you that she lives here too? Or is it just me?"

Monte shook his head and shrugged a bit. "I'm happy for her."

Dallas nodded. "Absolutely." He looked at the small door across from them. "I'll go tell the buildin' supervisor. You'll get the car?"

Monte nodded and started toward the main door. "I'll be at the curb."

Dallas half waved after him and started for the door that had a plaque:

Building Super

Dallas walked to the door and knocked. He leaned against the door frame for a moment and waited for an answer. His eyebrows knit and he knocked again. "Hello?" he wondered.

The door swung open a minute and two more sharp knocks later. A squat man with a bulldog face looked up at Dallas and tilted his head. "Whaddya want?"

"I'd like to request a new lock put on the door for apartment three twelve?"

"You live there?"

"No sir, I kno—"

"If you're not the resident, I'm not going to change anything for you."

"I don't want it changed. I want it replaced."

"What's the difference?"

"The difference is the lock that's on the door is currently broken." Dallas shrugged a bit. "Which makes it a little hard to function as a lock."

"Who broke it?"

"I was hopin' that you might be able to tell me." Dallas shifted his weight a little. "Hear anythin' strange comin' from the third floor at some point?"

"The residents like to be left alone. I don't interrupt them."

"Did you notice anyone else that was up there? Someone who didn't belon'?"

"You don't belong."

Dallas looked at him for a moment and resisted the urge to sigh or roll his eyes. "I see. So there was no one hangin' around at some point yesterday that you saw?"

"I already told you no."

"And you didn't want to think about it for a half moment longer?"

"Don't need to."

Dallas grunted and shook his head a little. "All right. Thank you for your time. Could you still please put a new lock on the door?"

"Which apartment?"

"Three-twelve."

"I'll see what I can do. I've got a lot on my plate."

Dallas looked at him and then back at the building at large. "I appreciate it."

"But not until the person who actually lives in three-twelve asks."

"Do you know who that is?"

The bulldog head swung back and forth. "I don't mix with the tenants. We're not from the same places in life."

Dallas couldn't argue that point. "And if I told you that it was a friend of mine who lived there and I'm worried about her apartment being one slight breeze away from being completely open for the whole world to see, would that change things?"

"Where's your friend?"

"Not home."

"When your friend gets home, and asks, I'll change the lock on the door."

"Hey." Dallas stuffed his foot into the opening between the door and the frame. "My friend is gone currently. An unknown amount of time."

The bulldog turned to look at him and sighed. "Fine. But if that's the case, then I have to call the cops."

Dallas pulled the wallet out of his pocket and flipped it open. "I'm a detective at Wainwright detective agency."

"So, you're not a cop."

Dallas didn't know how to respond to that. The man wasn't wrong. Technically. "No?"

"Then I'll just call them and get them to sign off on the lock change."

Dallas nodded slowly. "I'll just call them myself, then. Save you the dime." He walked toward the front door.

CHAPTER 7

THE ONE WITH THE CALL TO THE POLICE

"Miss Dee?" Dallas wondered, pulling the right side of his collar up.

"*What is it?*"

"I'm goin' to need some police here." Dallas pushed the door open just enough that he could step two steps out of the building. "Monte? We're goin' to be a bit."

Monte nodded.

"I'll call you back?" Dallas wondered.

Monte offered a thumb up before walking to the driver's side of the hack.

Dallas watched as the hack started and drove away from the curb. He turned and stepped back into the building. "Dee?"

"*I've called them, Dallas. They should be to you in a couple of minutes.*"

Dallas nodded once. "Thank you. Tell them which apartment I'll be in, will you?"

"*You've got it.*"

Olli shifted in her bed and huffed quietly under her breath. She took a heavy breath and blinked a couple of times. A quick shifting stretch, and Olli gave up completely on trying to keep her eyes closed.

She felt restless. She wanted to keep sleeping. Everything was tired and felt heavy. Better than before, but still tired. Her brain was the problem. Racing hither and yon trying to figure out what was happening, why she and Gloria were targeted, why they just left her there instead of taking her too...did they drug Gloria? If they didn't, why would they drug her, but not Gloria?

There were too many questions. And it wouldn't be easy to answer them here.

Olli rolled over and looked up at the ceiling above her bed. She stared at it for a moment, trying to will herself to close her eyes and leave them closed. She knew that Dallas would want her to stay where she was. The second that her father knew, he'd order her home. And, as the man in charge of Wainwright Detective Agency, it was his call to make.

Maybe if she hurried, she would make it to the office before Dallas would be able to tell Alan about what had happened. If she was <u>there</u> and looked like she was doing better, Al would surely let her stay.

Modified assignment was better than having to lay in bed and try to keep her eyes closed. At least in the District Detective Office, she would be able to do paperwork and try to piece together what had happened last night.

She <u>hated</u> nothing more than paperwork, and yet it was preferable to laying here and trying to get her eyes closed.

Olli tossed her hands up in the air and let them fall down onto the bed and her stomach loosely. "Aces. Fine." She sat up and ignored the slight swirl of disorientation. She blinked and swung her feet over the edge of the bed and stood up.

The dizziness wasn't too bad this time. She shrugged a little and walked over to the closet quickly. Time to change into something a little better for work.

Olli opened her closet door and looked back at the bed, smiling a little. She couldn't believe that Dallas had been able to find her jacket.

It didn't take Olli long to get dressed. She sat on a deep-toned walnut chest to pull on her backup pair of knee-high, lace-up motorcycle boots. They were a few years older than the boots that she had been wearing the day before. The ankles were a little more wrinkled, and the soles were a bit more worn, but they were good enough to survive another day. And that's exactly what she needed them for. Olli patiently pulled the laces snug, starting in the middle of her upper foot and working her way all the way up her shin right up to the base edge of her kneecap. She gnawed on the inside left corner of her bottom lip and tied the laces off. Olli stood up and pushed her deep blue, wide-legged pants over her knees. She took a step and shook her foot with each step as she walked toward the door.

Olli grabbed her jacket as she walked through the door. It was time to get to the office.

Dallas rubbed his thumb up the top edge of his nose and rested the bottom ridge of his eyebrow bone on the tip of it for a moment while taking a slow even breath and closing his eyes. He blew the breath out between his lips, trying to let out the frustration and impatience out with it. His head tipped back up and he dropped his hand as he opened his eyes.

Olli was right.

Mackenzie had swooped in and instantly started to big-foot around, acting like Dallas hadn't been waiting for him, asking the same questions that Dallas had asked the building super.

If the irritation at the questions being asked—despite the fact that Dallas had told Mackenzie the answers that he had been given already—was bad, Dallas was becoming downright ornery at the questions that Mackenzie was asking <u>him</u>.

"I'm sorry, Detective." Mackenzie looked at him. "Am I boring you?"

Dallas folded his arms and narrowed his eyes at him. "I already told you. We've been through <u>all</u> of this, just three hours ago. And, last time I checked, you were furious that you even had to listen to what we were sayin'. <u>Now</u> you want to listen?"

Mackenzie looked insulted. "I listened the first time."

Dallas tilted an eyebrow. "Worried that I'm going to tell a different story this time?"

Mackenzie shook his head. "More like hoping that you don't. Look. I know that Olivia and I don't get along very well, but I saw the papers. The Silencer and Cross Bay Louie put away in the space of a year...she must not be a <u>terrible</u> detective."

"I'll make sure to tell her that you said so," Dallas mused dryly.

Mackenzie looked at him for a moment and then shrugged like he wasn't the least bit concerned if Dallas was offended or not. He rubbed the outside edge of the first knuckle of his left hand against the left side of his nose. Up and down once.

Dallas' eyebrow tipped slightly. It wasn't the first time that Mackenzie had made the motion since he arrived at the apartment. Curiosity crossed his mind again with the motion. It seemed like a habitual motion when Mackenzie was frustrated. "Listen, Mack—"

"Mackenzie."

Dallas held up a hand and nodded in an allowing way. "My apologies." He looked at Mackenzie seriously and cleared his throat. "Mackenzie, if you don't mind tellin' the buildin' super to change the lock on the door, Olli and I will handle the case."

"Whoa, whoa, whoa." Mackenzie held his hands up and looked at Dallas, insult washing over his face. "What makes you think that you're going to be heading up this case?"

"The fact that you wouldn't even know there was a case if I hadn't called you down here? Since you didn't believe Olli when she told you that Gloria was missin' back at the dance club."

Mackenzie rubbed his knuckle up and down his nose.

Dallas' eyebrow dropped slightly. So <u>Olli</u> was the trigger. That was interesting. Something he'd have to ask Olli about at a later time.

"Look. I don't know why Olivia still spends time with that Gloria. I doubt she's missing. She probably ran off again. She's done it half a dozen times."

Dallas looked over at the mess in the living room and tilted his head. "You think that she did this? Before she ran off...again?" he wondered, looking at Mackenzie.

Mackenzie stared at him for a moment. "Are you done?"

Dallas tilted his head slightly. "So...yes?"

"Are you doing this because of what I said about Olivia?" Mackenzie tilted his eyebrow.

"Feelin' guilty about what you said about her when she couldn't defend herself?" Dallas countered, watching him.

Mackenzie rubbed his knuckle against his nose. "No."

Dallas grunted. "Look, you don't want the case, anyway. We both know it. And if you <u>do</u> take it, that means that you're goin' to have to work with Olli. At least a little bit. She's all messed up in it." Dallas shrugged.

Mackenzie looked at him for a moment. "Are you serious right now?"

Dallas nodded, choosing to ignore the tone that Mackenzie had used. He switched his fedora from his right to his left hand. "Let us run with it. Olli's so close to it, she's goin' to want to have her nose buried in it, anyway. It won't bother me. But it <u>will</u> bother you. I don't know Gloria all that well, but I get the feelin' that you don't like her all that much. I think she deserves a fair shake. Can you give her that?"

Mackenzie looked at him for a long moment.

Dallas held out his hands and swung them back, his left hand dropping the fedora onto his head as one motion. "You know what? This is our case. You can tell the super to replace the lock on your way out. Tell your boys not to touch anythin'." He walked toward the front door.

Mackenzie looked after him for a moment and narrowed his eyes. "I didn't agree."

"You also aren't goin' to actually try to work this case. And it's not somethin' that Olli's goin' to be able to let go of.It's better this way. You know it is."

Mackenzie nodded once and shrugged, not seeming to care about the conversation or his involvement in the case any longer. "Have fun. It's going to be a bit of a snore."

Dallas opened the mangled front door with a nudge of his foot and gestured for him and the three cops with him to walk out. He followed them and closed the door gently.

It didn't close completely, and rocked back open a few inches.

Mackenzie stopped in front of the bulldog-faced man and spoke to him quietly for a moment, gesturing toward the door as he talked.

Dallas stood next to the door, waiting to see what happened.

"He says I gotta change the lock? And you're in charge here now." The bulldog man walked up to the door and half pointed at it.

Dallas looked at the door and nodded once. "I would really appreciate it."

"We'll see you around, Stowe. Good luck with that girl. She's trouble." Mackenzie shrugged and walked to the stairs and started down them, his cops in tow.

Dallas nodded and grunted once. "And there's the difference between us. I think she's brilliant, and I really enjoy the trouble we get in."

Mackenzie made a scoffing noise that echoed up the stairwell.

Dallas shook his head. He leaned against the wall, just to the left of the door frame.

Bulldog looked at him and then the door. "What are you doing?"

"Waitin' for the new lock."

"But that'll take me a few hours..."

"I got all day."

"You want me to run to the hardware right now?"

Dallas pushed his hat up a little and half smiled with a firm edge. "If you don't mind."

Bulldog sighed like it was the largest inconvenience of his day.

Dallas smiled tightly, though it wasn't completely able to reach his eyes. "I'll be right here."

Bulldog sighed dramatically and nodded once. "I'll just go now then."

"I appreciate it."

Bulldog turned and walked away from him, his jowls moving a little as he walked.

Dallas adjusted his weight against the wall and settled himself into the wait that was about to happen. He checked his watch.

It was going to be a long afternoon.

Olli stepped out of the hack and adjusted her jacket down a little lower on her hips. She closed the door behind her without looking back at it and started toward the front steps.

Up three tiers of concrete steps, right up to the right revolving door of the two that were set into the building at the top of the landing.

She pushed through the door, not moving fast, but keeping herself at a steady pace. Her eyes slid up to the large clock face bolted to the soaring stone wall to her left, out of sheer habit.

Almost two.

She must have slept longer than she thought. That was good. Hopefully, Dallas would forgive her for showing up to work at all today.

Olli walked through the lobby, not bothering to look at the front desk, or the detectives that were sitting at desks scattered around the room to create space and keep the whole room tastefully full of people.

There were a few desks that were empty, proof of hard times everywhere. The Depression hadn't slowed crime down, but it certainly had taken a bite out of people spending money to figure out whatever it was that bothered them about their lives.

Alan had been very careful to only get rid of the detectives that were ready to retire or move onto something else. And when they had left for greener pastures, an attractive severance package following them through the door, no one was hired on to fill their spots.

Olli glanced over the lobby one more time before trotting up the stairs that dug into the left wall of the lobby and started toward the second floor. She trotted up the stairs, slowing down as she reached the top.

This floor was quieter, only a couple dozen desks.

Olli raised her right hand in a small greeting to the men that were working behind the desks.

Two of them smiled and nodded in a friendly enough way. A couple actually waved.

Olli walked around the corner to the last flight of the steps in the stairwell. She walked up, zipping her jacket down. It was a little too warm now that she was three flights up and the air was still. Olli shrugged out of it and hooked it over her left elbow as she walked down the hallway to the left of the stairwell.

This floor was the quietest so far. There was a conference room and three offices.

The president's office, where Al spent most of his time, the office that belonged to Al's partner, Jake, who was in charge of the detectives on the bottom two floors, answered to Al, and kept things moving along smoothly; and the last office which was the biggest on the floor. It was behind that door that Olli spent nearly all of her time.

The District Detective office.

The brass plaque on the door was eye level. Below it were Olli and Dallas' names. Each on a separate plaque and riveted to the door.

Olli smiled to herself and walked up to the door. She brushed through it and walked into the room. "Dee? I'm here. Is Dallas back yet?"

Dee appeared just a couple of feet away from her, dressed in a snappy bright green business suit. She smiled in relief and looked over Olli like she was inspecting her for injury. "Where have you been? You're so late! Are you all right?!"

Olli held up a hand and nodded a little. "I'm just fine, Dee. Just had to sleep it off."

"Dallas told me what happened. Are you sure that you're not hurt?"

Olli looked at the girl that appeared to be her age, though completely holographic and could be foiled by a power outage. She smirked and shrugged a little. "Nothing that I can't handle. Is Dallas back yet?"

"No? I thought he was with you?"

Olli tilted her head and then shook it. "No. Aces...did he not tell you what all happened?"

Dee huffed and shook her head. "I have no idea what all I know and what I don't know."

Olli walked to her desk and sat on the front edge. She hefted her weight up and back with her palms. She hooked her ankles together and swung her legs a little. "All right. Since he's not here, I'm assuming that it's because he's still stuck at Birdie's apartment."

Dee held up a hand. "Why is he at Birdie's apartment? He _knows_ where she lives?!" she looked at Olli and pointed her finger at her pointedly. "Do _you_ know where it is?"

Olli nodded. "I know her real name, too. Dallas does now too."

Dee stood where she was for a moment and then took a small breath while shaking her head. "I have so much more to learn, apparently. What is he doing there?"

"Someone took her, Dee. And they tossed her place too."

Dee pressed her hands against her cheeks and gasped sharply. "Gracious. But why?!"

Olli shrugged. "I don't know. Yet."

"Is she all right?"

Olli frowned a little and shrugged her shoulders. She picked her hands up off the desk and folded them in her lap. "I honestly don't know, Dee. I'm hoping so. We're going to find her, though. One way or the other."

Dee nodded. She pulled her hands away from her face and smoothed her skirt a little. "How can I help?"

Olli stared at the floor-to-ceiling windows to her left.

Dee stood where she was a couple more seconds before she cleared her throat. "Olli?"

Olli blinked and looked over at her. "Hm?"

"You're staring out the window again."

Olli blinked again and tilted her head. "Sorry. What did you say?"

"How can I help?"

Olli took a long breath and scrubbed at her face. "I really don't know yet."

"All right. Let's start at the beginning." A chair appeared just behind Dee, and she sat down on it primly. She adjusted her skirt. A disappointed look crossed her face and the chair under her got taller, so she was eye level with Olli. "All right. Tell me everything that you can remember. Nothing is too small."

Olli took a breath and closed her eyes for a minute. "There was an Auburn. Couple of years old—"

"An Auburn?" Dee glanced up at her, a notepad blinking into her right hand and a pen into her left. She wrote on the pad and then glanced at Olli. "What's the significance?"

Olli watched the wall across from her split down the middle and start to open up. She shrugged a little and watched the note that Dee had just made on her pad get printed out like an invisible typewriter was moving. "I'm really not sure, honestly. But for some reason it followed us around for most of the afternoon."

"Tell me where you first saw it," Dee instructed, pen scribbling a couple of notes. "You know that you're going to want to have it."

Olli nodded. Dee was right. "All right. I met up with Gloria just out side of The Corner Diner. After I had lunch with Dallas..." Olli talked for a while, her legs swinging together, apart and one-at-a-time as she ran through the events that she could remember. Her eyes went between watching out the window at the skyline and running over the notes that were typing out across the computer screen.

Dee scribbled out everything, her pen hand racing across the notepaper and resetting quickly. She didn't look at her hand, she watched Olli's face and nodded a couple of times. A few well-placed questions kept the information flowing. The notes on the computer screen readjusted themselves and organized so that like information was together.

Olli shifted a little and looked impatient. She stood up and started to pace the width of the computer screen as she talked, not watching the information adjusting and moving itself around. She ticked off thoughts on her fingers as she talked. Her focus shifted to Dee and back to the windows or the wall that she was facing.

Dee glanced at her and then back to her notepad as she pivoted the chair she was sitting on to face Olli better. The chair perfectly changing mid-shift to a rolling, pivoting office chair to suit her needs.

Olli frowned a little as she talked and looked at the office door.

"What is it?" Dee wondered, her tone soft.

"Why isn't Dallas here?" Olli tilted her head and looked at Dee curiously.

Dee shrugged a little. "I'm not sure, Olli."

"Should we call him?"

Dee looked at her and shrugged one shoulder slightly. "If you want."

Olli made a grumbling noise and looked over at her. "I wouldn't even know where to call him."

"Where did you see him last?" Dee wondered, folding her hands in her lap, the notebook and pen blipping away from her hands in the middle of the motion.

"Gloria's place."

"Maybe he's still there?"

"Why would he still be there?" Olli tilted her head.

"Why would who still be where?" Dallas wondered, swinging the door open and stepping into the office in one motion.

Olli pivoted to look at him and smiled a little. "Dallas."

Dallas smiled at her and pulled his fedora off his head. "Afternoon, Fox." He set it on the top hook of the hall tree and unzipped his brown leather jacket. "I didn't know if you were goin' to be here."

"I couldn't sleep anymore." Olli shrugged. She shifted a little on her feet. "Where've you been?"

"Where have I been?" Dallas repeated, hanging up his jacket on the hook next to Olli's. "The apartment."

Olli's eyebrows jumped. "You only just got back?!" She shook her head and scoffed. "<u>Aces</u>!"

Dallas grunted and pulled his tie loose a few inches. He undid the top two buttons on his neck and looked at her like he was half exhausted. "So, I spent some more time with your friend Mackenzie."

"He is <u>not</u> my friend," Olli scoffed, half laughing as she talked.

"No, he is not," Dee echoed, her eyebrows going up as her chin tipped down and she discreetly scratched her head behind her right ear, her eyes flaring a little.

Olli looked over at Dee and frowned a little at the tone that she used. She shrugged and shook her head. "Why?"

"I just thought that it was such a good time at the dance hall," Dallas quipped, rolling the sleeves of his shirt up to the middle of his forearms.

Olli watched the movements, a little bit of her body language relaxing at the habitual movements. "Oh. I see. You're just a glutton for punishment."

Dallas snorted. "I just wanted to have a new lock put on the door. The super wouldn't do it without the police sayin' that he could."

Olli tilted her eyebrow and leaned against one of the black leather chairs facing her desk. She shifted her weight against the top edge and folded her arms. "I don't understand...did he not know that you work here?"

"I told him." Dallas shrugged. "He insisted that he would only do it for a cop."

Olli closed her eyes and shook her head a little. "All right. So you had him call the police?"

Dee cleared her throat. "Or me."

Olli glanced at Dee, slightly to her left, and a few inches more toward the windows. "You called them?"

Dee nodded. "I didn't ask for Mackenzie, to be clear."

Dallas shrugged. "Don't worry about it, Miss Dee."

Olli sighed and shook her head. "Honestly, he probably heard about the call and inserted himself."

Dallas shrugged. "Either way. There's a new lock on the door, so Miss Gloria won't have to worry about someone walkin' into her place uninvited for the time bein'."

Olli grunted. "Unless they're inclined to kick the door in again."

Dallas looked semi-corrected and nodded. "True."

Olli took a beat and pursed her lips. "Aces...I don't even know why it was tossed in the first place."

"Would she be keepin' somethin' there for someone?"

Olli looked at him for a moment, her expression thoughtful. "I don't think so."

"You don't think so?"

"I don't know for sure, but she's smart enough not to hold things for people."

Dallas looked at her for a moment and tilted his head. "Are you sure?"

"Yeah." Olli tilted an eyebrow. "Aces, why?"

"I'm just checkin', no need to get up in arms about it."

"But why."

"How much time do you really spend with her, Olli?" Dallas looked at her seriously.

Olli pursed her lips and adjusted her arms a little, like she didn't want to process the question for a minute. She folded them tightly over her ribs and her eyebrows knit.

"She wouldn't take anythin' right?"

Olli sighed like she was suddenly tired, and half shrugged, half shook her head. "Honestly, Dallas...you're right. I haven't spent a whole lot of time with her."

"You don't have any ideas why?"

Olli's arms unfolded and her hands came up to her face. She rubbed her fingers up her nose, across her eyebrows, down her eye sockets, across her cheekbones, down around the front of her ears, along the underside of her jaw and off her chin. The movement slow, like she was trying to massage the thoughts in her head out of her mouth. She sighed softly and shook her head. "Honestly, tonight is the first time in probably...seven months that I've spent time outside of her cage-dressing room-with her."

Dallas watched her and bobbed his head. "I'm just tryin' to help you get to the bottom of this."

Olli looked at her feet, kicked out almost too far in front of her, right ankle over her left. "I know."

"Anythin' that you can think of."

Dee cleared her throat. "I have notes."

Dallas leaned a little to look past Olli. "You have notes?"

Dee stood up and nodded. "Olli just finished debriefing me on everything she remembered. I'm sure she's a little braindead." Dee glanced at her and smiled like she was looking out for her. "Olli, why don't you take something for that head, and I'll fill Dallas in on what you told me?"

Olli blinked her eyes a couple of times and looked at Dee. "Hm?"

"Why don't you just relax for a minute?" Dee wondered, her tone gentle.

Olli licked her lips a little and nodded slowly. "Right." She stood up and walked around the edge of the chair that she was half sitting on and skirted the edge of her desk. A small sigh escaped her as she settled into the black leather office chair. Olli picked up her left foot and set it on her desk, then dropped her right ankle over her left. She sunk a little lower in her chair and closed her eyes.

"Are you tired, Fox?" Dallas wondered, looking at her in concern.

Olli nodded. "Mmmhm."

"You didn't overdo it, did you?" Dallas walked a few more steps toward the desk and looked at her closely.

Olli opened one eye and nodded. "I just wanted to close my eyes for a minute. I'll be listening."

Dee stood up and zapped to stand next to Olli. She reached out and set her hand on her head. "You're sure, Boss?"

Olli opened her other eye and looked at her with a small start. "Aces. You're a lot closer than I thought you were going to be."

Dee smiled at her. "You're sure you feel okay?"

Olli scoffed. "It's not the first time I've been drugged, and I slept all morning after I went home."

Dallas sat on the arm of one of the nearest chairs facing Olli's desk and rested his arm on the back of the chair. "All right, Miss Dee. Time to stop fussin'. Tell me what she told you. Maybe somethin' will jump out at her while you're talkin'."

Dee looked at him and nodded sharply. "Right. On it, Boss." She stepped around the corner of the desk and walked to the middle of the open space of the room.

The chair that she had been sitting on disappeared, and a small notepad appeared, cradled in her arms.

Dee pulled a pencil out from behind her ear and tapped the top of the notepad. "All right. If you turn your attention to the screen, we'll start working through this, one point at a time." She gestured with the pencil-holding hand toward the computer screen.

Dallas shifted in the chair so he was facing the computer and smiled at her a little. "All right. Tell me everythin'."

CHAPTER 8

THE ONE WITH THE STORY RECAP

Dee smiled at him and nodded. "All right. So. You and Olli went to lunch at the Corner Diner. That part, you know."

Dallas nodded and shifted the way that his jaw sat on his hand. He watched the screen as the bullet points appeared while Dee expounded on them. After a bit, Dallas peeled his eyes away from studying the screen. He swung his head around to look at Olli.

She was sitting in her chair, eyes closed, hands folded over her hips. It would almost look like she was sleeping, if it wasn't for the movement on her lower lip. She was gnawing at it, probably processing what she heard back.

Making sure that it rang true with what she remembered.

"Miss Dee? Could you pause for just a moment?" Dallas wondered a minute later, his voice quiet.

Dee paused and looked at him. "What is it?"

Dallas smiled and nodded once. "Thank you. Fox?"

"Hm?" Olli wondered, not opening her eyes.

"Everythin' all right? How are you feelin'?"

Olli opened her eyes slowly. "Fine."

"You don't look like you feel fine..."

Olli shifted and shrugged a little. "I just want to remember more."

Dallas frowned a little and pointed toward the computer screen. "Fox...most people wouldn't remember this much if they <u>hadn't</u> been drugged. Cut yourself a little more slack."

Olli frowned and rolled her eyes. "I know."

Dallas looked back at her and then toward the computer screen again. "You see all of this, right?"

Olli looked at the screen and nodded. "Yeah. Yeah, I see it, Dallas. Aces...I should have known better."

"You couldn't have known," Dee protested.

Olli gnawed on the inside left corner of her bottom lip. She sighed and blew a second long breath out between her lips.

Dallas watched her and nodded slowly. "I know that you know. But I'm goin' to say it, anyway."

Olli looked at him slowly. "That would be?"

"It's not on you that she was taken. It's not somethin' that <u>you</u> did."

Olli's eyebrows jumped up fractionally and tilted a bit. "I wish that I could believe it."

"He's right, you know," Dee looked at her and nodded.

Olli sighed a little. "Just because he is doesn't mean that I feel better."

Dallas made a face like he completely understood and bobbed his head a little. "All right." He gestured to Dee. "Go ahead. Tell me what else she said."

Dee nodded and pivoted on her heels to face the computer again. She talked her way through the rest of the notes and finally ended. "That's all she told me."

"Nigh on word-for-word," Olli grunted, sitting up a little straighter.

Dallas nodded a little as he processed the information that he had just heard. "I'm goin' to ask somethin'. And I don't want you to get frustrated with me, all right?"

Olli's eyebrows knit together for a moment, before her chin tilted up and to the left a bit while her head pulled back. "Aces, with a windup like that, how could I say anything but all right?"

Dallas smiled a little, like he was expecting her reaction. "I know that you are very firmly of the opinion Miss Birdie didn't run off and leave you at the dance club. The state of her apartment is also a pretty hard mark in your column. Now, Mackenzie-"

"Aces. What did he say?" Olli growled a little.

"You know, someday one of you two is goin' to explain to me what it is about the other that makes the two of you hate each other so much."

Olli shot him a bland look and folded her arms.

"All right. Can I just tell you what I heard? What he said? Things that I observed from talkin' with him? <u>Without</u> you bitin' my head off?"

"Good luck."

"Aces! <u>Dee</u>!" Olli looked at her secretary and frowned. She turned her attention to Dallas and smiled a little. "Yeah. I'll listen."

Dallas smiled at her a little. "He made it seem like she had a habit of duckin' away from real life. That true?"

Olli rolled her eyes and half shook her head. "Not that I've ever seen."

"How'd she end up at The Phoenix?"

"She's a singer?"

"There's <u>nowhere</u> else in this city that needs a singer?" Dallas wondered, his tone skeptical.

Olli took a breath and started to answer before her mouth slowly closed. She looked thoughtful and gnawed on the inside lower left corner of her bottom lip for a bit.

"You don't know?" Dallas' eyebrows jumped.

Olli looked a little insulted. "I didn't see the point in asking."

"You didn't see the point in askin' why your friend was workin' at a <u>well-known</u> speakeasy?"

Olli covered her face with her hands and took a slow, heavy breath. She blew it out between her fingers in a heavy sigh. "Aces." The word came out between her fingers in a tight sigh. She pulled her hands away and looked at him. "I don't know why. It...never..." Olli's voice trailed off. She pursed her lips and looked slightly irritated. "I've got to be the worst detective ever. She's been my eyes and ears for so long, I didn't even stop to think how it was that she ended up in that position in the first place."

Dallas clicked his tongue and shifted on the arm of the chair that he was perched on. "Olli," he admonished. He folded his arms and looked at her closely. "You've had a rough day. Don't be so hard on yourself. You're a brilliant detective."

Olli huffed and pursed her lips.

Dallas looked at her and shook his head. "Come on, Fox. It's not somethin' to worry yourself over. But I think that it does give us a place to start, don't you think?"

"Find out why she sings there and then maybe why she disappeared will stumble out of the shadows?" Olli wondered, looking at him like she was frustrated and tired at the same time.

Dallas nodded. "Actually, I thought that we would start somewhere else?"

Olli tilted her head. "Like where?"

"I know that you don't think that she just left you there and went about her life, but we have to check." Dallas shrugged. "Let's start at her dressin' room."

Olli looked at him for a moment and pursed her lips. "You believe him."

"I don't disbelieve him."

"Then you don't believe me."

"It's not that simple." Dallas shook his head.

"Aces, that was a diplomatic way to say that you agree with him but don't want to let me know that you're doing it." Olli looked at him blandly.

A look of insult crossed Dallas' face. "Olivia Wainwright." He shook his head. "I thought that you would know me better than that."

Olli half shrugged. "Everyone always sided with Mackenzie. I was the bad kid."

"Now see, that I believe," Dallas smirked.

Olli shot him a dull look. "Shut up."

"Allow me to explain why it's complicated?" Dallas tilted his head a little.

Olli sighed and nodded. "All right. That's fair enough."

"I might not know why the two of you hate each other, but I do know that both of you ended up on the job. And I hear that you're not the only one to follow daddy's footsteps and be successful at it."

Olli grunted.

"Which means that, whether you like it or not, we have to look at this logically and that means takin' everythin' off the table."

Olli shifted how her arms were folded and sighed a little. "I know. And he thinks that she was a flake and took off. Which means that you want to go to make sure that he's not right. Because if he is, then there's no case. And if he isn't, then we know for sure that something terrible happened to her and that I was drugged for a reason."

Dallas tapped his nose a little. "Exactly. I don't know why you would be drugged otherwise, and it's somethin' to look into as part of kickin' off this case—"

"Wait. This is our case?" Olli sat up a little straighter.

Dallas smirked and nodded. "I talked to Mackenzie. Convinced him to let us have it while I was waitin' for the door to be fixed at the apartment."

Olli smiled a little and nodded. "So, you do believe me."

"I never doubted you. You're my partner. You say somethin' is off...somethin's off."

Olli bit her lips together and nodded slightly. "Thanks."

"Dallas shook his head. "It's not somethin' that you have to thank me for. You've toed a much heavier line for me. And we didn't know each other nearly as well as we know each other <u>now</u>."

Olli smiled and blew out a small breath. "That was a while ago."

"Doesn't mean that I've forgotten it."

Olli smiled and made a small humming noise. "Well. I guess we have a trip to make."

Dee looked between them and cleared her throat. "I'm going to store these notes for later?"

"That would be great. Thanks, Dee." Olli pulled her feet off her desk and sat up straight.

Dallas pushed up and off the arm of the chair and looked at her closely and held up his hand. "Hold on just a second. Are you sure that you want to do this right now?"

Olli stood up out of her chair and shrugged a little. "Why not? Her show is supposed to go on in a couple of hours. If she's there, we can catch her before she goes out on stage. Maybe she can fill in gaps and I'll be able to figure out what happened last night."

Dallas nodded slowly. "And you're feelin' up to it?"

Olli looked confused for a moment. "Why wouldn't I?"

"Because you were drugged last night?"

"And slept most of the day away."

"And—"

"Aces, <u>and</u>?!"

"<u>And</u> you look a little pale still."

"He's right, Olli."

Olli looked over at Dee and tilted her head, her look dry and half irritated. "I don't want to be pitied or pampered or pandered to. I'm fine. I'm a <u>detective.</u> That means something to me. It means that I have to keep going even when I don't feel one hundred percent."

Dallas pushed his hands into his pockets and looked at her softly for a moment. "All right. I agree. This job isn't for the light of heart. Or those without grit. However, you're not alone anymore. And this little adventure to The District can wait a couple more hours. Rest a bit. Maybe have a cup of coffee. Honestly, better yet, tea. Let your head clear a bit more."

Olli looked at him for a moment. "You know, you're getting dangerously close to smothering me." She wrinkled her nose. "And I don't drink tea."

"You have though." Dallas tilted his head.

"That was different." Olli sat on the corner of her desk and allowed herself to look a little tired. "Cross Bay wouldn't let me drink coffee. Said it was…" Her voice trailed off while she thought. "Worker's swill."

Dallas blinked a couple of times and snorted. "Why am I not surprised?"

"Because he's incredibly pretentious?" Olli looked at him and smirked.

Dee smiled to herself and blipped out of sight.

Dallas chuckled softly. "You're not wrong. How about some water, cup of joe, and you sit for another hour or so. We'll do some paperwork or a crossword."

Olli looked at him for a moment.

Dallas waited patiently, a small smile on his face.

Olli's shoulders dropped a little. "All right, fine." She stood up.

"Whoa there. Where do you think you're goin'?" Dallas shook his head. "I'll get it. You sit down and close your eyes until I get back."

Olli opened her mouth and started to make a protesting noise.

Dallas pointed at her chair. "You know that you want to. Go on."

Olli sighed and walked to her chair again and dropped into it with less grace than usual. She sunk a little lower in the seat and rested her head back on the top edge. Her eyes closed slightly and a small sigh escaped her.

Dallas smiled and nodded. "I'll be right back."

Olli grunted softly. "Sure, Dallas." She kept her eyes closed and set first her left foot, then her right foot, onto her desk. Her right ankle adjusted to rest across her left.

Dallas smiled and left her quietly. He walked down to the second floor and started to get together some coffee for her. He was honestly surprised that she hadn't fought him more on sitting still.

She must have been tired.

Olli zipped up her jacket and shifted in it slightly. "All right. Are you ready?"

Dallas swung his jacket on and smiled at her. "I'm ready." He zipped up his brown leather jacket.

Olli picked up the fedora that sat on the top hook of the hall tree. She offered it to him and smiled. "Dee, we won't be back tonight. We'll see you tomorrow morning."

Dee blinked into the room again, just a few paces away from them. "The both of you? All right."

"Thank you, Fox." Dallas took the fedora and pushed it onto his head.

Olli looked at her and nodded. "Why wouldn't I be back?"

Dee looked caught for a moment and tugged on the top edge of her smart black skirt. "No reason."

Olli sighed softly. "I was drugged a little. I'm all right. I slept most of today after all. I'll be just fine to come in tomorrow morning."

Dee nodded once. "Yes, Boss."

Dallas opened the office door and gestured with his left hand. "Fox? Shall we go?"

Olli pivoted on her toes and nodded. "Dee, call Monte?" she requested as she breezed through the door.

"Already taken care of. He should be downstairs waiting for you."

Dallas smiled at her. "Don't fret, Miss Dee. I'm sure she'll be fine." He followed Olli out the door and gently pulled it closed behind him.

Olli stood a couple of paces down the hallway and smiled at him slightly.

"Not goin' to make me run after you?"

"I'm a little tired today. Thought I'd give us both the break." Olli smirked, pushing her hands into the pockets of her jacket.

Dallas chuckled and walked up to her. "Well. It's a nice change of pace, and I wouldn't mind if it happened a little more often."

Olli made a thoughtful noise. "I'll take that under advisement." She pivoted on her heel and walked with him, her hands still in her pockets.

Dallas chuckled softly and matched her pace down the first flight of stairs. "Do you have any idea what you're goin' to say to her if she's there?"

Olli stepped off the last riser. Her boot heels made a soft scuff-clicking noise as she walked across the tile underfoot. She took a long breath and blew it out between her lips. "I'm really not sure. I just don't see how she could do something like that to me. I'm pretty much her only friend."

"And that sort of thin' isn't somethin' to be taken lightly." Dallas looked at her and started to walk down the next flight with her.

Olli pulled her right hand out of her pocket and ran it along the polished mahogany handrail that ran down the middle of the flight. She shrugged a little.

"You think that she had a good reason."

Olli nodded and stepped onto the floor of the lobby. She walked a few more steps before shrugging. "I suppose I do. Gloria isn't that type of person. I know she looks like a ditz. But...She's sweet and kind."

"I was meanin' to ask. Why do you call her Gloria?" Dallas dropped behind her half a step so they could skirt a couple of people walking in a slight angle compared to them.

Olli glanced over at him when he stepped up next to her again. "Why wouldn't I?"

Dallas looked at her, confusion on his face. "I thought that her name was Birdie..."

Olli gripped his arm a little and pushed him off in a quiet corner not far from the doors. She opened a small, unassuming wood door. She walked into the room and gestured for him to close the door.

Dallas stepped into the room and pushed the door closed with a half-stunned look. "I've worked here almost a whole year, and I never noticed this door before."

Olli smiled and nodded. "This used to be a staircase." She half gestured around the narrow room. "Granddad had it. When he worked here he would use this to come and go without being seen. Or hardly seen."

Dallas looked at the walls around them and nodded slowly. "What is it now?"

Olli shrugged. "A dust closet."

Dallas chuckled. "What? No secret staircase to the big office upstairs?"

Olli shook her head. "No." She laughed a little. "No, not right now." She gestured around. "They had the stairs taken out."

Dallas looked around and looked at the wall to his right, furthest from the door. He turned his gaze to Olli and tilted his head. "Really? That's not a fake wall?"

Olli shrugged and shook her head.

Dallas didn't look convinced, but let it go. "All right. Dust closest secrets. I can't wait to hear this."

"Her name is Gloria." Olli shrugged and pushed her hands into her jacket pockets again.

Dallas nodded slowly. "All right. Birdie would be a...stage name?"

Olli made an impressed noise and nodded, tapping her nose. "Exactly. I never really asked, but I get the impression that it's because of the way that she sings."

"Like a bird," Dallas supplied.

Olli grunted and shrugged. "Yeah. Probably."

"Did she come up with it herself?"

Olli half shook her head and shrugged. "It's probably more likely that someone gave it to her."

Dallas made a thoughtful noise. "Right. Like most nicknames."

Olli nodded.

Dallas waited a few minutes and reached up to adjust the way that his fedora sat on his head. He dipped his head a little. "Fox?"

Olli took a small breath and blinked a couple of times before focusing on him. "Hm?"

"Tryin' to burn a hole in the wall behind me?" Dallas wondered, a slight smirk tugging at the corner of his lips.

Olli tilted her head for a moment, trying to understand what it was that had him smirking. Realization dawned a moment later. "Oh yeah, just like the first time we met."

Dallas nodded and pivoted his shoulders slightly as he turned his head to look at the wall behind him. "Huh. Look at that! There's a little singe mark right there, see it?"

Olli rolled her eyes and scoff-laughed softly, under her breath. She shook her head and jutted her jaw to the side. "Yeah, I see it."

Dallas smirked and looked at her pointedly. "Fox, are you all right?"

Olli's eyes went back and forth and she tilted her head slightly. "Aces. Why?"

"Because you were just starin' into middle distance and didn't realize what I was doin' for a solid three seconds. You're out of it. Just a little bit. Whether you like it or not, you're...not yourself." He held up his hand. "Now, don't get upset. I'm just worried about you. You're normally sharp as a tack."

Olli took a small breath and nodded. "I know. I know. I'm all right."

"I don't think so. I think you're a lot more tired and hazy than you want to admit."

Olli pulled her hands out of her jacket pockets and looked at him slowly. "What do you want me to do? I need to do my job! My _friend_ is missing, Dallas!"

Dallas gently set his hand on her arms, just a few inches below her shoulders. "I know. I'm worried about her too. Let me go to the club. You rest. If she's not there, then we know for sure that there's somethin' wrong."

Olli pursed her lips tightly and looked at him in a half-exasperated way. She looked at him closely. "You're not going to let this go, are you?"

Dallas smiled at her in a proud and bright way. "Look at that. You're already getting' sharper!"

Olli smiled brilliantly and pivoted on her right heel and took two steps toward the door to her right. "Let's go."

Dallas hurried after her and shook his head. "No. No, I'm still going alone. You're still not yourself. And I don't feel like gettin' caught tonight." He rushed after her and reached for the doorknob.

Olli's hand closed on the doorknob the same time that Dallas' hand closed around hers. She looked at their hands and tilted her head a little. Her head pulled back a little, and she tilted an eyebrow at him. "Wouldn't I have to come along to make sure that you _didn't_ by that logic?"

Dallas shook his head. "You're not completely you. That's when mistakes happen. He slowly pulled his hand back from hers, but made sure to lean against the door with his shoulder to keep her from yanking it open right away. "You've taught me a lot, Fox. I'll be just fine for one adventure without you."

Olli looked at his hand, just a few inches past her shoulder. "Let me get this straight." She shifted to face him a little better. "You're forbidding me from going into The District this time?"

Dallas looked at her for a moment and nodded when he realized that she wasn't just asking a rhetorical question. "Yes."

"Aces! <u>Why</u>!?"

"I've <u>told</u> you why!"

Olli sighed, irritation crossing her face. "You <u>do</u> realize that you really don't have a right to tell me what I can and can't do."

"I do."

"And yet you are."

"More like suggesting strongly that you don't do somethin' that could hurt you more and possibly cloud your judgment."

Olli looked at him for a moment, clearly processing. "All right."

Dallas blinked a couple of times. He took half a step back and looked at her like he had never seen her before.

"What?" Olli tilted her head.

"You just...giving in?"

"You had a good point."

Dallas reached over and laid the back of his hand against her forehead. "You <u>must</u> be sick."

Olli clicked her tongue and smacked his hand away. "Aces. If you're going to be that way, I'm going to go; anyway."

"Nope. You agreed. No takin' it back now."

Olli sighed and shook her head. She sighed a little and pulled the door open. "<u>Aces</u> fine! But I'm going back upstairs. I'm not going home. I can't lay in that bed anymore today while it's light out." She breezed out of the doorway and walked into the lobby.

Dallas followed her out and closed the door behind him. "Well. Considerin' the fact that you are the <u>most</u> stubborn person that I know...I'll take it."

Olli looked unsure for a moment before blinking and shrugging. "Well. Aces. I don't know whether to say thank you, or to be insulted. So, I'll just go back upstairs and see if I can make myself remember more things." She pointed toward the stairs that would lead back up to the upper floors.

Dallas smiled at her and nodded. "Thank you, Fox."

Olli started to take a breath and then shook her head. "All right. I'll be there when you get back."

Dallas stood where he was, watching her walk through the lobby back toward the main stairway. He waited until she was past the wall up the first flight. He waited just a few more seconds and then walked toward the revolving door. Dallas pushed through the left revolving door and walked down the concrete steps quickly.

A bright yellow hack pulled up to a soft stop at the curb, so close that it nearly hopped it.

Dallas smiled a little and walked across the sidewalk that was between the steps and the road. He opened the front passenger door and dropped into the passenger edge of the seat. "Evenin', Monte."

Monte smiled at him and dipped his chin a little. "Evenin'."

"Up for a run?"

Monte grinned and nodded. "Sounds like fun."

"I need to check on somethin' at The Phoenix."

Monte made a grunting noise and barely checked his mirror before pulling away from the curb. "You go' it. We gotta change wheels firs'."

Dallas smiled and nodded. "I figured as much." He rested back against the seat in a loose way. "Have a good afternoon?"

Monte's eyes half slid toward him. "Are we doin' this?"

"Why not?"

"Why don' you tell me how she's doin'?"

"She's in the office. She went through the wringer."

"How cranky is she?"

Dallas snort-chuckled. "Sounds like you have a pretty good handle on who she is as a person."

Monte made a long humming sort of noise in the back of his throat. He looked at him and dipped his chin.

Dallas watched the world pass by for a moment before pivoting slightly to look at Monte. "Tell me about Mackenzie."

Monte glanced at him and blew through the light that had just turned red. "In wha' way?"

"Every way. Why does she hate him? Why does his hatred for her extend to me?" Dallas tilted his eyebrow and looked at him closely.

"Why do you think I know?"

"Because for some odd reason you have your finger on her pulse. You know things that by all logic you shouldn't."

"Thankee?"

Dallas chuckled a little and bobbed his head. "I know. It doesn't sound good out loud. But seriously, Monte. I know that she tells you things. She trusts you more than anyone else that I know." He shrugged a little again. "Plus, you're the one that's known her the longest outside of my boss."

"An' you don' think he'd tell you?"

"I don't think that he really noticed it all. And honestly, I'm not entirely sure that he wouldn't be surprised that the little feud that they had in high school has continued to this day."

Monte chuckled quietly to himself as he shook his head and smirked. "High school. Didja forge' when she told you how she me' me?"

Dallas thought for a moment and then clicked his tongue. "That's right. Elementary school." He made a thoughtful noise. "How many times you figure she beat him up?"

Monte laughed quietly and shrugged. "Knowin' Oliver...too many times."

Dallas grunted. He let the silence stretch for a bit longer before he cleared his throat. "What about Birdie?"

"Wha' abou' her?"

"How long has Olli known her?"

"I'm no' really sure. At least as long as I've known her."

Dallas looked at him and pulled his fedora off his head. "So. They've been friends for a long while."

Monte grunted and bobbed his head.

"So...they're really good friends." He shook his head a little. "Why does she let her friend sing in a speakeasy? She got you a better job."

Monte stopped short for a red light. "No. She go' me a differn' job. And it was her father. Olli didn' have much more than a pout t' sway him a' tha' poin'."

Dallas caught himself on the dashboard with his left hand and slowly pushed himself back into his seat. "Sorry."

Monte shook his head. "I'm not upset. I jus'...there are some weeks...las' year I wasn' sure how I was goin' t' afford t' pay for my house."

CHAPTER 9

THE ONE WITH THE REALITY CHECK

Dallas frowned and looked over at him. "Monte, I—"

"Oh, no. I don' say tha' t' ge' yore pity."

Dallas clamped his mouth shut. "Right."

"I made it. For th' record. And I made it honestly. Before you ask."

Dallas smiled at him and made a quiet humming noise in the back of his throat. "I never doubted it. I know that you weren't gettin' paid for the runnin' you did for Razor." He smiled at him.

Monte scoffed. "Still worth it."

Dallas nodded a little. "You're a good friend."

Monte smiled and turned to head to the neighborhood where he lived. "She's offered, ya know. A differnt job. Th' girl won' take it."

Dallas grunted and bobbed his head. "Seems strange to me."

Monte shrugged a little. "It's complicated."

Dallas spun his hat in his hands a little while, he thought.

It wasn't more than ten minutes later and the two of them were back on the road, heading toward The District in the black Pierce Arrow Coupe.

Monte's spirits seemed to have lifted the moment he was behind the wheel of the powerful straight eight. He smiled brightly and regaled Dallas with stories from when he was running moonshine, before he had met Olli.

Dallas listened and asked a few questions here and there, curious and trying to understand. He brought up Olli and what she was like when she had decided that she wanted to follow her father's footsteps.

The Pierce Arrow rolled to a soft stop a few blocks from The Phoenix's back alley.

A slight drizzle had started just a few minutes after they had crossed The Line into The District. The buildings segregated to the dangerously quiet part of Big Town, turning dark more from the constant mist than the amount of water coming down.

Monte shifted his weight in the seat and looked over at Dallas quietly for a moment.

Dallas paused in the middle of pushing his fedora onto his head and tilted his head a little. "What is it?"

Monte sighed like he was frustrated and then shook his head a little. "I'm usually sittin' here tellin' _her_ tha' she needs t' be careful. Needs t' watch her back."

Dallas smiled a little and nodded. "Promise I'll be careful."

"I mean it." Monte rested his right elbow on the top of the backrest. "All righ'? Don' forgit, th' last time you were in here alone—"

"I got jumped," Dallas finished the thought. He smirked a little and chuckled. "And I met Olli." His eyes focused on something in the middle distance, a soft, fond smile on his face to match his tone.

Monte watched him and snapped the fingers on his left hand twice. "Hey. I need t' know tha' you're goin' t' focus. If you don' you're goin' t' end up in trouble again, and I don' know this place like she does."

Dallas blinked and shook his head. "Monte, if I get captured, tell her I ran away. It'll be easier for both of us that way."

Monte scoff-chuckled and bobbed his head a little. "You're no' wrong. I'll make sure she jumps off from here."

"You'd _tell_?!" Dallas looked at him, askance.

"Why no'?! She's no' goin' t' be mad a' _me_!"

"Why not?!"

"I'm her favorite."

Dallas stared at him for a moment and slowly shook his head. "You're terrible."

Monte snorted. "Go on. Git."

Dallas plunked his fedora on his head and shook his head a little. "I can't believe you're dismissin' me."

"If I si' here much longer, someone's goin' t' notice."

Dallas pulled on the door handle and leaned the door open with his weight. "There's not even anyone around, Monte. You're gettin' paranoid."

"That's what _you_ think." Monte shook his head and shooed him with his hand. "The buildin's have eyes."

Dallas swung up and out of the Pierce Arrow. "Which way is The Phoenix?" He pointed the complete wrong direction with a soft smirk.

Monte looked at him dryly. "_Go._"

Dallas laughed quietly and started toward The Phoenix at a brisk, purposeful walk. He adjusted his fedora a little as he walked.

Monte watched him walk and ducked his head a bit to watch under the top edge of the windshield.

Dallas paused just before he turned the corner and half waved.

Monte held up a hand in a small returning gesture.

Dallas took a breath and turned to walk toward The Phoenix. It was odd, walking to a known speakeasy without Olli.

It took Dallas a bit longer than he remembered to get to the back entrance of The Phoenix.

Without Olli around to be the unofficial, walking, talking map, Dallas got turned around a couple of times and almost ended up in the wrong building. Twice.

Once he had found the correct building, and the way in that he was looking for, Dallas started to relax a bit.

He stopped once he was through the doorway and gently pulled the door shut with a gentle snick. Dallas felt the wall for a moment.

A string of dim, half glitchy light bulbs started to light up overhead.

Dallas blinked a couple of times against the half-light and adjusted the way that his fedora sat on his head. He walked through the tunnel at a brisk pace. Down a short set of five stairs and a sharp right, three short stairs up, and Dallas pushed his way through the side wall of the dressing room.

He pushed a few costumes aside and stepped through the clothes rack that had been shoved up against the side wall.

Dallas looked around the dressing room and frowned. The only lights on in the room where the frosted glass lamps that rimmed the middle mirror of the three running along one wall of the dressing room.

The seat facing the mirrors was empty.

Dallas tilted his head and looked around the room, trying to suss out if there was any movement in the room.

The door yanked open and a sharp-dressed man breezed through it so fast that he almost ran Dallas down.

Dallas stepped back two steps.

"Oh, good gracious." Razor looked at Dallas and tilted his head. "Dallas! What...how...did you get into my best singer's dressing room?"

Dallas took a breath and held up a hand. "Evenin'."

Razor smiled a little and gripped his hands together. "Oh! Well, this is a wonderful surprise. I had no idea you were popping in for a visit!"

Dallas cleared his throat. "I just..."

Razor tilted his head. "Have you got time for a coffee? Or are you more of a tea man?"

Dallas shook his head. "No. No, I'm workin'."

Razor looked a little disappointed, and then glanced around the room. "Where's Olli?"

"The office."

"Alone?" Razor wondered, concern lacing the word. "Is she all right?"

Dallas bobbed his head back and forth. "She's all right."

Razor's eyes narrowed a little. "What's going on? She's not all right."

Dallas waved his hands.

Razor looked around the room and half cleared his throat. "Where's my singer?"

Dallas pointed at the room vaguely. "You haven't seen her yet tonight?"

Razor slowly shook his head. "No...I've been told that she missed the first two songs. I came up from my office to see if she was all right."

Dallas' eyes narrowed for a split second and pursed his lips. "She's not here."

"I can see that. Thank you, Detective."

Dallas pulled his head back. "Ah. <u>Now</u> I understand why the two of you have the relationship that you do."

Razor chuckled a little and tilted his head. "Why is my singer missing?"

"Who says she's missin'?" Dallas tilted his head and pushed his hands into the pockets of his leather jacket.

"You're here." Razor looked at him shrewdly. "And Olli's not with you. Which means something happened to her, too."

"Maybe I'm just on a solo run tonight?"

"She'd never allow it."

"She's not my <u>boss</u>." Dallas scoffed.

Razor smirked a little and chuckled. "I see. So there is something wrong. For how long?"

"I don't really know. I was mostly comin' to check that she was actually gone."

Razor's eyebrows knit together a little. "I don't understand."

Dallas sighed tightly and shook his head a little. "I'm not sure that I should tell you."

"Why not?"

"Because—"

"Because I'm her boss?"

"More like you're a different kind of boss."

Razor sighed a long note of understanding. "She would be terribly proud of that answer."

Dallas bobbed his head. "I think so too."

"So." Razor pushed his hands into the pockets of his pants and rocked his weight off his heels and up off the balls of his feet before slowly dropping down onto his heels again. "My singer is missing for a long while now if you're here looking for her. And you're here looking for her because our favorite detective is convinced that she's missing."

"How do you know that Olli thinks that?"

"Because I know they were out together last night."

"You know they're still friends?"

Razor shrugged and bobbed his head. "Well yeah. Sure. Of course. They went to school together. They're quite close still, from what I understand."

Dallas grunted. "I don't suppose that you would know of anyone that would want to take her?"

Razor touched a couple of the outfits like he was trying to keep his fingers busy and shrugged a little. "I can't think of anyone off the top of my head currently."

Dallas nodded a little and looked around the room. He shifted his weight, unsure of how to proceed, and looked back at Razor while taking a slight breath. "You'll let us know if something springs to mind?"

Razor nodded and glanced around the room again. "Of course I will. And in the most discrete way possible."

Dallas scoff-chuckled and pursed his lips. "I didn't think you did discrete."

"I do many things, Detective. It's part of my edge." Razor tapped the top right edge of the tip of his nose softly.

Dallas' eyebrows went up fractionally and he nodded once. "I'll keep that in mind."

"Tell Olli I hope that she's feeling better soon?"

"I will." Dallas shifted his weight back toward the way that he had come in, but caught himself before he fully committed to the movement. If Razor didn't know about the tunnel into the dressing room, there was no need to tip that hand.

Razor looked back at the main door to the dressing room that was mostly behind him and cleared his throat. "Well. I guess I can go back and tell my guests that it'll only be instrumental music entertaining them tonight." He stepped back toward the door and rested his hand on the doorknob. "Oh, Dallas?"

Dallas froze and looked at him, half caught, not knowing what made him feel that way. "Yes?"

"Do me a favor? Go back out the way that you came in? I don't need the mess of trying to explain your appearance here tonight. And locking you up in one of my cells would only cause drama."

Dallas stared at him for a minute and nodded slowly. "Understood."

"Good." Razor nodded and smiled at him in the way that one would smile at an old friend. "Have a good night. And be safe. The District is rarely safe, but it's even worse after dark."

Dallas nodded slowly, suddenly feeling like his mother was telling him to walk home from school safely. "Right."

"You have a way back, I assume?"

"Plannin' on loanin' me a car?" Dallas smirked.

Razor shook his head. "Certainly not. If you didn't, then I'd probably lock you up, but since you do..." He shrugged like the option was out of his hands.

Dallas stared at him for a moment.

Razor smiled at him brightly and opened the door just enough to slip through.

Dallas watched the door gently close and stood where he was for a moment, completely unsure what he should do next. He had always watched the interactions between Olli and Razor; he had never really been a large part of them.

If he had thought that they had a strange relationship before, knowing that the friendly respect that Razor had for Olli extended to him as well had him completely flummoxed.

Dallas shook himself and pivoted toward the secret door.

Monte looked up when the passenger door opened. He smiled and dipped his chin. "Righ' on time. Mind teachin' Oliver how t' do tha'?"

Dallas laughed and shook his head. "I'm still trying to teach her to tell me before she goes running off into the night."

"A simple no would be fine." Monte smirked. He started the Pierce Arrow and shifted it into gear.

Dallas snorted and pulled his hat off his head.

Monte turned onto a slightly wider road and started to build speed. He glanced at Dallas and frowned a little. "Lemme guess. Oliver was right. She's no' there."

Dallas shook his head. "She is not. Razor was."

Monte side-eyed him. "Was he."

Dallas grunted and stared out the window for a minute before shifting to face Monte almost three-quarters of the way. "Has he always been like that?"

Monte looked at him and then back to the road in front of them. "I'm goin' t' need more."

"He acts like we're friends." Dallas half took a breath and shook his head a little. "In fact, he acts like we're better friends than some of the friends that I've had for my entire life."

Monte sighed and shifted in his seat. "I really don' know wha' t' tell you."

Dallas pursed his lips, scrubbed his face with his right hand and ran his fingers through his hair. "Think he does it because he likes Olli so much?"

"Prolly." Monte shrugged.

"Does he treat you like that?"

"Me?"

"Yea. You."

Monte shook his head. "Las' time I talked t' him, he jist wanted me t' run for him."

Dallas made a thoughtful noise. "So yes."

"I don' know how he talks t' you and Oliver."

"He said he'd let us know if he thought of someone who would want to take Miss Birdie."

"Sounds like him," Monte's tone was dry, like the very thought didn't remotely surprise him.

Dallas bobbed his head a little. "Do you?"

"Do I wha'?"

"Do you know who would want to snatch her?"

Monte drove across The Line and tapped his fingers on the steering wheel for a moment while he thought. He shook his head and glanced at Dallas. "Sorry. I've been outta th' game for t' lon'. An' even when I <u>was</u>...I was runnin' lon' hauls. Otta state. So your guess is goin' t' be much better than mine."

Dallas sucked on his teeth for a moment and nodded.

Monte turned at the next corner and started to work his way back to WDA. He let the silence stretch, sensing that Dallas had a lot on his mind and needed to process it.

"How am I goin' to tell her that her best friend is missin'?"

Monte looked at him but didn't offer a comment.

"How am I supposed to make her believe that it isn't her fault?"

"Oliver is smart. An' she has a good heart. She already blames herself, wha' makes you think you tellin' her is goin' to make her stop?"

Dallas pursed his lips together and grunted. "I just don't want it to cloud her thinkin'."

"She'll be all righ'. She's a tough one."

Dallas looked at the front of WDA as the Pierce Arrow rolled to a stop and nodded slowly. "Thanks for the ride."

"Anytime. My pleasure."

Dallas pushed his fedora back onto his head and reached for the door handle without looking. "I'll see you soon."

"Plan on it. I wan' t' brin' her home."

Dallas nodded again and pushed the door open with his bicep and shoulder.

Monte watched him go for a moment before pulling away from the curb.

Dallas started to climb the steps to the revolving doors and looked back to check if the Pierce Arrow was still at the curb when he didn't hear any horns.

He wasn't sure why it amused him that Monte had managed to pull the car out into traffic in a space the proper size, but it did.

Dallas pushed through the left of the two revolving doors and habitually looked at the right door, waiting for Olli to step through. A moment later, he blinked and started toward the stairs that would eventually lead him to the third floor.

Odd how habits snuck up on you when you weren't expecting them to.

Olli shifted her weight in her chair and leaned over the right arm almost too far to snag the hand of her coffee mug. She pulled herself back upright and wrapped both hands around the outside of it while she read the page of the file in front of her. She shifted her hips out a little further in the seat and allowed her back to slide down deeper into the chair. Once she had leaned it back a little further, Olli switched her ankles so her left was over her right.

A quick sip from her coffee, and Olli reached a hand out to turn the next page in the file.

She started and choked on her next sip when the office door opened.

Dallas froze, halfway into the office, and looked at her, unsure of what was going on. "You all right, Fox?"

Olli dropped her feet off the desk and leaned forward in one motion, still coughing a little. "Aces." she ground out between coughs. "Yes. Yes, I'm good."

Dallas slowly stepped into the room and pushed the door mostly closed. "You're sure?"

Olli nodded again and coughed hard one last time. "Yeah. You just surprised me."

"You get surprised?" Dallas wondered, taking off his fedora and dropping it on its customary upper hook on the hall tree.

Olli shrugged and bobbed her head. "It can happen."

Dallas made a thoughtful noise and hung his jacket up. He turned toward her and took a long breath before sighing it out slowly. "I have news."

Olli looked at him and grunted. "I was right."

Dallas pushed his hands into his pants pockets and nodded slowly. "You were right."

"She's really missing then..." Olli bit her lips together and made a thoughtful noise in the back of her throat. "Any ideas?"

"I didn't find anythin' there, if that's what you're askin'."

Olli shook her head. "I'm not surprised." She scrubbed her face with both of her hands and sighed a little. "Aces! I knew something was up last night. I should have made her come back here. Or come home with me...the station."

Dallas clicked his tongue. "Olli," he chided. "You know very well that you're not to blame." He walked into the office a little more and sat down in one of the black leather chairs facing her desk. After folding his hands together and setting his elbows on the arms of the chair. "You know as well as I do that you would have looked insane."

Olli shrugged a little and flared her eyes minutely. She took a breath. "I don't know about that."

"I do. She would have been irritated. You would have questioned your judgment."

"Would not!"

"You are now."

"That's because my best friend is missing!"

Dallas tilted his head and shook his head a little. "Oh come on. I thought that I was your best friend," he teased gently, a smirk crossing his face.

Olli rubbed the dark circles that were under her eyes, the color getting a little dark. "Sure, Dallas. You're my best friend."

Dallas grinned at her brilliantly. "And as your best friend, I just want you to know..." He paused and moved his hands around a little like he was trying to gather his thoughts. "I don't think that they would have given up if they didn't succeed last night."

Olli pursed her lips and bobbed her head. "I know you're right." She reached over to the top drawer on the right side of the desk and pulled it open a few inches. She slipped her hand into the drawer and pulled out a round compact that was about the size of her palm. It had a mother-of-pearl face that had an off-set, long-tailed obsidian square set into the bottom left side of the face.

Dallas looked at her over the top edge of his coffee mug and lifted an eyebrow. He had never seen that compact before, honestly, he was quite sure that he had never seen Olli open that drawer of her desk before either.

Olli didn't notice the look, busy popping the compact open and flipping one of the sections over so she could pick up a small round of fluffy cotton. She held the compact up to eye-level and started to dab white powder under her eyes.

"What...are you doin'?" Dallas wondered after she switched to dabbing under her left eye.

Olli froze like she had forgotten she wasn't in the room alone and looked over at him, leaving her hands where they were and barely turning her head to look at him. "What?"

"That's what I asked. What are you doin'?"

"It's powder?" Olli tilted her head slightly, her tone completely confused.

"I know what it is, I'm just shocked that you have it in your desk." Dallas looked at her closely.

"I keep it around for the days that I don't look like I've been sleeping." Olli shrugged and went back to dabbing the powder under her eyes. She snapped the middle of the compact shut and picked up a bright-pink fuzzy piece of cotton and touched it against the apples of her cheeks a couple of times each side.

Dallas blinked a couple of times and watched her. "You...wear makeup when you're not in court?"

Olli snapped the compact shut and dropped it into the drawer carefully. She pushed the drawer shut and looked over at him with a shrug and a dry smile. "Never let them see you have a bad day."

"Everyone is allowed bad days, Fox." Dallas looked at her and smiled. "_Everyone_. Who told you that?"

Olli shrugged and set her heels on the corner of her desk comfortably. "Gloria said it once, and it stuck with me for some reason. It's something she would do in a situation like this..." her voice trailed off as she stared off into the middle distance.

Dallas looked at her for a moment and pursed his lips. "I wouldn't think less of you if you took a day, Olli."

Olli blinked and focused on him. "I would."

Dallas nodded, not surprised at the statement. "Good."

"That doesn't make it any easier to let it go."

"You did your best. We'll find her."

"It's been almost a full day. We're so far behind. And we have nothing new to go on either."

Dallas tilted his head and looked at her for a moment, like she had suddenly grown a second head. "You're just givin' up?"

A look of insult crossed her face. "No."

"All right. Where do you want to start?"

"What happened while you were looking for her?"

Dallas took a long breath and bobbed his head. "He knows."

"Razor knows she's missing." Olli closed her eyes and slowly shook her head. "If it wasn't bad enough that they have a twenty-four-hour lead on us, now Razor knows. Which means that we might as well be thirty-six..."

"That bad, huh?"

Olli grunted. "You've met him."

Dallas narrowed his eyes a little and tilted his chin up to the left a little. "I'm not entirely sure that I have. I've been in the same room. But I can't..." He splayed his hands out a little and moved them like he wasn't sure that he could find the right word.

"Get a handle on who he is?"

"Exactly."

"He is confusing. But they don't call him Razor for no reason."

"How _did_ that happen? I'm assumin' that he isn't the type to get an ironic name. And last time I checked, Anthony doesn't shorten down to Razor very well."

Olli snorted and shook her head. "He was younger than me when he appeared in Joey's family. Al said he just seemed to appear out of nowhere. He wasn't born here, but he went out of his way to make it sound like he was. Rose through the ranks rather quickly. He's wicked smart. By the time I was around...ten—he had Joey's ear. I guess that was only five years after he showed up."

"So he's _very_ smart."

"Incredibly."

"Which is why the sudden jump in the number of hours we're behind."

Olli tapped the end of her nose. "Exactly." She covered her face for a moment with both of her hands and blew a long breath through her lips and between the edges of her palms. "And she's his singer."

"Personal and razor sharp," Dallas nodded slowly. He held up one finger. "Although, he did promise to call if somethin' came up."

Olli looked at him dryly. "We _may_ have a strange relationship, but we're not _that_ close."

"You don't think he'd call when he promised to?"

Olli pursed her lips and shook her head a little. "No. I really don't. He's going to want to settle the score."

"Seems messy for him."

"He has men for that."

"The dirty jobs."

Olli nodded. "Oh yeah. He's smart _and_ ruthless."

"Why'd he save you then?"

"I was a kid? He had a strange attack of good conscience?"

Dallas didn't know what to say to that, so he simply grunted and bobbed his head. "So. Smart and ruthless. So what? He's goin' to have his boys go find her?"

Olli nodded. "There's a very real possibility that could happen." She pursed her lips and looked out the window for a bit. After a small breath of frustration, she turned to focus back on Dallas. "He probably has already."

"How do we beat him?"

"Beat Razor?"

"To findin' Miss Birdie?"

Olli shifted her weight a little. She tented her fingers and stared out the windows for a while.

Dallas sat where he was, patiently waiting for her to tell him what was running through her mind.

Olli watched the world outside the windows for a while. "I think..."

Dallas waited a few minutes, hoping that there were more words forthcoming. After the silence stretched a little too long, he leaned forward and cleaned his throat. "Olli."

Olli didn't move for a moment. The next second, she yanked her feet off the top of her desk and stood up in almost a singular movement. She rushed around the near corner of her desk, squeezing between the edge and the wall.

Dallas watched her and held up his hands slightly. "Whoa. Whoa, where are you going?"

Olli raced to the door of the office and yanked it open. "I have a theory." She stepped out of the office and took a sharp right.

Dallas stood up and hurried after her. "Hold on now. Care to share with the class?" He hurried to the office door and managed to catch up to Olli after jogging a few steps down the hallway after her. "Where are we goin'?"

"To talk to Al."

Dallas nodded slowly and then looked at her skeptically. "Why?"

"I just realized that maybe she didn't start working for him. Maybe there's someone who wrote her checks first. And if <u>that's</u> the case..."

"Then there's someone to start with?" Dallas offered.

Olli smiled and nodded a little. "Exactly." She walked up to the office door that was mostly closed and knocked on it."

"Well, you must not be in too much of a tizzy," Dallas mused. "Usually you just burst your way in and worry about knockin' later."

Olli shot him a dry look and half shrugged. "Maybe you're starting to rub off on me."

"Enter." Alan's voice drifted through the few inches of space between the door frame and the front edge of the door.

Olli smiled at Dallas and brushed the door aside as she walked into the office. "Hi, Al."

Alan looked up from the paperwork spread out in front of him. He smiled a little in a friendly way. "How are you feeling?"

Olli dropped into the first chair that she reached and shrugged a little. "I'm feeling more like myself every minute."

Alan nodded and glanced at Dallas, looking for his agreement. "Good."

Dallas half shrugged and bobbed his head.

Alan's focus went back to Olli. "I didn't expect you to come to me and tell me how you were feeling."

Olli smiled and folded her hands. "Actually, we came here because I have a question, and Dallas just tagged along."

"Is that so?"

Dallas nodded. "That's pretty much the way it happened."

Alan made a thoughtful noise and focused back on Olli again. "Ask away."

CHAPTER 10

THE ONE WITH THE HISTORY LESSON

"Who'd Birdie work for before Razor opened The Phoenix?"

Alan blinked. "Going to be honest, Olli, that wasn't the question that I thought you were going to ask."

Olli tilted her head. "Why?"

Alan shrugged. "Not important, I suppose." A thoughtful look crossed his face. He leaned back from his desk and tilted his chair back a bit. "And you think that since she was nabbed right out from under your nose that she's been taken by the person that Razor stole her from."

Olli nodded. "I figured, even if it's not the <u>actual</u> person..."

"At least we have a place to start." Dallas smiled and stepped over to sit on the arm of the chair next to the one that Olli was currently sitting in.

Alan made a thoughtful noise. "True. Apparently, sitting still for an entire afternoon is good for you." He smirked in Olli's direction.

Olli frowned a little and clicked her tongue. "Aces."

Dallas chuckled a little and instantly sobered when Olli shifted her whole body to look at him.

Alan smiled a little and then looked thoughtful again. "All right. Let's see if I can remember the first time that I saw her singing..."

"We were about sixteen the first time that she started to sneak around."

Alan pursed his lips and shook his head a little. "So young." Alan pursed his lips and shook his head a little. "So young." He blew a breath out between his lips slowly. "Were you really sixteen? I thought it was before that..."

Olli shrugged a little. "That's when I remember her talking about it the most. And it's right about the same time that she started to talk about cutting her hair."

"Gloria had long hair?" Dallas looked at Olli, and one eyebrow went up slightly.

Olli glanced at him and nodded. "Up until just a couple of years ago, yes."

"It was quite a shock the day that she came for dinner with a bob and bright blonde hair." Alan looked at Dallas insightfully. "I started to worry that Olli was going to do the same thing."

"Wait..." Dallas shifted slightly and slid his hands into his pockets. "She's not naturally blonde?"

"She has dark hair like me." Olli nodded.

Dallas' eyes blinked-flared. "She was a <u>brunette</u>?! Is?!"

Olli looked over at him and smiled. "Yes."

Dallas blinked a couple more times and shook his head. "But she's...so blonde?"

Alan looked between them, amusement on his face.

"There are ways to change that, you know." Olli shrugged.

"I can't even imagine her without that hair."

"It used to be long, too. Longer than mine now." Olli touched her elbow and looked at her father, waiting for him to remember.

Alan nodded. "I remember."

"That must have been a shock to see her with such short, blonde hair..." Dallas shook his head slightly and scoffed.

"She got three days of detention from our teacher." Olli smirked.

"What's she's not telling you is that she also had those three days for missing so much class." Alan pinned Olli with a disapproving look.

Dallas looked at Olli and shook his head slightly.

Olli shrugged. "Worth it."

"Was it?" Dallas wondered, his voice pitching sharply.

"I got the job that I wanted!" Olli defended.

"In hind sight I might have made a few errors..." Alan looked at Dallas and shrugged slightly. "But she's a good detective, so I'm not too upset about it anymore."

Dallas looked between them and shook his head slightly. "All right..."

"Anyway—" Olli leaned on the word before clearing her throat. "Do you remember when she started to sing for Razor at The Phoenix?"

Alan thought for a moment. He shook his head and shifted in his chair. "No. No, Razor didn't recruit her to sing at The Phoenix. She started to sing there before he took it over."

Olli sat up a little straighter and looked at him in surprise. "He didn't?"

"He wasn't much older than you are now. And at that point, he was new here and to Joey's Family."

"When did she cut her hair?" Dallas wondered.

"I think it was almost the end of summer that year," Alan answered for Olli, starting to pick up steam as the memories came back to him. "She came over just a couple of weeks before school started."

Olli nodded and smiled a little. "It happened on a weekend. I spend the night at her house on a...Thursday?"

"It was a Friday. She came over on Monday," Alan corrected.

Olli nodded slowly and then it picked up faster. "Aces. That's right. And somewhere between our slumber party and Monday night dinner, she had cut her hair short. Right up to her jaw. Just like she has it now."

Dallas whistled softly. "Did she explain why?"

Olli closed her eyes and pursed her lips together tightly, trying to remember. "There were a few different explanations...now that I think about it." Her eyes blinked open, and she looked between Alan and Dallas. "The one that she told me the most was that she got gum in it."

"She chewed gum a lot?" Dallas tilted his head.

Olli shook her head. "I didn't believe her."

"You didn't?"

"I thought she wanted to be a flapper." Olli shook her head and looked at Alan. "I was so insulted that she wouldn't tell me the actual reason I just...stopped talking to her for almost a year." Her eyes flared. "You don't think that I was the reason that she started to sing in a club...do you?"

Alan shook his head slightly and held up a hand. "You're getting ahead of yourself, Olli. And you didn't shove her onto that stage. She chose to step onto it."

Olli pressed her left hand against her forehead and stared at his desk for a minute.

Dallas watched her and glanced at Alan. "Olli?"

Olli blinked and pulled her hand off her forehead and cleared her throat. "Right. I know. It's just hard to not. I know it's not my fault for last night. Or back then—"

"It's all right, Olli. Take a breath." Alan looked at her for a moment. "You're getting yourself worked up. You won't think clearly."

Olli looked at her father squarely and nodded a couple of times. "Yessir."

Dallas looked between them.

Alan nodded. "Good. I don't remember ever seeing a brunette girl singing at any of Joey's clubs."

"Clubs?" Dallas tilted his head. "Plural?"

Alan nodded. "He had half a dozen back then."

"That's a lot of clubs for there only to be one now. What happened?" Dallas wondered, tilting his head a little and looking between Olli and Alan curiously.

Olli shrugged and looked across the desk at her father. "I don't know. Do you?"

Alan shrugged slightly. "Consolidation. It's easier to keep tabs on raids for only <u>one</u> club."

"How very logical and business smart..." Dallas mused in a dry tone.

Olli scoffed a little. She rolled her eyes and half shook her head. "That's Razor all right."

"So. Which club was she singin' at?" Dallas wondered. "The first time that you saw her?"

"That would be..." Alan scrubbed his chin and cheek. He stared into the middle distance, his eyes focused somewhere on the wall behind Olli and Dallas' head.

Olli waited patiently for a couple of seconds. When the silence started to stretch a little further than she thought it should, her right knee started to bounce. She glanced at Dallas and then looked back at Alan. "Dad."

Alan blinked. "I don't remember exactly what it was called. But it was where that big fire was last May."

"Over by the department store? The big one that opened a couple of years ago?" Olli pointed vaguely in the direction that she was talking about.

"I've seen that place!" Dallas piped up. "It's just a big grassy lot. I wondered what happened there!"

"It used to be a very large theater. Joey swooped in while it was failing and renovated it to be the best worst kept secret speakeasy in Big Town. It was very upscale. Only the richest and most influential got in." Alan shrugged a little. "As you can imagine, only the best acts would play there."

"And she was on stage there?" Dallas' eyebrow jumped slightly. "That must have been quite the shock for you."

Alan shook his head a little. "I didn't realize it was her at first."

"Why?" Dallas tilted his head.

"The last time I had seen her she was a brunette. I didn't realize it was her until she walked into my dining room for dinner a couple of days later with bobbed blonde hair to match her personality." Alan flared his eyes a little and shrugged.

Dallas looked at Olli and tilted his eyebrow.

Olli shrugged a little and shook her head. "She didn't tell me she was going to, but I wasn't really surprised she bobbed her hair."

"And the blonde?" Dallas' other eyebrow jumped to match the first.

Olli's shoulders dropped a little, and she snorted a little. "Aces, <u>that</u> was a shock."

Dallas sat quietly for a moment and then he took a breath. "I have a question."

"What's that?" Olli asked, the tone and reaction time habitual.

"How did she get on the stage of the best club?"

"Velvet Nightcap!" Alan tossed his hands slightly as he finally recalled the name.

"I thought that speakeasies weren't supposed to have names...Then I moved here." Dallas scoffed.

"They have names." Olli shrugged. "Only the worst-kept secrets are the ones that everyone knows."

Dallas grunted. "I see."

Alan pursed his lips, the memories starting to come back from the past. "I'm really not sure how she ended up on the stage of The Velvet Nightcap. I would have thought that she would have started on the smaller stages and worked her way up."

"Before you ask, I don't remember her saying that she was singing at any clubs in the weeks before she cut her hair." Alan shook his head a little and shrugged.

Olli shook her head. "I don't even remember her telling me that she liked to sing. Aces!" She scrubbed her face and groaned into the palms of her hands. She pulled her face out of her hands and sighed tightly.

Dallas looked over at her and shook his head. "Don't do that to yourself, Olli."

Olli looked over at him for a minute. She took a long breath and blew it out between her lips tightly. She sat perfectly still for a moment, not saying anything.

Dallas tilted an eyebrow and glanced over at Alan. He tilted his head.

Alan glanced at him and then looked back at Olli expectantly.

"Al?" Olli asked, after almost two whole minutes of silence, suddenly looking like she might have a thought.

"Yes, Olli?"

"Did Joey run the Velvet Nightcap himself?"

Dallas looked at her and tilted his head curiously.

Alan thought for a moment, the fingers of his left hand splayed over his lips and chin. "I'm assuming you're asking if he was the manager and not just the owner?"

Olli nodded.

Dallas held up a couple of fingers on his right hand.

"Yes, Dallas?"

"Why wouldn't he run his own club? Especially if it was his best club?"

"Joey wasn't the type to be floating around doing the day-to-day." Alan shook his head. "At least, not at that point."

"And what point was that?" Dallas tilted an eyebrow.

"That would be before Razor came to town and established himself as Joey's advisor."

"What did he do instead?" Olli wondered.

"He was mostly the type to want to mesh in with the people that had a lot of money. I think that he just wanted to be seen."

"Who handled the boring day-to-day?" Dallas tilted his head.

"Two-Timer."

"Was he good at it?" Olli tilted her head, her tone heavily skeptical.

"Why did you use that tone?" Dallas looked at her.

"I just...have a really hard time imagining him managing a few nightclubs. It's not really his style."

"I would have thought that numbers were very much his style?" Dallas mused.

Alan snorted. "A bookie and a club manager are two very different things, Dallas. Sure, Two-Timer's your man if you want to place a bet. He knows that world in and out."

Dallas nodded a little. "Fish outta water, huh?"

Alan nodded. "He didn't take it well when Razor was handed the reins, though."

Dallas looked at Olli like he was hoping for an explanation.

"Razor's younger. And extremely business smart." Olli shrugged. "And a con man."

Alan grunted. "Two-Timer had been in Joey's family for years. Worked his way up. Brokered the trust that it took to run the clubs."

"Why exactly do they call him Two-Timer?" Dallas held up a hand. "I know we're gettin' a little off track. But...that's what they called him? Of all the names that he could be called?"

Alan shrugged. "I really don't know. It was something that Joey called him. It seemed to stick. Honestly, I was a little surprised that he kept it after Joey died."

Dallas grunted and shrugged. "Back on task, then." He looked over at Olli.

"She started to sing before Razor came to town, right?" Olli wondered, tilting her head.

Alan nodded. "Couple of years, yes."

"So. Two-Timer is in charge of this swanky club...everythin' is goin' beautiful for him. He's important. He's the man of the hour." Dallas made a thoughtful noise.

Alan nodded with him as he talked. "That's about how it went, yes."

"So...how did thin's go while he was in charge? Did thin's run smoothly?"

Alan nodded. "As far as I knew."

"And you said," Dallas pointed to Olli, "That Razor didn't show up for a couple of years..." his voice drifted off as a thoughtful expression crossed his face.

Olli nodded when he pointed at her and then tilted her head, waiting while he thought.

Dallas blinked and looked at Alan. "Who did the recruitin' for the clubs?" He sat up, suddenly looking a bit more excited, as his idea started to take shape. "Was...was it <u>him</u>?"

Alan rubbed his forehead and temples like he was trying to massage the memories to the forefront of his brain. "I don't know. It wasn't something that came up." He sighed and shook his head a little. "Honestly, it wasn't even something that I thought to ask."

Dallas nodded slightly and made a thoughtful noise. He turned to look at Olli and started to take a breath.

Olli shook her head. "No. I know what you're thinking, but Monte wouldn't know. He didn't mess around with what's going on <u>in</u> the buildings. Just ran the 'shine." She shrugged a little. "Plus, he was usually on the long runs, remember?"

Dallas sighed the breath out and nodded. "That's right. He did say that."

"I'm not even sure if he was working for the family at that point. It's hard to know for sure, since we didn't even know he was a problem until he almost ran Olli down all those years ago—"

"And he's so good at not getting caught..." Olli mused, smiling, clearly proud of her best and oldest friend.

"I'm not sure that's something to be proud of, Olli," Alan pointed out in a dry tone.

Olli shrugged a little, a small smirk on her face.

"Gettin' back around to the point at hand..." Dallas cleared his throat. "Is there someone we could ask? Someone who was around at the time?"

"You could ask him." Alan shrugged.

"Two-Timer?" Olli scoffed a little. "It's still too soon to get caught by him. And he's not <u>any</u> fun to talk to."

"We're <u>not</u> askin' Razor." Dallas shook his head. "He wasn't even here at the time."

Olli shrugged. "He'd at least answer them."

Alan frowned a little. "Have you been going to see him again?"

Olli took a breath and pursed her lips. "It's not like I walk into his office and sit down..."

"Funny. He comes to <u>our</u> office like he owns the place." Dallas mused, his tone dry.

"That was a long time ago."

"A long time ago?" Dallas snorted. "Olli, that was less than a year ago."

Olli shrugged and held her hands out a little. "I was just as surprised as you were."

Alan sighed a little. "You can't go hanging around him like he's your favorite uncle. You're supposed to try to arrest him."

Olli looked over at Dallas and then looked back at her father. "I know, Al."

Alan looked at her for a moment and nodded slowly. "Good. Ask someone else."

"<u>Is</u> there anyone else?" Olli wondered, tilting her head.

"What about her parents?" Dallas spoke up, breaking the awkward feeling in the room. He had been dutifully ignoring the growing tension between the Wainwrights. It wasn't too difficult, since his brain was going a mile of minute, trying to figure out where all the information was leading them to.

Alan and Olli both turned to look at him at the same time.

Dallas glanced between the two of them. "Her parents. They had to know."

Olli made a noise like she wasn't sure. "I'm not sure that's completely true."

Dallas' eyebrow dipped. "You're tryin' to tell me they didn't notice that somethin' was different until she suddenly showed up at home blonde and in slinky dresses?!"

Olli shrugged. "She didn't really have the best relationship with her parents."

Dallas grunted slightly. "So, they probably won't know then?"

Olli shook her head. "No." She looked thoughtful for a moment and then glanced at him. "I'm not even sure where they are."

"What...they...died? Or...?" Dallas tilted his head.

"They disappeared," Alan spoke up. "She lived with us most of the last year the girls were in school."

"And you just let her leave willy-nilly? You didn't ask where she was goin' or who she was with?" Dallas demanded. He sat up a little straighter, and a horrified expression washed over his face. "Uhmm..." He cleared his throat. "Sir."

Alan looked at him and nodded a little. "Honestly, Dallas. I could barely keep Olli in the house when she was supposed to be there."

Olli looked at Dallas and nodded a little. "It's true. I was a terrible kid."

"But she was livin' with you?" Dallas looked at them and frowned a little.

Olli half shook her head. "More like...she would pop in for a few days here and there when she needed it. Most of the time Dad didn't even know."

"That's not even remotely true," Alan admonished. "I knew. But I wasn't about to stop her from having a safe place to stay."

Olli blinked and looked at her father for a moment, processing the new information.

"So..." Dallas mused. "Basically, there's no one that we can ask. No one that would know...except Razor."

Alan frowned. "I'll keep thinking. If I come up with a name, I'll let you know."

Olli rubbed her face and then combed her fingers through the top half of her hair. "Did Razor steal Birdie from someone? Did...Did they take her back?"

Alan blinked and thought for a moment. "I don't know if that's what happened."

Olli pursed her lips and looked at him for a moment. "But what you just said—"

"Two-Timer managing the clubs, Razor taking over," Dallas interrupted quietly, like he was finishing her thought.

Alan looked between them. "You don't really think he would, do you?

Olli smirked a little and nodded. "Yeah, Al. I really think that he would."

"All right. Tell me why you think that Two-Timer suddenly decided to start up a speakeasy right under Razor's nose and we haven't heard about it," Dallas instructed.

They had left Alan's office almost twenty minutes before and had been in their office nearly that whole time. Olli had left for a brief few moments for a coffee run, and was now pacing in the middle of the room.

Olli unwrapped her left hand from her mug and took a sip as she paced from the door toward his desk. "You know why they call him Two-Timer?"

"I'm assumin' that it has somethin' to do with a backstabbin' personality trait." Dallas leaned against the front edge of his desk and watched her.

Olli nodded. "That's a good way of putting it, actually."

Dallas grunted. "Which begs another question."

"What's that?" Olli wondered, turning her back to the door and starting another pass toward him.

"Why did he wait so long?" Dallas tipped his head slightly. "How long ago was it that Razor came to town again?"

Olli paused in the middle of her pass, just a few feet from him and looked thoughtful for a moment. She sipped her coffee and folded her left hand around the mug. "Fifteen, twenty years ago?"

Dallas nodded a little. "And how long was he here before he took over for Two-Timer?"

Olli shrugged a little. "Maybe a year after he got here."

"So you're tellin' me, the backstabbi' man who earned a name like Two-Timer waited <u>this</u> long to enact some sort of revenge?" Dallas looked at her skeptically.

Olli shrugged again and turned to walk back toward the door. "Sure."

Dallas watched after her. "<u>Why?</u>"

Olli pivoted on her left heel and looked at him for a second. "Why?"

"That's what I said," Dallas agreed. "It just doesn't make sense to me. If he's that much of a retaliatory person, why not open up his own speakeasy right away? Take back all the people he lost from Razor and Joey?"

Olli pointed to him with her right hand and mug, tapping her nose with her left first finger. "You just said the reason."

"Joey?" Dallas assumed, his voice going up slightly.

"Exactly him." Olli nodded, starting to walk toward him. "He wouldn't have done anything while Joey was still around. It would have meant certain death."

"As opposed to <u>now?</u>" Dallas wondered, tilting an eyebrow.

"Razor's not really the murdering type." Olli shrugged, pivoted on her right toes, and walked back toward the door.

"All right, fine. Sure. But how long has Joey been gone?" Dallas held out a hand and tilted his head slightly.

Olli froze for a second and made a thoughtful noise in the back of her throat.

Dallas' eyebrow rose fractionally. "Do you not know?" His head pulled back slightly, and he tipped it slightly to the right. "Oh...goodness gracious. Have I finally asked a question that the great Olivia Wainwright doesn't know the answer to?!" He slowly started to smirk as he talked, his tone going up with his shock.

Olli clicked her tongue and shook her head. "I...I <u>know</u> this." She stood where she was, half-staring at the floor a few paces in front of where she was standing, her coffee mug halfway to her mouth.

Dallas waited patiently for a minute or two, watching her process. He let a few more minutes pass before he cleared his throat. "Olli."

Olli blinked and looked up at him, finally pulling the mug up to sip from it. "Hm?"

Dallas held his hands out and tilted his head. "You all right?" he wondered, a chuckle in his voice.

Olli sipped her coffee again and shrugged. "Yeah. I don't remember."

"You don't remember if you're all right?" Dallas tilted his head slightly and pulled it back.

Olli sent him a bland look and huffed. "Aces, Dallas."

Dallas chuckled and shrugged a little. "Just tryin' to snap you out of it."

Olli sipped her coffee and nodded a little. "All right. Consider me out of it."

"To the library?" Dallas offered.

Olli nodded and took another sip. "I think I know an easier way."

"Olli...normally I'm a fan of your...out of the box thinkin', but I feel like this is a bad plan."

Olli looked at him and then back at the door they were standing in front of. "Why?"

"Because I'm pretty sure that if we were goin' to ask someone about when Joey disappeared from the picture, it would be Al."

"Why?" Olli tilted her head.

"He's our boss. For starters?" Dallas looked at her and raised an eyebrow.

Olli frowned. "He's busy."

"Then let's just check the library."

"Why?"

"What is that supposed to mean?" Dallas looked at her like he was starting to lose patience.

"Aces, Dallas. It's just a couple of questions. Why is that such a bad thing?"

The door in front of them pulled open suddenly. "Because he doesn't trust me, Olli," Jake informed, smiling at her.

Olli looked at him and then looked over at Dallas. "Is that true?"

Dallas shrugged, and half shook his head. "We're here now, I suppose."

Olli frowned a little before she pushed her way into the office, past Jake, and through the door.

Jake stepped to the side a little and offered for her to go ahead. Just a couple of seconds too late. "Dallas?" he wondered, not looking the least bit offended.

Dallas shrugged a little and walked into the office after Olli. "We're here now."

"So you've mentioned." Jake chuckled and closed the door before walking back to the chair behind his desk. "What is it, kids?" he wondered, looking at Olli.

"When did Joey leave?"

Jake looked at her for a moment before getting thoughtful. "Gee, kiddo, right out of the gate without a hello."

Olli shrugged a bit. "I'm in a hurry."

Dallas looked between her and Jake with a watchful eye.

"I see. Your friend, right? The missing girl?"

Olli nodded.

"And what does that have to do with Joey?" Jake wondered, looking between them.

"We're just lookin' for how lon' grudges might have been runnin'." Dallas shrugged.

Jake nodded. "I think it's been about fifteen years or so now."

"You're sure?" Dallas looked at him closely. "That's almost as long as you were out of town."

Olli looked at him sharply. "Dallas," she hissed.

Jake nodded and shrugged a little. "I still heard things."

Dallas didn't look convinced, but let it drop for the time being.

Olli sat where she was for a second, looking like she didn't know what to do. "So. Any ideas why Two-Timer would hold a grudge this long?" She changed the subject sharply, pulling the attention back to the subject she wanted to talk about.

Chapter 11

THE ONE WITH THE LONG-HELD GRUDGE

"I imagine because it took him this long to come up with." Jake shrugged, not insulted by the question.

Dallas tilted his head. "I'm not sure that I understand."

"He's not exactly the most clever person I've ever met." Jake shrugged, looking at him with a slight smile.

Olli snorted and rolled her eyes.

Dallas looked at her and then back at Jake. "So, there's more than <u>one</u> reason Razor worked his way up the ranks and took over Two-Timer's spot so quickly."

Jake nodded. "That's exactly right."

Dallas looked at him and then at Olli. "All right. Now I have another question. I'd even argue it's the elephant in the room."

Two sets of eyes turned to look at him.

Olli's eyebrow dipped slightly. "What is it?"

"If he's like you say," Dallas looked between them again and shifted in his chair. "How did he end up a boss of one of the three factions?"

Olli looked at Jake, clearly waiting for an answer.

Jake cleared his throat and shrugged a bit. "Honestly, Al and I never really figured it out—"

"But you have a theory," Dallas interrupted, looking at him closely.

Olli looked over at him and frowned a little. She didn't say anything, but looked back at Jake, suddenly calm.

Jake shrugged, no feathers ruffled by the interruption. "Honestly, there's <u>one</u> thing that Two-Timer and Razor share in common...two things."

"Cryptic," Dallas mused dully.

Olli glanced at him and frowned.

Jake chuckled. "They are both <u>ruthlessly</u> self-serving and unafraid of doing whatever it takes to get what they want."

Dallas nodded. "Understood."

"There is one thing that's different," Olli mused softly, her voice low and quieter than she normally talked.

Dallas looked over at her and tilted his head. "What would that be?"

"There are <u>some</u> lines that Razor won't cross."

Jake grunted. "I'm not so sure about all that, Olli."

Olli looked at him and tilted her head a little. "I am."

Jake scoffed a little and shook his head. "I'm not sure why he saved you, Olli, but you don't owe him any kind of allegiance for that."

Olli's eyes narrowed for a split second. She started to take a breath before pursing her lips closed and rolling her eyes.

Dallas stood up stiffly and offered Olli a hand.

Olli looked up at his hand and took it before standing up. She smiled a little at Jake and started toward the door of the office. "Thanks for the insight, Jake."

Jake smiled warmly and nodded. "You're welcome, kids."

Dallas smiled and half-dipped his head before opening the office door for Olli. He looked at Jake for a moment longer before following her out.

Jake waved a little and went back to working on the papers in front of him.

"Olli?"

"Hm?" Olli looked up and over at Dallas and tilted her head a little.

"You've been really quiet." Dallas leaned slightly and looked at her closely. "What's going on in your head?"

Olli shook her head. "I'm just...thinking over last night." She picked her feet up and set them, one at a time, and rocked back into her chair a little deeper.

Dallas stood up and walked over to her desk. He walked to the back corner and leaned against the back edge, nearly at her ankles.

Olli looked up at him and tilted her head. "What?"

Dallas lightly tapped her booted ankle. "You keep beatin' yourself up..." He shook his head. "You know that isn't helping."

Olli sighed. "We were being <u>followed</u>, Dallas." She shrugged a little and half-tossed her hands. "I noticed. I said something a couple of times. She blew me off. Yelled at me, even. Told me we 'were out to have fun'." Olli scoffed and rubbed her temples. "She begged me not to work."

"And you think that because you allowed yourself to be persuaded that you're what? Suddenly bad at your job?" Dallas shook his head and clicked his tongue a couple of times. "You're allowed to not constantly work, Fox."

"But that's not the only thing!" Olli protested. "There was one time that I dragged her out the back door."

"You told me," Dallas agreed, nodding a little. "I remember you tellin' me."

"I should—"

"Olli. We're going to find her. I'm goin' to need your help. You keep dwellin' on what happened..." He raised an eyebrow. "You're not goin' to be able to help me now."

Olli looked up at him and nodded slowly. "Yeah. All right." She rubbed her temples a little again. "Aces. I know you're right."

Dallas smiled at her a little and nodded. "You're a good detective <u>and</u> friend, Olli."

Olli shifted which foot was on top of the other and nodded a little. "I know."

"Then stop beatin' yourself up. Let's get thin's goin'." Dallas stood up and playfully knocked her heels off the top of her desk.

Olli squeaked a little and pitched forward before her heels hit the floor with a loud thunk. She gripped the top of the arms of her chair, looked at Dallas like a cat that had just slid <u>back</u> down the tree a couple of feet.

Dallas chuckled and smirked at her. "Time to go home."

"But I just got here."

"No. Fox." Dallas shook his head. "You're goin' home."

"I don't want to."

Dallas pointed toward the door. "Olli. Don't make me carry you out of here."

Olli huffed and stood up. "Fine. All right. I'll go home. But I'm coming back here tomorrow morning."

"I wouldn't have it any other way." Dallas walked to the hall tree and scooped the black leather jacket up and held it out in a silent invitation.

Olli stood up slowly and walked over to him, looking completely resigned. "All right. I'm here."

Dallas chuckled and helped her thread her arms into the sleeves. He pulled the jacket up gently and draped it around her shoulders. "That's my girl."

Olli looked at him over her shoulder for a second and then shook her head. She stepped over to the door and pulled it open. "I'm only going because I'm exhausted."

Dallas smirked. "Right. I didn't think it had anythin' to do with me."

Olli pointed at his brown leather jacket. "Make sure that you put that on and follow me out?"

Dallas nodded. "I plan to."

The sun hadn't even really started to start to crest the shortest buildings when Olli stepped out of the hack and onto the sidewalk directly in front of WDA. She smiled and closed the door. "Thank you." Olli smirked and knocked on the roof. "Have a good day." She pivoted on the heel of her left boot and walked toward the low, wide, circular steps that led up to the front two revolving doors. She was up the first two sets of steps before she really noticed. Olli pushed through the right revolving door.

A quick glance up at the wall clock made her smile. It wasn't even six yet.

Dallas walked into the office, the morning's first cup of coffee in his hand. He loved getting into the office early in the morning; it was always so quiet. And the coffee room wasn't crowded at all.

"Morning, Dallas."

Dallas jerked to a stop in surprise. He closed his eyes and sighed between his pursed lips when coffee sloshed over the edge of the mug and down his right hand. "Olli," he blinked his eyes open and looked at her, eyebrows up like he was pleasantly surprised. "You're here...early."

Olli shrugged a little and nodded. "I guess that's true."

"Are you sure that you're all right?" Dallas switched which hand was holding his coffee and shook the coffee off his half-burnt fingers.

Olli tilted her head. "Why wouldn't I be?"

"How long have you been here?" Dallas' right eyebrow jumped up a couple of inches.

Olli shrugged a little. "Maybe an hour?"

Dallas grunted. He walked to his desk and set his mug on it. He turned and rubbed the hand that still stung from the surprise-slowsh. "All right. Who are you, and what have you done with my partner?"

Olli pivoted and looked at him for a minute. "What?"

Dallas held his hands out a little. "Olli, I've known you for a while now. You are not a mornin' person. And yet, here you are, and extremely coherent."

Olli snorted and pointed at the wall to her right. "I did a lot of thinking last night."

Dallas looked at the wall and wasn't surprised when he saw a map of downtown on it. "Downtown?" he asked, allowing her to work through her thoughts while she did so.

Olli looked over at him and nodded. "Downtown."

Dallas twisted slightly to pick up the mug from where he set it down on his desk and folded one arm over the other before taking a small sip of his coffee. "All right. I'm listenin'."

Olli pivoted to look at him and pointed at the map. "All right. Try to keep up—"

Dallas tipped an eyebrow. "You are very awake this mornin'. How many cups of coffee have you had?"

Olli looked at him and pursed her lips together for a second before she shook her head. "Nope—" She popped the 'p' noise with her lips, "I'm just feeling really excited about this thought process."

Dallas nodded. "And how many cups?"

"Four. Why?" Olli looked at him after walking within touching distance of the computer screen.

Dallas held up his mug a little and shook his head. "No reason. Just have to know how many more cups I'll need before I catch up to you." He set one foot on the fore-edge of the chair facing his desk and refolded his arms. "Go ahead, I'm listenin'."

Olli shook her head a little and turned toward the computer screen again. "See, at first I thought that the Auburn was following me. But the more I think about it...I didn't see it before lunch."

"We were talkin' while we walked," Dallas pointed out, sipping his coffee again in a careful way.

Olli nodded and looked over at him. "Well yes. Sure. But I didn't even catch sight of it in one of the windows."

Dallas nodded a little. "All right. Show me where you saw it the first time."

Olli stepped up to the computer and touched a point on the map. "Here. This is the first time."

Dallas made a thoughtful noise and sipped his coffee. "What store were you in?"

Olli carefully circled a building on the map. "This one."

"And the next place you saw it?"

Olli touched a point on the map and drew a short line. "This is where we were walking."

Dallas nodded and grunted. "Mmmhm."

"This store right here I saw the car twice—"

"Twice?" Dallas tilted his head and one eyebrow went up. "Why?"

"Drove by once. And then, when we walked out, I saw it sitting in a parking spot a couple of places down from the door." Olli looked at him before lightly touching the computer screen.

Another light-blue dot appeared on the map.

Dallas bobbed his head a little before sipping his coffee. "All right, I'm trackin'."

Olli glanced at him and then pivoted to look at the computer screen again. "There were three other stores. Here, here and...here." She touched three more places on the map. "I pushed her out of the back door of this store—" l—Olli circled one of the dots, the line a bright orange—"and we walked down this alley here." She drew a line as she talked, this one green. "Practically had to drag her. She was so upset that I was working."

"She thought that you were working?" Dallas held up a hand when a mildly irritated look crossed Olli's face. "I know, Fox. I know we've gone over it so many times, you think I should know the story better than you. You have to know why I'm doin' it."

Olli huffed and bobbed her head. "I might have forgotten something."

"Or just remembered somethin' else." Dallas nodded. "I <u>know</u> it doesn't feel like it, but I'm <u>tryin'</u> to help get to the bottom of this." He smiled at her a little and cleared his throat. "She thought you were workin'..." he lead her in back to where they had left the conversation.

Olli looked at him and shrugged a little. "Honestly, Dallas, she wasn't wrong. The only reason that I was dragging her all over back here was because I noticed that Auburn."

"That's not so much workin' as it is self-preservation, Fox." Dallas shrugged and fully sat on the top of his desk.

Olli glanced at him and licked her lips. She huffed a little and bobbed her head. "You're not wrong."

Dallas smirked. "I love it when you say that I'm right."

Olli looked at him and scoffed a little. "This is where things get a little..." She waved her right hand a little and pursed her lips. She cleared her throat, and half-closed her left eye.

Dallas looked at her and tipped his chin up. "This is where you tell me thin's get messy..." he offered. "This is where that 'but' I've been waitin' for is."

Olli opened her left eye and dropped her hands. "Yeah. That's about right."

"Talk me through it." Dallas picked up his mug, looked in it and frowned a little before setting it back down on the desk next to him.

Olli lightly gnawed on the inside bottom left corner of her lower lip. She folded her hands in front of her at about chest height and rolled her knuckles back and forth a little. "I'm not sure how they found us."

Dallas looked at her for a moment. "You didn't see the Auburn again that night?"

Olli shook her head. "No. We came down this alley and got into a hack right here." She touched the computer screen, leaving a soft pink dot. "We took that to the dance hall. When I got out, I checked. I couldn't help myself."

Dallas smirked a little. "Can take the girl out of work, but not the work out of the girl."

Olli glanced at him and tilted her head. She shook her head a little and rolled her eyes.

Dallas cleared his throat. "Olli, what I mean—"

"I'm extra careful, ever since Cross Bay got the jump on me and Monte," Olli offered with a rueful smile.

Dallas nodded. "I am too. We'd be foolish not to be."

"Getting kidnapped and held against your will tends to do that, I suppose." Olli looked at the map and frowned a little.

Dallas made a small humming noise and looked at her quietly. "So, what's got you all twisted up in knots, Fox?"

"How did they know?" Olli turned and looked at him seriously. "How did they know where we were?"

Dallas loosened his tie a little and hooked his arms together over his chest. "They didn't see you get into the hack?"

Olli pursed her lips together and thought for a second, her eyes roving back and forth a little. She shook her head a little. "No. No, I remember checking to make sure."

Dallas nodded slowly. "What about when you got there?"

Olli shook her head. "No way. I wouldn't have let her get out of the hack if the Auburn was there."

"You're goin' to hate me."

Olli looked at him and tilted her head slightly. "Why?" she wondered, one eyebrow moving up slightly.

"How do you know it's the same car?"

Olli looked at him for a moment before putting her hands on her hips. "What?"

Dallas held up his hands. "Think about it, Olli."

"Are you asking me because I'm a <u>girl</u>?"

Dallas laughed and shook his head. "Now, Fox…when have I <u>ever</u> slighted you for being a girl?" He scoffed. "I'm askin' because sometimes our minds can trick us into thinkin' that we've seen somethin' that isn't there…"

Olli pursed her lips. She sighed tightly and folded her hands just about neck height. After a second, she lightly bit her left thumbnail.

Dallas waited patiently, leaning his hands on the edge of the desk.

Olli shook her head and pulled her thumbnail out from between her teeth. "No. It was the same car."

"You're sure."

Olli nodded. "Very."

"Care to explain?"

"Auburns aren't very popular as a general rule in Big Town." Olli shrugged. "I don't know why." She glanced out the window and then back at him. "It's the reason that I noticed it in the first place."

Dallas bobbed his head. "That's true. I haven't seen many."

"They're flashy. A statement car." Olli scoffed and half-rolled her eyes. "Aces…it's almost like they wanted to be noticed."

Dallas made a small thoughtful noise and bobbed his head. "All right. Let's say they did."

Olli took a large breath and huffed a little. "To what end?" she wondered.

Dallas shrugged. "Usually this is where you tell me that it's some sort of…flamboyant, crazy mobster's attempt at calling attention to themselves."

"Razor doesn't have an Auburn." Olli looked at him and shook her head.

"I didn't think he did…" Dallas tilted his head. "Why?"

Olli half shook her head and started to pace again. "No reason."

"It's not like he would do this anyway," Dallas pointed out, watching her. "It really doesn't make any sense for him to do this."

Olli pivoted by the door and started to walk toward him. "It's true."

"She's <u>his</u> singer already." Dallas shifted a little. "And apparently, he knows that the two of you are friends."

Olli bobbed her head, pivoted, and walked back toward the door again.

Dallas watched her pace a couple of times. "Know somebody?"

Olli froze and looked at him. "What?"

"Do you know anyone?"

Olli pivoted at the door and shrugged. "I'm not sure."

Dallas tilted his head. "Fox. Focus."

Olli froze and looked at him sharply. "I'm listening."

"We agree that we have our <u>main</u> suspect, correct?" Dallas wondered, tilting his head slightly.

Olli's eyes roved back and forth as she thought.

Dallas tilted his head slightly. "Well?"

"Hm?" Olli blinked and looked at him. "Yes."

Dallas nodded slowly and looked at her closely. "Where'd you go?"

"But it just doesn't make sense."

"Explain."

"I don't think he did it."

"What? But we just agreed not that long ago that Two-Timer's our man." Dallas held out his hands slightly, his tone and look protesting all at once. He waited a couple of seconds.

Olli stood where she was and looked out the windows that created the wall behind Dallas' desk. Her eyes glazed over and she stared at the skyline, completely entranced.

Dallas watched her for a minute more before he cleared his throat. "Walk me through it, Fox."

Olli blinked a couple of times and focused on him. "Right. Sorry."

Dallas shook his head. "You don't have to be." He tilted his head. "Who is it?"

Olli walked over and leaned her forearms on the top edge of the backrest of the chair that faced his desk. "I think Two-Timer's behind it."

"Right." Dallas nodded. "We agreed on that."

Olli looked at him squarely for the first time in a bit and pursed her lips for a moment. "But I don't think that he's the one that _did_ it."

Dallas looked at her and nodded slowly once. "All right. Why?"

"He was the manager that picked her up first, right?"

"Accordin' to what Al told us." Dallas nodded slowly, not sure where she was going with her train of thought, but not willing to interrupt it, either.

"He's a bookie. He runs rackets that pull in almost as much money as Razor does with The Phoenix."

Dallas held up a finger and tilted his head. "Not to slow you down and rain on your parade..."

Olli pursed her lips and raised an eyebrow. "But..." she offered.

"Why would he need her?"

Olli started to take a breath. She shook a finger at him a little and bobbed her head while pursing her lips. "That's where things get a little more complicated."

"Explains why you kept starin' out the windows." Dallas grunted. "If he's makin' money, he doesn't need to have a singer around. Especially one that is so close with you."

Olli gnawed on the inside left corner of her bottom lip. "That's another thing. I'm not sure how Razor knows about us."

Dallas tilted his head. "Meanin'?"

"I thought that we were being sneaky enough that she wouldn't get caught telling me things."

"Maybe he doesn't care."

"She's my...our—ticket to taking him down."

"He's a bit more arrogant than that," Dallas pointed out, shrugging. "The man came here to report a murder."

Olli grunted a little and bobbed her head a little. "True..."

"And if it _isn't_ arrogance, it's an astounding level of brazenness." Dallas shrugged a little. "_If_ he knows. I don't think he cares."

Olli snorted and rolled her eyes. "You're right. I don't think he's ever been worried that he'll be arrested."

"Which means he really has no reason to snatch Miss Birdie off the street." Dallas looked thoughtful for a moment and then pursed his lips. "And, what little I've seen of the two of you interactin'...I find it hard to believe that he would do somethin' so rash as drug you."

Olli tilted her head a little. She started to take a breath to protest and then nodded slowly. "I suppose that's true."

"Now. Who do you know that _would_ do somethin' so stupid as druggin' you less than a year after Cross Bay Louie did the _exact_ same thin'?"

Olli gnawed on her lip for a moment and shrugged a little. She glanced out the window and then looked at him.

"Spit it out, Fox."

"Two-Timer."

"Good. We're back to our original suspect." Dallas nodded. "That means it's solid."

"But."

Dallas nodded and grunted. "But you don't think that he did it."

"Not directly."

"Think he'd drug you?"

"Drugging and poisoning really isn't all that far apart..." Olli shrugged a little.

Dallas shook his head. "That's not what I asked, though."

Olli looked up at him and tilted her head slightly. "What?"

"Would he drug you?" Dallas repeated. He held up a hand. "Wait. Before you answer that..."

Olli tilted her head and hummed slightly in the back of her throat. "All right...?"

"Why did you say that?" Dallas tilted his head and looked at her closely.

"Say what?" Olli half shook her head.

"Poisonin' and druggin' aren't that far apart?" Dallas' eyebrows jumped up.

"Oh." Olli shrugged a little. "I'm pretty sure that he's poisoned people before. Or at least <u>had</u> them poisoned."

"You're—" Dallas held up the first two fingers of both his hands and moved his fingers slightly, "<u>Pretty sure</u>."

Olli half shrugged slightly. "I've heard stories."

"From who?" Dallas wondered, his tone dipping skeptically. "Al? Or <u>Jake</u>?" his tone dipped down a bit.

Olli's eyebrows knit together slightly. "What was <u>that</u> tone?"

Dallas frowned, and half shook his head. "Nothin'. Don't worry about it."

Olli's left eyebrow dipped slightly. She looked at him for a moment and then half shrugged. "All right." She searched his face for a minute. When she didn't find what she was looking for, she shook herself ever-so-slightly and blinked. "Both of them. And my granddad too."

Dallas grunted. "So he's been around for a bit."

Olli nodded and perched on the arm of the chair.

"Your granddad,"

Olli tilted her head a little. "What about him?"

"He came right out and told you that Two-Timer poisoned someone?"

Olli laughed. "No."

"No," Dallas repeated. He shifted his weight on his desk a little and one eyebrow went up. "Beg pardon?"

"Before you ask, I'm not making it up."

Dallas shook his head. "I didn't ask. And I've known you long enough to know you don't make things up."

"I inferred."

Dallas scoffed and half-clapped his hands a couple of times. "Well done on that sidestep."

Olli pursed her lips and snorted. "Aces, Dallas!"

Dallas chuckled and raised his eyebrows. "Come on. How did you...<u>infer</u> it?"

"Some of the stories that he told. He would talk about how fast Two-Timer walked <u>right</u> up the ladder of Joey's organization."

"Sum it up in a couple of sentences?" Dallas leaned his hands on the desk edge next to him.

"Started from the middle bottom, made a few enemies—probably where he earned the name—and suddenly he was high middle and one of his biggest..." Olli paused while she fumbled for a word, "enemy was suddenly dead. Wasn't shot. Granddad only stumbled on the body by pure accident a few weeks after Two-Timer was suddenly in his spot."

"Rinse and repeat?" Dallas assumed, tilting his head slightly.

"Half dozen different stories. All with the same general feel." Olli nodded, her lips pursed slightly.

"So, you're sayin' there's a pattern."

Olli looked at him and nodded. "Exactly." She pushed back into the chair and rested her head on the front edge of the top of the chair, after sinking down deeply into the chair.

Dallas watched her scoot half out of the chair before half staring at the ceiling. "You're..." he let his voice fade slightly. He cleared his throat. "Fox. Do you remember when the night started to get hazy?"

Olli opened one eye and looked at him for a moment. "Yeah. I remember. I was three drinks deep—"

"What were you drinkin'?" Dallas interrupted, looking at her closely.

"Why does it matter?" Olli opened her other eye and tilted her eyebrow.

"If it's water, it's a <u>whole</u> lot harder to spike than somethin' that has a lot of flavor already."

Olli grunted. "South Side."

Dallas looked thoughtful. "Remind me again...what's in a South Side when there's not anything'...booze related in it?"

Olli started to take a breath and then looked thoughtful. She pursed her lips and made a thoughtful noise.

"If I may?" Dee wondered, suddenly appearing not far off the far left corner of Dallas' desk.
Dallas looked to his right and raised an eyebrow. "Miss Dee."
Olli looked to her right and nodded. "Go ahead, Dee. You're better versed than I am."
Dallas looked at her and smirked before turning his attention back to Dee.

THE ONE WITH THE COCKTAIL INGREDIENTS

D ee cleared her throat and fussed over her short, swinging, heavily pleated skirt, this time a bright blue. A matching knit sweater was tucked in perfectly. She looked at them and smiled. "A South Side you said, correct?"

"That's right." Olli nodded.

Dee cleared her throat and clasped her hands behind her back. "A South Side was made popular in the south side of Chicago. According to what I can find, usually it has some sort of gin in it—"

"Unless it's made at a club like the one that I went to last night." Olli pointed out.

Dee looked over at her, nodding slightly, barely acknowledging the interruption.

"What else is in it, Miss Dee?" Dallas looked back over at her, bringing her to the center of attention again.

"Simple syrup, lime and lemon juice. It is also worth mentioning that there is a variation in which soda water is used to make it fizzy."

Olli's mouth dropped open slightly. "You're telling me I could have had a fizzy drink last night?!" she protested.

"Olli...I don't think that's the point." Dallas looked at her and tilted an eyebrow.

Olli snapped her mouth closed. "Right. There you have it. It's sweet, sour, has a little kick."

"Ah." Dallas smirked. "So it's the Olli of the fake booze drinks." He looked over at Dee and his eyebrow went up fractionally.

Dee chortled a little and nodded. "Exactly."

Olli wrinkled her nose a little and shook her head slightly. "Aces, Dallas. That's not weird at all."

Dallas smiled a little and shook his head. "I mean no offense, Fox."

Olli shrugged a little, like she was already over it, and smirked. Her smirk fell slowly, and she tilted her head. "I...don't remember tasting anything different in the last one...or the third one?"

"Do you remember how many you had?" Dallas tilted his head.

Olli folded her hands and held them up to her mouth. She set her lips on her knuckles and made a thoughtful noise. "Three. That I remember."

Dallas smiled at her. "And nothin' tasted different?"

Olli shook her head. "No. Whatever they used had to be really good."

Dallas grunted. "And that's his thing, hm?"

Olli nodded a little. "I didn't see anyone that I recognized either."

Dallas smiled. "I suppose it only made sense that I ask that question next."

Olli nodded.

"I have another one."

Olli tilted her head. "What's that?"

Dallas shifted a little and pursed his lips. "Do we <u>actually</u> know who's in his employ now?"

Insult crossed Olli's face. "Of course we do."

Dallas' eyebrows went up, and he cleared his throat. "Olli. I've been here for a while, and I'm goin' to be honest, I don't really know...<u>anythin'</u> about Two-Timer or his organization. In fact," Dallas looked thoughtful and his eyebrows worked a little—"now that I think about it, I don't really know a whole lot about Ace's organization, either."

Olli shrugged a little and made a soft grunting noise. "I guess...that's true." She shrugged a little. "In my defense, we have been a little busy."

Dallas scoffed a little and nodded. "I'm pretty sure I know more about Cross Bay and his habits than I do about The Big Three."

Olli frowned a little.

Just the mention of the kidnapper that had snatched them both off the street tended to bring a dark cloud over the District Detective office. It was still a bit of a sore spot on Olli's pride. Getting caught off guard wasn't in her nature. Dallas still had moments where he felt like he had let her down, despite the fact he had spent months pouring through old case files trying to find her.

Dallas held up a hand and shook his head. "Sorry about that."

Olli shrugged and grunted quietly. "I suppose my training has been lacking."

Dallas shook his head. "I don't think so." He chuckled. "I've learned a <u>lot</u> since I came here. About how the mob views kidnappers, how to make Prussian Blue...and if I ever need a bogus prescription for booze." He smirked at her. "I'm sure that'll <u>all</u> come in handy at one point or another."

Olli scoffed and laughed a little. "I guess."

"Oh! And to never assume I'm trapped in <u>any</u> room. There's almost always a tunnel somewhere nearby."

Olli snorted a little and shook her head. "Well. At least I haven't completely neglected your Big Town specific training then."

Dallas shook his head. "Not so much that I can't do my job."

Olli nodded and half-smiled. "Well. Good." She looked at him square. "What were you going to ask me before?"

Dallas looked confused for a moment before he nodded a little. "Right. Is Two-Timer like Razor?"

"How so?"

"Does he just...let new members into the family without question? Or does he test them?"

Olli half shook her head. "He doesn't really let new people in."

"There wouldn't be someone trying to impress him by doin' somethin' stupid like druggin' you?"

"I wouldn't say that either." Olli shook her head. "There's plenty of guys that would do something dumb like that."

"Any up-and-comers you can think of?" Dallas wondered, tilting his head.

Olli frowned. "Not...that I can think of."

Dallas knit his eyebrows together slightly. "Not a single person that you can think of?"

Olli folded her hands together and her eyes closed for a second. She took a few breaths, her eyes still closed.

Dallas waited for her patiently. He didn't want to push her; it was the longest he had seen her concentrate on a single thing for so long. Usually she dove headfirst into things and never paused to think about things before they happened.

The knock at the door startled them both.

Olli physically started and gripped the arms of the chair as she flailed slightly to look over her shoulder at the door.

Dallas blinked and looked up at the door sharply. He stood up and cleared his throat. "Who is it?"

Olli scrambled out of the chair and turned around to face the door in practically one motion. She glanced at Dallas and started toward the door.

"Detectives? It's Iris Stanton? From Reception? Downstairs?" the female voice drifted through the door.

Olli shared a confused look with Dallas and stopped between their desks. "Come in?"

The door swung open quickly. A girl around Olli's age and height—with her three-inch heels—walked in like she was two minutes late. She had a smart, dark-silver dress suit on and her deep brown hair was up in a flawless French Twist.

"What can we do for you, Miss Iris?" Dallas smiled at her quietly.

Iris smiled at him in a flirty way and offered an envelope. "This came for you. Just now." She didn't look away from him.

Dallas looked at Olli and tilted his head a little. "For...me personally?" he tilted his head.

Iris smiled brightly. "It says District Detective Office."

"Oh. For us then." Dallas smiled and took the envelope from her. "Thank you for bringing it up, Iris. You didn't need to rush it up here." He pivoted and offered the envelope to Olli.

Olli took it and smiled. "Thanks for rushing it up, Iris."

Iris watched the envelope transfer from her to Dallas, and then to Olli. Her smile fell fractionally, and she nodded. "You're welcome, Detective." She focused on Dallas and lightly touched her hair. She pivoted and walked back to the door. "Door open or closed, Detective?"

"Just leave it open please, Ms. Iris." Dallas smiled at her.

"Iris?" Olli spoke up, her voice full of confusion.

Iris finally looked at her. "Yes?"

"There's no stamp?" Olli tapped the top left corner of the envelope after turning it so Iris could see. "Did this come in the mail?"

Iris looked where her finger was and then shook her head. "No. The mail came this morning."

"But this came just now?" Olli tilted her head. "How?"

"Messenger?" Iris shrugged, a tight smile on her lips. "Was that not clear?"

"Sorry." Olli smiled in a fake way. "Silly me must have missed it when you didn't mention that."

Dallas clicked his tongue and looked at Olli like he was slightly disappointed.

Olli pursed her lips and half rolled her eyes.

Iris flushed a little and looked scolded. She pivoted on the toes of her high-heeled shoes and walked away sharply.

"That was rude," Dallas mused dryly.

"I know! This has been my office a lot longer than she's been here." Olli agreed, turning the envelop around in her hands. "And she acted like I wasn't even here!"

"I was talkin' about you," Dallas looked at her sharply.

Olli looked at him sharply. "Me?!"

"You snapped at her," Dallas pointed out, looking at her pointedly.

Olli looked up from the envelope and wrinkled her nose. "Dallas..."

"You didn't need to."

Olli sighed and walked to her desk. She pulled a letter opener out of the small secretary station and slit the top of the envelope open. "This is so strange. We never get messengered here."

Dallas allowed her to drop the subject of the receptionist and walked to her desk. "Used to be able to say that a mobster has never stepped foot into this room either..."

Olli grunted a little and pried the envelope edges apart. She fished out a soft white piece of paper. "Aces...what is...this?" she wondered, slowly setting the envelope down.

Dallas tilted his head and stepped forward another step. "Is that paper?"

Olli shook her head. "I think it's...it feels like a cocktail napkin?" She pondered it a bit as she started to unfold it. "But it doesn't seem like there's anything on it..."

A single, deep black feather floated out and lightly kissed the floor between their feet.

Dallas watched the feather and stared at it for a moment. "What kind of feather do you think that is?" He pointed at it.

Olli blinked a little. "Looks like one from a feather boa."

Dallas nodded a little and tilted his head. "A feather boa...or headpiece of a singer, perhaps?"

Olli's mouth was still hanging open a little. She blinked and shook herself a little and snapped her mouth closed. "Birdie!" she whispered. She started to inspect the cocktail napkin closely, turning it this way and that.

While Olli dissected the folds of the napkin, Dallas knelt down and picked up the feather. He stood up and twirled it between the first two fingers on his right hand. "She found a way to let you know where she is." He grinned a little. "Good girl."

"She did," Olli agreed.

Dallas looked up from the feather. "What did you find?"

Olli turned the napkin a little and pointed at some bright red, messy letters.

Olive,
Shipped out with the old man

Dallas looked at the words a little more and then changed his gaze to Olli's face. "What does that mean?"

"I don't know." Olli shrugged.

"She must not have had a lot of time..." Dallas mused. "Is that lipstick?"

Olli turned the napkin around and looked at the words again. She nodded. "That's her shade too."

"You would know better than me on that." Dallas twirled the feather in his fingers again. "Shipped out...with the old man..."

Olli grunted and blindly sat on the top of the desk. She stared at the note a bit more. "I'd be willing to bet that the old man is Two-Timer."

Dallas nodded. "I'm guessin' he has her singin'?" He hefted the feather as his evidence.

Olli looked at him and nodded. "She didn't have a boa on when we were dancing."

"You danced?"

"No."

"She moves fast." Dallas nodded. "It hasn't even been two days."

"Birdie has no fear," Olli agreed. "Gloria never had a good sense of self-preservation either." She looked at him dryly.

"You talk like they're two different girls." Dallas looked at her, past the feather.

"They are. At least to me." Olli shrugged.

"How is that?"

"Gloria is a carefree girl. Nice, but a little too easy to dazzle with shiny things—"

"How is that different than Birdie?" Dallas tilted his head. "She's a singer in a speakeasy. Now, quite possibly in the second speakeasy since I've known her. All she has is shiny dresses and things."

"Birdie looks out for Birdie." Olli shrugged. "Gloria wants to make sure that everyone is included."

"Then why does she tell you anythin'?" Dallas looked at her skeptically.

"Because Birdie and Gloria love to gossip. And Birdie doesn't stop being my friend. I just...s how up from time to time and give her the chance to gossip."

Dallas looked at her for a moment and made a thoughtful noise. "Sounds like you're describin' two sides of the same exact coin." He smirked. "A six of one and half dozen of the other, if you will."

Olli bobbed her head and shrugged. "You're not wrong. It is still the same girl."

Dallas grunted and nodded. "All right. Any guesses on the 'shipped out'?" he wondered, tilting his head a little. He stepped forward and offered Olli the feather.

Olli took it and set it next to her on the desk. She looked at the note again and shook her head a little. "That's the part the really doesn't make sense to me."

"There's not any chance that it's some sort of code?" Dallas looked at her closely.

"I'm sure it is. The problem is…I don't know what she's trying to say." Olli made a frustrated noise and shrugged.

"You two didn't talk in a code?"

"Well sure. Just girl stuff, though. Mostly her way of letting me know which guys she thought were a catch or little things like that. And mostly when we were teenagers—"

"You say that like it was such a long time ago." Dallas chuckled.

Olli shrugged. "Either way. This doesn't have a hidden meaning as far as I know." She frowned and looked at the message again. "She never writes things down…" Olli mumbled softly.

"What was that?" Dallas looked at her and raised an eyebrow.

"Birdie never writes things down." Olli's eyes pulled up off the note and met his. "She just gossips and I listen, hoping for something I can use in a case."

Dallas nodded a little and made a thoughtful noise. "Why is that important?"

Olli pursed her lips and shook her head a little. "I don't know yet."

"Could it be just as simple as…what it says?" Dallas tilted his head a little, half pointing at the napkin.

Olli's eyebrows knit together. "She left? Why would she drug me just to duck town?"

"I don't think she drugged you to duck town." Dallas tilted his head. "Seems to me she would have just left if she wanted to leave."

Olli grunted a little and bobbed her head. "True."

"Somehow I get the feelin' that Gloria wouldn't do that to you." Dallas smiled a little. "And I don't think Birdie would either."

Olli shook her head. "Nah." She set the napkin down on her desk and wandered over to the middle of the room. She half wandered back and forth where she had been pacing just a few minutes before. Her heart wasn't in it though, it seemed she was doing it just to fidget.

Dallas turned and watched her. "Penny for your thoughts, Fox?"

Olli glanced at him. "Shipped out…"

Dallas grunted. "It's cryptic. I agree."

Olli wandered back and forth a few times. "Maybe she's down river?"

"What river?" Dallas tilted his head.

"The one that empties into The Harbor." Olli pointed vaguely toward The Harbor as she walked.

Dallas tilted an eyebrow. "Wouldn't that be…up river?"

Olli looked at him. "Technically."

"What's up that way?" Dallas wondered, clearly unconvinced that something would draw Birdie that way.

Olli pulled a small face and shook her head. She gnawed on the inside left corner of her bottom lip and shrugged. "Basically nothing." She walked a few more steps. "There might be a riverboat or two on the river. But none of them are big enough to draw Birdie away from the Phoenix—" She stopped short.

Dallas looked at her closely. "Shipped out," he repeated.

Olli stared into middle space for a moment and then looked at him. "She's on a boat!"

Dallas stepped toward her a few feet and grinned. "Okay. So…she's on a boat…" A little of the excitement drained out of him. "But where? The river?" He held up a hand. "The Harbor?" He pointed in that direction. "The ocean?" He flung his arm completely out and pointed.

Olli nodded slowly. "I don't know."

"Okay…all right…" Dallas looked thoughtful for a moment. "Who can we ask?"

Olli sucked on her teeth. "I don't know."

"Monte?" Dallas wondered hopefully.

Olli snorted. "No. No, he wouldn't know about a boat."

"Ten bucks says he might know someone who knows." Dallas raised an eyebrow at her.

Olli looked at him like he had grown a second head. "<u>Ten</u>?!" She laughed. "Who are you? Rockefeller?!"

"What?! Too rich for your blood? You? A <u>Wainwright</u>?! Didn't your family build this town?"

"I'm just a <u>detective</u>!" Olli protested.

"Fine." Dallas smiled at her. "Lunch tomorrow says he'll know someone."

Olli nodded and offered her hand. "Yeah. Let's go see Monte."

Monte pulled into his driveway, letting the hack idle up his driveway. He started slightly and huffed when both District Detectives stepped out of the deep shadows of the garage.

Dallas waved once and pulled the garage door open on the large garage. He smiled and gestured for Monte to drive in.

Olli pushed her hands into her jacket and smiled tightly.

Monte idled the hack into the garage and turned the motor off. He pulled the keys out of the ignition and reached for the door.

The door disappeared away from his reach before he got his hand on the handle.

Olli was there, leaning on the door edge. "Hiya, Monte."

Monte looked at her for a moment before stepping out of the hack. "Oliver...Dallas." He looked over at Dallas and half smiled. "Sneakin' up on me?"

"We have a question." Dallas smiled.

"We brought dinner from the Corner Diner," Olli piped up.

Monte looked between them and nodded slowly. "Must be a heavy ques'ion."

"Why do you say that?" Dallas wondered, tilting his head slightly.

"You brough' me dinner." Monte gently pulled the hack door out from under Olli and closed the door. He shooed them both toward the open garage door. "Clarence doesn' usually let food walk ou' th' door. Which means...you asked for it special. Mus' be a <u>doozy</u>."

Olli looked at Dallas and bobbed her head a little.

Dallas chuckled. "You sound like you know us too well."

Monte grunted and swung his arm around Olli's shoulders, pulling her out of the door and onto the driveway. The movement was that of an older brother being friendly with a preferred little sister. "Come on now. I'm starvin'. And I'm sure food's get'in' cold."

Dallas pulled the garage door down and fell into step behind the two of them.

Monte walked Olli up to the back porch steps. "Where's th' food?"

Dallas paused by the gate and picked up a box. "I've got it."

Monte nodded and walked up the three steps to his back porch. He unlocked the back door. "Come on, kids."

"Told you the door was locked." Olli looked back at Dallas and smirked.

Dallas shrugged. "You did."

"Told 'im what?" Monte looked at her, opening the back door.

"I just figured that your back door wouldn't be locked."

Monte chuckled. "She broke in las' time, eh?" he paused and waited for Olli to walk through the door.

"I wouldn't...say...that..." Olli faltered, just about to step through the doorway.

"But, yes. Apparently, she did." Dallas smirked. "Go on, Fox. Food's getting' cold."

Olli looked between the two of them and shook her head a little before walking through the door.

Dallas looked at Monte and smirked. He walked through the door, careful to turn the box a bit to fit through the door with no problem.

The smell of warm beef and vegetables wafting on the soft breeze.

Monte sniffed a little and made a noise of happiness. "Beef stroganoff?! Is tha' wha' I smell?!" He pivoted and followed Dallas through the door. He let the screen door close behind him with no regard to how it bounced and chattered off the door frame.

Olli looked back at him and shook her head. "No. I'm sorry, Monte. It's just beef stew and some bread."

Monte shrugged and didn't look the least bit torn up about the information. "Works for me. Grab some bowls, Oliver."

Olli nodded and walked to the kitchen, her steps confident and practiced from years spent treating the house like it was her own. She fished out three bowls and opened a drawer a few steps down from where she had been, rescuing three spoons from the holder.

Dallas opened the box and unloaded the contents onto the table carefully. "Hope you're hungry Monte. We told Clarence it was goin' to be the three of us." He chuckled. "I think he heard make sure we have enough for three blocks."

Monte chuckled softly and bobbed his head. "Tha' sounds like Clarence."

Olli stepped into the dining room and set the bowls out in front of the chair where Monte usually sat, the one she preferred when she ate there, and the chair that Dallas usually ended up occupying. She laid out the spoons and smiled at them. "There. Now we can eat."

Monte pulled his chair back and sat down heavily. Like his bones were suddenly too heavy for him. "All righ'. Let's have it." He waved his hand a little. "Wha' could be so big, tha' beef stew was required?" he looked at the food on the table and then at Olli like he expected her not to lie to him.

"Beef stew is always good." Olli smiled at him brilliantly.

"He only makes it on Mondays durin' the win'er."

"Point?" Dallas tilted his head.

"It's May." Monte looked between the two of them. He zeroed in Olli, like he blamed her specifically. "And <u>Friday</u>."

Olli looked at him innocently. She shrugged a little. "It sounded good."

Monte grabbed the big bowl that Dallas had pulled from the box it traveled in. He started to serve himself and didn't say anything for a moment. "You know..." He adjusted how he was holding the bowl and carefully served a bit more into his bowl. "Las' time Clarence made this, he told me it's a three day even'. He starts it Friday nigh', and doesn't star' t' serve it until Monday for dinner." He looked at Olli pointedly and offered her the large bowl. "Which means...you've been stewin' on this ques'ion for three days a' leas'."

Olli didn't move for a moment, looking at him like she was weighing her options. She blinked and slowly took the bowl from him. "Did he."

"He did." Monte picked up his spoon and inspected it, front and back, before dipping it into his bowl. He slowly stirred the stew before looking up at Olli again. "I seem t' recall <u>you</u> were there tha' nigh'."

Olli served herself some stew and shrugged a little. "Mmhm. I guess I was."

Dallas looked between the two of them. "Is this...Is this why you said we had to wait for Friday night?" he looked at Olli.

Olli looked up at him. "Okay—fine." She smiled a little. "All right. Aces. Yes. I asked Clarence to whip up a batch of this. And I knew it would take three days." She looked at Monte and pursed her lips. "It <u>is</u> a big ask."

Monte reached forward and grabbed a piece of bread. He looked at her and tilted his head. "Well? Go on then."

Olli offered the bowl to Dallas and smiled tightly. "We think we might have figured out where Birdie ended up."

"Where?"

"On a boat."

"Monte looked between them for a moment and nodded slowly. He stood up and walked to the kitchen. "I don' really understand why this is considered a big ask..." He pulled out a small dish of butter and walked back to the table. After he set the dish in the middle of the table, he sat back down in his chair.

Olli reached forward and grabbed a piece of bread and the dish of butter. She used the back of her spoon to spread a bit of the butter over the bread and shrugged. "We were wondering if you knew of any..." her voice trailed off as she looked at his face. "So that's a no, then?"

Monte stared at her dryly. He clicked his tongue sharply a couple of times. "Well, gee, Oliver, it didn' exac'ly come up las' time I was a' Th' Pheonix."

Dallas chuckled and reached for a piece of bread. "Don't blame her, Monte. I thought you would know. And that she should be the one to ask if you didn't."

Monte looked at him and shook his head a couple of times. "You two. I swear..." he took a bite of the bread in his hand and thought while he chewed. He shook his head again. "I'm really sorry, kids. I haven' heard any whisperin' about a boat."

"Know anyone who might have?" Dallas wondered, pausing to blow on his bite.

Monte chewed on the next bite of his bread and absentmindedly stirred his stew.

Olli took two bites before her spoon clanked against the edge of the bowl. She blinked and then looked at Monte.

Monte shook his head. "I don'." He looked over at Olli sharply when the spoon clanked against the bowl again. "Oliver..."

Olli was resting her elbows on the table, rubbing her temples with two fingers of each hand.

"She's havin' a hard time with it," Dallas informed quietly.

Monte nodded slowly and reached over to rub Olli's near shoulder a little. "Hey there, Oliver. Ea' your stew."

Olli picked up her head and sighed a little before she nodded. "I know. Aces...I swear I know it's not my fault she's missing."

Monte smiled at her in a quiet, but tight, way. "It's no'."

Dallas took another bite before he cleared his throat a little. "Monte?"

"Yes?" Monte took another bite and looked at him.

"What do you know about Two-Timer?"

Monte looked at him for a moment in complete confusion. "Two-Timer..."

"That's what I said, yeah." Dallas nodded.

Monte shrugged a little. "No' a whole lo'. I don' even think I've really seen him."

"Razor didn't talk about him much?" Dallas wondered, glancing at Olli, surprised she hadn't jumped on the bandwagon of questions.

"Ne'er men'ioned him." Monte shook his head. "And I wasn' around very much either. Like I've said before. I was off on the long hauls. I didn' spend a lo' of time around town before I me' Oliver." He looked between them. "Why?"

"We think he's got her." Olli looked over at him.

Monte looked at her and knit his eyebrows for a moment. "Tha' is n' good." He took a bite, chewed, and swallowed. "He took Ms. Birdie...ou' from under th' Con Man's nose..." He looked between the two of them and shook his head. "Tha's no' goin' t' end well."

Olli grunted. "We talked about asking him some questions...but the problem is—"

"We ask questions, Razor realizes what happened..."

"Th' clash would be...terrible."

Olli nodded. "They already hate each other. It wouldn't take long for it to spill out of The District and into this side of town."

CHAPTER 13

THE ONE WITH THE STUPID PLAN

Monte grunted quietly and took another bite. "Yore a fan of stupid plans." He looked at Olli. "Have you considered askin' him?"

Olli's spoon froze halfway between her mouth and the bowl. She stared at Monte and only blinked when some of her stew dropped off her spoon and back into the bowl. "Did you hit your head today?" she wondered, blinking again. "Aces, Monte. There's stupid and then there's absolutely <u>insane</u>."

"I haven't been here very long, but I'm pretty sure I'm not goin' to be ready to be in that office again." Dallas shook his head. "Somehow I get the feelin' he won't be so generous as to let us wander out again."

"Not without a hail of bullets." Olli shook her head. "No way."

"Well. If you decide t' do somethin' insane…lemme know. I'll be around th' corner with th' fas' car." Monte winked at her.

Olli scoffed a little and shook her head. She stirred her stew and took another bite. "I'll keep that in mind," she mused, after swallowing her bite.

Dallas took another bite and looked thoughtful. "We're goin' to have to do somethin'. We can't just sit on our hands."

Olli shook her head. "We're not going to do nothing. She sent us a message. That means she wasn't in on it and she's in trouble. We need to get her back." She paused with just the tip of her spoon lightly touching the top of her stew. "And Monte's right. Razor finds out that Two-Timer scooped Birdie…"

Dallas grunted and nodded. "We do not need a war between the two of them."

Monte snorted and shook his head. "Tha' will turn this place int' a bloodbath."

Dallas leaned back in his chair and rested his hands on the table for a moment. "You know.. .just once since I got here, it would be awful nice if everythin' didn't end up as a literal do-or-die situation for the whole town."

Olli smirked and shook her head a little. "Sorry, Dallas. That's part of what makes our job so important."

Dallas nodded and shrugged a little. "I know. We worry, so no one else has to realize they're in trouble."

Olli grunted and took another bite of her stew. After a couple more bites, she looked at Dallas. "I think tomorrow we're going to have to pack a lunch."

Dallas looked at her and smirked a little. "Time for a stakeout?"

Olli nodded. "I think it's time we start watching to see what's going on over at Two-Timer's place."

"Gonna need a car?" Monte wondered, glancing between the two of them, hope leaking into his tone.

Olli pursed her lips a little and made a thoughtful noise. "Maybe?"

Monte looked at her and pursed his lips. "You don' wan' me there."

Dallas scoffed.

Olli stared at him, aghast. "Montana Dirks! How could you say something like that to me!?" She shook her head. "I would love to have you there to take us after Two-Timer if he leaves. The problem is that if. I'd hate for you to miss out on a day or two's worth of hacking."

Monte frowned a little. "I could use a break."

"Does he leave often?" Dallas wondered.

Olli shrugged a little. "I'm not sure. I haven't watched him in a while."

"Who were you watchin' lately?" Dallas tilted his head.

Olli shrugged a bit. She swirled her spoon in the little bit of stew left in her bowl. "Before you showed up?"

"That long ago?" Dallas' eyebrows jumped.

Olli laughed a little. "We've been a little busy since the day we met, in case you didn't notice."

Dallas scoffed and nodded. "That's a good point. Who were you watchin' before we met?"

"Ace."

Monte clicked his tongue a little and took a bite. He ignored the look Olli shot him, choosing instead to take another bite of his stew.

Dallas glanced at Monte and then looked back to Olli. "Why's that?"

"He's a killer."

"One she's been obsessed with since I've known her." Monte looked at Olli, concern and disapproval in his eyes.

"I never got close enough. He knew what I was doing."

Dallas nodded a little. "I see. Not Razor?"

Olli shook her head and scoffed a little. "I have Birdie for that."

Monte shot Dallas a pointed look and took another bite.

Dallas waved his hands a little and nodded. "All right. How long has it been since you checked on Two-Timer?"

Olli thought for a moment. "Couple of years."

"So you really have no idea what his day-to-day looks like." Dallas nodded a little slowly. "Monte?"

Monte looked at him and raised an eyebrow. "Mmhm?"

"We're not goin' to need you right away. You'll have to keep yourself company if you take a day off."

Monte looked at him for a second before turning to focus on Olli.

"He's right," Olli agreed. "We're going to have to spend a couple of days just sitting and watching. We can't risk following every car when we have no idea who's in them or what the normal schedule looks like."

Monte dipped his chin once and grunted softly. "You go' it. Jist le' me know when you need me."

"The second we know," Dallas promised.

Monte looked between the two of them and bobbed his head. "Good 'nough."

Olli smiled a little and took another bite. "It's settled then. Bright and early tomorrow morning we head into The District and settle down for a watch party."

"Why is it so <u>bright</u> this early in the morning?" Olli grumbled a little, rubbing under her eyes. She stepped out of the hack she took to WDA. She offered a couple of bills to the hackie. "Thank you." She walked up to the front stairs of WDA and stretched her arms a little.

"Mornin', Fox. Ready to get started?"

Olli stopped less than halfway up the first set of concrete steps. She looked up at him. "You're...here..."

Dallas nodded, trotting down the steps to meet her. "I'm glad you're here. Ready to go?"

Olli stood where she was, a single foot on each step. "Aces...but I just got here."

"Perfect timin' then." Dallas smiled a bit.

Olli stood where she was for a moment longer before she nodded a little. "We need to pack a lunch, at the very least."

Dallas shook his head and joined her on the step that her left foot was on, half a step closer to the road than she was. "I called Clarence just a couple of minutes ago. He's goin' to have some lunch for us."

Olli looked at him for a moment before pivoting and starting down the steps with him. "Aces, Dallas, how long have you been here?"

Dallas looked thoughtful and adjusted his fedora on his head a bit. "Maybe ten minutes."

Olli looked at him skeptically and then shook her head. She made a soft scoffing noise and walked with him. "I don't suppose you made sure that Dee knew we were going to be out all day and called Monte to get us a ride across The Line too while you were upstairs?"

"Monte'll meet us there. Breakfast and then we go across The Line." Dallas nodded, offering his near elbow to her as they walked toward the Corner Diner.

Olli snorted and slid her hand into his elbow lightly. "Busy ten minutes."

"I figured you'd want to get as much time there as we possibly can. Figured I'd make myself useful." Dallas smiled at her.

Olli nodded and looked up at him with a small smile. "Thank you, Dallas."

Dallas smiled and dipped his chin once. "I want to find her as much as you do, Fox."

Olli looked around a little and sighed. "I don't like this...at all."

"We'll find her. We've got a good start." Dallas paused at the corner and checked traffic.

Olli nodded and looked the opposite way that Dallas did, both directions. She stepped off the sidewalk the same time he did and crossed the road with him. "Hopefully." She walked up to the front door of the Corner Diner.

Dallas smiled at her a little when she habitually stopped half a step shy of the door and looked up at him. He pulled the door open for her and tilted his head, encouraging her to go in first.

Olli pulled her hand out of his elbow and stepped through the open doorway. "Mornin', Clarence!" she called as she stepped into the small diner.

Dallas smiled a little and followed her in, pulling the door closed behind him.

Clarence, a middle-aged, portly man with a deep love for good food and a happy disposition, had owned the Corner Diner for almost twenty years, and usually saved a booth for the detectives every day around lunchtime. The same could be said for a stool about halfway down the bar where Monte had his breakfast after the morning rush hacking businessmen to work.

"Ah! My friends! Come in!" Clarence waved them forward, a large grin on his face. "Dallas! Lock the door behind you."

Dallas froze where he was and walked back to the door. He turned the lock under the door handle. "The top lock, too?" He looked over his shoulder at Clarence.

Clarence shook his head a little. "That is enough. It will keep the others out until I open." He walked up to the long counter and smiled at them in a happy way.

Dallas smiled and turned back to the main room. "Monte here yet?"

Clarence shook his head. "No. He should be here soon." He looked up at the clock on the wall and nodded a little, like it had confirmed the statement. "Perhaps ten more minutes."

Olli smiled and sat on the stool to the right of Monte's stool. "Thank you, Clarence."

Clarence beamed at her and walked over to her. He leaned across the counter and cupped his hands around her cheek for a moment. "What do you want for breakfast, my friend? Anything. You tell Clarence and I make you smile and your heart sing for the food I bring you."

Olli's lips smushed together slightly as he squeezed her cheeks gently. "Uhm..." She smiled as much as his hands would allow before gently pulling his hands away. "French toast and hash browns? Couple of eggs? Oh! And do you have any icebox sweet rolls?"

Clarence grinned and nodded. He reached forward, gently clasped her neck with both hands and pulled her forward to kiss both cheeks. "Of course. You want them over medium, yes?" He looked at her pointedly.

Olli blinked a couple of times and nodded a little. "Yes, please?"

Clarence grinned at her and kissed her cheek again. "You have such a simple request. Of course I do this for you." He smiled and turned to Dallas, eyebrows going up with the unasked question.

Dallas dropped onto the stool to the left of Monte's favorite. "I'll have the same." He smiled a little and leaned back a little while taking off his fedora, almost acting like he was worried Clarence would kiss his cheeks as well. He dropped his fedora on the bar top in front of him and to his left.

Clarence looked at the hat like it had affronted him and then back at Dallas. "No—no. My friend. You must tell me what you would like for breakfast."

Dallas caught the look and picked up his fedora. He walked it to the hooks by the doorway and set it on one. "I'm serious. Olli has good taste in breakfast. I'd like exactly what she ordered, please." He walked over and sat back down on his stool.

Clarence looked at him for a moment, weighing his statement for truth before nodding. "All right. I will do this." He turned to the grill top behind him like a boxer sizing up for a fight.

The door clunked against the lockbolt. The next moment, there was a pointed knock on the glass.

Clarence turned and looked at the door, ready to scold whoever dared to rattle his lock in such a way. "Mr. Monte! Right on time! He rushed past the end of the bartop and hurried to the door. He unlocked it and pulled the door open with a large grin. "Good morning! Come inside. I have coffee ready for you. Come in! Come in!"

Monte smiled and pulled his cowboy hat off as he stepped across the threshold. "Morin', Clarence. Sorry I'm late." He looked a little deeper into the diner and smiled. "Well, hey! Mornin' kids!"

Olli smiled and waved at him. "Hiya, Monte. We saved you a seat." She patted the stool between her and Dallas with a smile.

Monte set his hat on the hook next to Dallas' and grinned. "That's sweet of you."

"Mornin', Monte," Dallas wished, smiling at him in a calm way.

Monte half-tossed a leg around the stool before he sat down. "Mornin'. You two been here lon'?"

Olli shook her head. "No. We just got here."

Clarence smiled and locked the door again. "Now that everyone is here, I get the breakfast going. You sit and talk. I cook. It'll be done before you know it." He walked past them and around the bar top. He grinned at them brightly and started to set plain, white ceramic mugs in front of them. "Would you like milk in your coffee?" He looked between them, trying to gauge their needs before they asked for anything."

"Black is fine for me." Monte waved his hand a little.

"I'll take a splash." Olli smiled softly.

Clarence smiled at her brightly and nodded. He walked over to a tall, large icebox just a few dozen steps away. "Fresh from the farm. Not just a half hour before you arrived." He walked back over and stopped in front of Olli. "Just a splash, you say?" Clarence's eyebrow went up slightly.

Olli nodded a little. "Please?"

Clarence obliged, pouring just a small, but healthy, splash of milk into the mug. "Dallas? My friend?" He hefted the milk bottle and raised his eyebrows slightly.

Dallas looked at the milk for a moment, weighing the question. "Sure. I'll take a little."

Monte set his hand over the top of the mug and shook his head when Clarence looked at him. "No thankee. Black. Like always."

Clarence shook his head and stepped two steps to pour a little milk in Dallas' mug. He bustled back to the icebox and stowed away the milk before scooping up the coffeepot as he walked back toward them. A broad smile crossed his face as he poured each of them a full, steaming mug. "There. You keep this. Help yourself." He set the pot down roughly in the middle of the three of them before turning to his grill.

Olli carefully wrapped her hands around her mug and laced her fingers together. She watched Clarence for a moment before half-standing up and reaching to the other side of the counter to pick up a spoon that sat in a wire tray on the half counter that ran under the bar top on Clarence's side. She sat back down on the stool and started to gently stir her coffee and milk together.

Clarence spent his time cooking, chatting at them over his shoulder, telling them all about the things he heard while dishing out food the week before.

Monte sipped his coffee and engaged with him more than the detectives, obviously more used to the bubbly personality so early in the morning.

Olli offered her spoon to Dallas without being asked and sipped her coffee. She smiled and listened as yet another story rolled out of the man across the way.

Dallas took the spoon without comment and started to stir the coffee and milk in his mug. He smiled a little at a joke that Clarence cracked in the middle of one of his stories. He glanced at Monte and chuckled at the look on his face.

Monte half-glanced at him and then turned his attention back to Clarence. He sipped his coffee and grunted.

Clarence didn't seem to notice how quiet his only guests were. He continued to chat away while he cracked eggs and tossed the shells to the far edge of the grill, where he kept all his food scraps for later.

Usually some sort of broth at the end of the week. Which was then used for soups or saved for winter weather in the deep freeze ice box that Clarence only opened when he needed to add ice.

Olli scoffed a little and shook her head. "Aces, Monte, you should have told me Clarence was such a riot this early in the morning. I'd have breakfast here more often."

Clarence turned around and looked at her brightly. "Olli! Do you mean that?!"

Olli looked at him and smiled a little. "Sure, Clarence."

"She's not a mornin' person. I wouldn't hold my breath." Dallas chuckled and sipped his coffee.

Clarence looked at him and pivoted to look at Olli. "Is that true?"

Olli wrapped her hands around the coffee mug and looked a little guilty. "He's not wrong."

Clarence made a small, thoughtful noise and bobbed his head. "Is all right. You come here for lunch and dinner." He smiled at her brightly. "That is important."

"You come here for dinner?" Dallas leaned on his arms and looked over at her.

Olli looked at him and nodded. "A couple of times a week."

"Why didn't you say something?" Dallas protested a little. "I would come with you."

Olli shrugged. "I don't know."

"She comes here to unwind after a bad day," Clarence soothed and looked at him brightly. "Much like you do when you come for breakfast before work."

Olli looked over at him and smirked. "You come here for breakfast sometimes?"

Dallas bobbed his head and nodded. "I do. Usually just before goin' to the office."

"Aces. That's why all you ever do is drink coffee. You're not even hungry!"

Dallas nodded and smiled a little. "Exactly."

Olli smiled at him and then looked at Clarence. "Well. Thank you, Clarence."

Clarence turned and looked at her and smiled brightly. "Of course! It is my pleasure. As always."

Monte smiled a little and sipped his coffee.

Breakfast passed quietly enough from the customer side of the bar top. Clarence took it upon himself to keep them entertained and their coffee full. While he waited for them to finish what they were eating, he put together sandwiches for lunch. He cut a couple of apples up and wrapped them in wax-dipped paper.

All the food was wrapped and placed into a paper bag, which was folded up tightly and placed on the bar top near Dallas, where it wouldn't be forgotten.

Olli reached into her jacket and dug into the inner pocket of her jacket. "Thank you for breakfast, Clarence." She smiled and dropped a couple of bills on the bar top next to her plate. "For everyone." She gestured to the three of them.

Clarence clicked his tongue a little and shook his head. "My friends!" he gestured to the money and then the food, looking insulted.

"Take the money, Clarence." Dallas dropped a couple of bills from his pocket next to the bag where their lunch was waiting for them. "Haven't you heard? There's a depression on."

Clarence looked at the money he dropped and started to protest.

Monte set a couple of bills down next to his coffee mug. "Close my tab, will ya?"

Clarence's shoulders dropped a little, and he shook his head. "This is too much!"

"Come on. We need to get going." Olli looked down the line, making eye contact with Dallas and Monte for a couple of seconds.

Monte smiled and stood up off his stool. "Time t' go, Clarence. Same time t'morrow?"

Clarence sighed like he was exasperated but couldn't find a way to protest. He gathered up the money and nodded. "Tomorrow, my friend."

Monte smiled and nodded once before walking over to the hook where his hat was hung. He scooped it up and dropped it on his head loosely. "C'mon, kids. Day's not ge'in' any younger."

Dallas grabbed up the bag that Clarence had set by him. "Thanks for breakfast, Clarence." He smiled a little and hefted the bag. "And lunch."

"Of course! You come back any time you need. I make you all the food you want." Clarence grinned at them brightly.

Dallas smiled and stood up off his stool and walked after Monte. "We'll make sure to."

Monte offered his fedora and smiled at him.

Dallas took it and smiled. He dropped the fedora on his head.

"You have a good day. And come back soon." Clarence smiled and waved at them a little, one hand wiping the countertop where they had been sitting.

Olli smiled and nodded a little. "Promise, Clarence. We'll be back soon." She smiled a little and walked toward the door, swinging her jacket up and around her shoulders, sliding her arms into the sleeves one after the other.

"Open sign, Clarence?" Monte wondered, tilting his head slightly as he stepped to the door and unlocked it.

Clarence nodded. "Thank you."

Monte flipped the small rectangular sign hanging from a light chain next to the door and unlocked it. "Have a good mornin'." He pushed the door open and stepped out.

Dallas looked at Clarence and nodded once, quietly echoing the sentiment. He gestured for Olli to go out in front of him and walked after her.

Olli smiled and waved a little. "Bye, Clarence. Have a good morning. Thanks for breakfast. And lunch."

Clarence smiled at her brightly and nodded. "Of course! It is my great pleasure!"

Dallas stepped out and around the door that Monte was still holding for him. "Let's get goin'."

Monte gestured to the black Pierce Arrow Lebaron sedan. "We're ready whenever you are."

Olli walked toward the car and smiled. "You brought Lightin'."

Monte smirked. "You said we're goin' t' Th' Distric'. Tha' means th' fast car."

Dallas chuckled and offered his elbow to Olli quietly as they walked.

Olli slipped her hand into the crook of his arm and pushed her other hand into the pocket of her jacket. She looked around at the foot traffic walking past them in a bored, curious sort of way.

"...That was a great party last night. We should go back." A young man, about the same age as Olli, looked at his friend with a bright smile as they passed the three of them, walking toward downtown.

"Who knew it would be such a good time partying on the water?!" his friend agreed.

Olli half-turned her head and looked after them. Slowing down enough, she nearly stopped.

Dallas took two more steps and was almost pulled to a stop. He looked back at Olli and tilted an eyebrow. "Comin'?" he wondered quietly.

Olli stood where she was for a moment longer, watching the two walk into the diner, laughing together. She blinked and shook herself slightly before turning to smile at him. "Yeah. Coming." She took a couple of steps to catch up to him and smiled a little. A thoughtful look crossed her face.

Dallas started toward the car again and glanced down at her. "Somethin' on your mind?"

Olli shook her head a bit. "No...just thought I heard something interesting."

"You did?" Dallas paused. "Like what?"

"One of them said something about a party on the water." Olli looked at him and shrugged. "It's probably nothing."

Dallas frowned a little and shrugged. He gestured toward the car with the hand that held the bag with their lunch bag. "Shall we? We have a long day of watchin' ahead of us."

Olli took a breath and nodded. "Yeah. Let's go."

Monte reached the sedan and set his hand on the handle of the back door. He looked over for the detectives and frowned when he was alone at the car.

Dallas checked for traffic and walked both of them across the road. "Sorry. Got distracted."

Monte shrugged a little and opened the back door as they got close. "Your timetable. No' mine." He smirked.

Olli snorted and stepped into the rear compartment of the car. She settled on the seat and smiled at him. "Thanks."

Monte nodded and winked. "I go' nowhere else t' be."

Dallas clapped his shoulder softly before stepping into the sedan and offering Olli the bag with their lunch at the same time.

Olli took it and set it on the bench seat next to her carefully. She smiled at Dallas and looked back at the Corner Diner through the back window of the sedan.

Dallas sat down next to her and raised his eyebrow. "What is it?"

Olli shrugged a little and grunted. "Just...really curious."

"Party on the water is a really interestin' sentence," Dallas agreed. "But are you really <u>sure</u> that it has anythin' to do with Miss Birdie's disappearance? They just said a party. That's all."

Olli grunted a little and bobbed her head. "If it was a few years ago, I'd probably agree. But people around here really aren't partying lately. I can't remember the last boat party I was invited to."

"You've been invited to boat parties?" Dallas looked at her like she had suddenly grown a second head.

Monte dropped into his seat and slid slightly to be more under the steering wheel. "She used t' go t' all sortsa parties."

Dallas looked at him and then back at Olli. "<u>You</u>?"

"Aces. What is that tone supposed to mean?" Olli wondered, tilting her head. "I come from a good part of town! And a very important family." She smirked. "Did you forget?"

Dallas scoffed and sat back a split second before the Pierce Arrow shot out of its parking spot and roared down the road. "Seems you have."

Olli stuck her tongue out at him. "I'm busy. I haven't really had the time to dress up for a party."

"Weren't you just complain' a few weeks ago about how bored you were?"

Olli shrugged a little. "All right fine. I've...avoided the last few parties I got invited to."

"No dress to wear?" Dallas smirked.

Olli half-shrugged one shoulder and shook her head. "I just...I have a hard time agreeing to a few lavish parties when...<u>this</u> is happening everywhere else." She pointed to the long bread line wrapped around the corner of the block from a soup kitchen. "Seems like a waste of time and money right now. People out here need help. And I can't do that in an evening gown and trying to choke down some sort of fancy-pants food that doesn't even taste that good."

Dallas watched the bread line for a moment and pursed his lips before looking back at her. "You're a good person, Olli."

Olli looked at him and smiled a little. "Thanks. That means a lot."

Dallas grunted and bumped his shoulder against hers. "I know you don't hear it very often. And I'm really glad you're my partner."

Olli looked at him and smiled a bit brighter. "I like having you for a partner, too."

Dallas smiled brightly and nodded a little.

Monte glanced in the rearview mirror and smirked to himself slightly. He rolled to a stop at a red light and waited patiently for the color to change, habitually watching traffic.

Not that there was any reason to suspect that something would happen—but—ever since Cross Bay Louie had snatched Olli and kept her for months, Monte had taken to watching traffic that much closer.

The detectives in the back seat had a dangerous job but Monte was determined to do his part to make sure it never happened again.

CHAPTER 14

THE ONE WITH THE DISTRICT RUN

Monte gently rolled Lightin' to a stop in a dark, dingy alley and pulled the brake. He draped his arm over the top edge of the backrest and looked at the back seat. "Las' stop on th' line, kids." He pushed his cowboy hat up a little and smiled. "Sure you don' need anythin' else?"

Olli grabbed the bag with their lunch in it and shook her head. "No."

"Thanks for the ride, Monte." Dallas smiled at him a little and scooted across the back seat to open the door.

Monte dipped his head deeply and smiled again. "You know I'd never have it any other way."

Dallas stepped out of the Pierce Arrow and offered Olli a hand.

Olli scooted across the back seat. She stepped forward a bit and dropped her hand on Monte's shoulder for a moment before setting the bag on Dallas' hand.

Monte smiled at her and nodded a little.

Dallas looked at the bag and blinked. He pursed his lips lightly and held the door open for her while she got out. "I'll hold the lunch while you get out?"

Olli smiled at him brightly. "Thanks."

Dallas sighed in a half-exasperated way before pushing the door shut. "Show me where we're hidin' out for the rest of the day?"

Olli nodded and started toward the back of the building they had parked next to, slightly tugging on the bottom of her black leather jacket as she walked.

Dallas looked at the bag in his hand for a moment longer before he shook his head and walked after her. "I'll just carry the lunch then." He walked after her.

Olli looked over her shoulder and smiled slightly. "All right." She looked a little confused but kept the smile.

Dallas scoffed to himself and jogged a couple steps to catch up with her. "How close are we to Two-Timer's headquarters? None of this looks familiar."

Olli pushed her hands into the pockets of her jacket and shrugged a little. "We're a few blocks East. There's a tunnel in the back alley here, runs this whole length of this street. The second to the last building is basically right on his front porch. I figure we find a good window on the top floor and see what there is to see."

Dallas nodded a little and adjusted his grip on the bag. "I'll just follow you then."

Olli looked back at him and smiled a little. "Sure. All right." She walked around the corner of the building they were next to and made her way down the back alley. When they were halfway down the alley, she stopped and looked over at him. "I'll slide in quick. You can drop the lunch to me and slide in yourself?"

"Slide in?" Dallas blinked and half started when Olli pulled the coal chute door open, sat down and pushed herself down and through the opening. Dallas stood where he was for a moment, sheer shock keeping him frozen.

Olli bent her knees and caught her balance well enough on the floor in the basement. She brushed herself off and pivoted to look up through the coal chute door. "All right! Toss the lunch down. I'll catch it."

Dallas blinked and crouched down next to the open door. He placed one hand on the pavement and tilted down until he was almost able to completely see through the opening. "What..."

Olli shrugged. "It's faster than walking all the way to the front of the building and trying to get through the door."

Dallas scoffed and shook his head. He set the bag down on the chute and dangled it down as far as he could reach before he let go.

Olli stepped a couple of steps forward and caught the bag. "Got it. Come on down."

"I'm not entirely sure I can," Dallas mused, looking at the chute and frowning.

"It's bigger than you think. I fit." Olli shrugged.

"You're smaller than me!"

Olli laughed. "We're not _that_ much different! I've worn your jacket. It's the _same size_ as mine!"

Dallas sighed and pursed his lips. He _really_ didn't think he would fit.

Then again...Olli was right. She wasn't much smaller than him. Only a couple of inches shorter, broad shoulders, beautiful long legs...

Dallas cleared his throat and shook his head. "All right. Back up. I'm comin' in."

Olli laughed a little and took a couple of steps back. "It's just a short chute, Dallas. Not a _slide_!"

Dallas sat down and carefully threaded his feet into the chute. "Still. I'm going to be hungry later. I don't want to ruin lunch."

Olli stepped back two steps and laughed quietly. "Right. Don't want to ruin lunch."

Dallas scooted a little more and shimmied closer to the building. "All right. Here I come..."

Olli nodded a little. "I'm out of the way. And lunch is perfectly safe."

Dallas took one more breath and shook his head a little. He pushed off and ducked a little.

One moment, he was sitting on the alley, the next he was stumbling across the floor of a basement.

"You made it!" Olli beamed at him, giggling a little. "The landing was a little shaky, but you didn't fall on your face!"

Dallas scoffed and stood up straight. "I lost my hat." He set his hand on his head and tapped it twice before looking back the way he came from.

Olli laughed a little and shook her head. "You did."

Dallas walked back to the wall and looked through the chute. "I can't leave that there..." He half-pointed and looked over at her.

His fedora was sitting on the pavement of the alley, upside down and rocking slightly.

Olli set the bag down on the floor carefully and walked to stand next to him. "Gimme a boost?" She smiled a little.

Dallas bobbed his head and threaded his fingers together. He bent down a little and held them out slightly.

Olli set her hand on his shoulder and carefully placed the ball of her right foot into his hands. She took a breath and bounced once on her left toes before straightening her right knee and half-bracing on his shoulder with her hand.

Dallas grunted and watched her, trying to anticipate where her weight was going to move so he could help her keep her balance.

Olli twisted a little as she stood up in Dallas' hand. She leaned forward and half-crawled her way up the chute. She reached forward and through the opening in the wall. It took a couple of tries and a lot of stretching to reach the nearest part of the brim. Olli pursed her lips a little and rocked forward a little further. "Almost...got...it..." she grunted, still trying to hook her fingers over the inside edge of the brim so she could pull it closer.

"Take your time. I've got you," Dallas grunted, holding her weight.

"Can you get me a little closer to the wall?" Olli half-pulled out of the chute to look down at him over her shoulder.

Dallas grunted and nodded a little. "Hold on." He shifted a little closer to the wall, pulling a face. He leaned his shoulder against the wall a little and pushed her foot up a little higher. "Got it?"

Olli ducked back into the chute and reached as far as her arm would allow her to. Her tongue slipped between her teeth and slightly stuck out of her mouth as she stretched her fingers as much as she could.

The fedora rocked a little and almost tipped onto the back brim when she was a little clumsy and bumped it a little awkwardly.

Olli's eyes flared, but she somehow managed to get her fingers inside the brim and managed to grab it. "Got it!" She pulled it back toward her and pulled out of the chute almost at the same time.

Dallas grinned and grunted a little as she moved. "Here. Step down now, nice and easy."

Olli half-stepped sideways and bounced a little on her left foot while catching her balance. "Here's your hat." She offered him the fedora. "Sorry about the brim..." her eyes darted down to the brim gripped in her fist and pursed her lips a little.

Dallas shrugged and took the fedora from her. "It's survived worse." He shook it slightly and whapped the wrinkled part of the brim against his thigh before dropping it loosely on his head. "See? Good as new." He tugged it down into place and smiled.

Olli nodded a little and smirked. "I see." She turned and walked back over to their lunch bag. After picking it up, she jerked her head toward her left. "Come on. We've got a long walk ahead of us."

Dallas smirked and walked over to her. "I'll follow you."

Olli nodded and started past a support pole. "This way." She walked forward to a jagged hole in a wall a few dozen yards ahead of them. "Sure you don't want to go first? There's some low ceilings in this place. What if you lose your hat again?"

Dallas scoffed and shook his head a little. "I think I can handle ducking."

Olli looked back at him and her eyebrows went up skeptically.

"You offered to get it!" He chuckled a little.

"That's because there was no way you were going to be able to reach up through the chute <u>and</u> be able to have enough reach to grab it. <u>I</u> was barely even able to reach it, and that was <u>with</u> you holding me up as far as you did."

Dallas nodded. "Thanks for that, by the way."

Olli nodded. "Can't have you losing that hat. You might lose some of your identity with it."

Dallas snorted and shook his head a little.

The wall ahead of them looked like someone had taken the time to remove the bricks and create a swinging door from them. If the door was shut, it would look like a solid wall. When the door opened, an odd rectangular opening would appear with some bricks swinging on the door, the rest staying in the wall.

"Why's the door open?" Dallas tilted his head, pointing at the door that was open about three feet.

Olli made an amused noise. She walked through the opening and grabbed one of the bricks on the door side. She threw her whole weight against it.

A loud groaning, scraping noise almost echoed in the silence of the basement. The door hadn't even moved a fraction of an inch.

"Best I can figure, the building settled. Or the floor heaved since they built it."

"Shouldn't have opened it so fast." Dallas smirked.

Olli shook her head. "It was open here when I found it."

"I didn't say you, per se." Dallas looked down the tunnel in front of him. "I don't suppose there's lights in this tunnel?"

Olli shook her head. "No. There's no power in these buildings. They were built before the electricity boom, and we're in the poor part of town right now."

Dallas looked at her and tilted his head slightly. "The...poor side?"

Olli nodded. "Back when Big Town was just on this side of The Line."

Dallas nodded. "Right. Tenement building?" He pointed up at ceiling above them.

Olli grunted and nodded a little. "Yeah." She bent down and picked up a half-broken hurricane lamp. "So, we have to make do with fire to see."

Dallas looked around a little and nodded. "Makes sense."

Olli fished her hand through the gap in the zipper on her jacket. She dug her hand into the inside pocket of her jacket. "I think there's still a few ounces of juice in this thing." She shook the hurricane lamp a little near her ear. "At least enough to get us through the tunnel right now."

Dallas looked down the tunnel and into the darkness that stretched in front of them. "There's no traps I need to worry about, is there?"

Olli snorted and shook her head a little. "We're near Two-Timer. Not Razor. He's a snake, but I doubt he's clever enough to come up with anything Razor-level."

"You haven't been here in a while then?" Dallas tilted his head.

Olli shook her head. "Not really. I was busy before we met. And you know the rest." She pulled a Zippo lighter from her pocket and flipped the lid up.

Dallas grunted and bobbed his head. "I suppose that's fair."

Olli spun the flint wheel and waited for the flame to start up. Once it was burning nicely, she tilted both hands and managed to get the wick to catch fire. "All right. Ready to go?"

Dallas smiled at her and gestured toward the tunnel in front of them. "Into the dark."

Olli nodded and started to walk with him. "Lamp or food?" she wondered.

"I'll take the light." Dallas held his hand out for the broken lamp.

Olli handed it to him and smirked.

It took them a few minutes of walking to get out of the first building. The tunnel seemed to run in a perfectly straight line, no matter what got in the way. There were more brick doorways, like the one at the beginning. Support poles would pop up every so often in the middle of the path.

They made it through the next few buildings—Olli indicating which brick walls were part of the structure of the buildings—and Dallas started to wonder how much longer they were going to be walking.

Olli finally stopped and pressed a hand up against the brick in front of her. "All right. Last doorway. There should be some stairs that come out right around here, and there should be a stairwell just to the left."

Dallas nodded. "I'm ready to get out of this basement."

Olli grunted a little and pushed on a few bricks. "Me too." She gripped a brick that pulled out of the wall slightly.

The door swung open with a loud creak and a few clicking groans.

Dallas held up the hurricane lamp and watched the door open slowly.

Just as the door opened, the flame in the hurricane lamp spluttered and died out.

Olli smiled back at him. "Just in time. That would have been really dark."

Dallas chuckled and nodded. "That is true."

Olli walked through the door and into the last basement. She gestured slightly to the stairs and walked toward it. "I want to get settled in quick. We don't have much time to get upstairs before the day really gets going."

"You're awful awake for someone who's not a morin' person," Dallas mused, trotting up the stairs after her.

Olli shrugged. "Clarence makes a good breakfast."

Dallas smiled and nodded a little. "He really does." He turned on the landing at the same time Olli started up the next flight. "How many flights up are we goin'?"

"I figure if we make it up to the fourth floor, we should be high enough up. We can see everything but not be within the line of sight." Olli shrugged, walking up the next flight purposefully.

Dallas nodded a little and trotted up after her. "Fourth floor."

The next few flights of stairs went smoothly enough. When they finally reached the floor Olli wanted to start on, both of them were ready to be done with the rickety stairs.

Walls groaned around them every so often. A thick dust covered the floor in the hallway. Everything around them looked dingy and filthy. There were a few doors missing into the sad-looking apartments. What doors weren't missing were mostly hanging off-kilter on their hinges.

"Well...this is cheery," Dallas mused to himself dryly.

Olli looked at him and grunted. "I don't think this building ever looked bright and shiny."

Dallas shook his head and frowned. "Who lived in a place like this?"

Olli shrugged a little. "Mostly hard workers, I'm sure." She frowned a little. "Dock workers mostly, I'd bet."

Dallas clicked his tongue a little and shook his head slightly. "Pity."

Olli looked at him and shrugged slightly. "I don't like it either. Just the fact of life, unfortunately."

Dallas' head bobbed slightly. "Are you plannin' on settin' up in the left apartment or the right?"

Olli looked back at him and shrugged a little. "Whichever one we can get into."

Dallas snorted. "Right. Which would you prefer?"

Olli pointed to the last door on the right side of the hallway. "That one. It'll be better as far as viewpoint. Harder for them to see us, too."

Dallas nodded and walked with her to the end of the hallway. He stepped up to the door and jiggled the doorknob. "It's...locked?"

Olli shrugged. "It happens."

Dallas frowned a little. "All right. Step aside a little, I'll knock the door open."

Olli looked at him and stepped off to the side a couple of steps.

Dallas stepped up next to the doorjamb and donkey-kicked it open. He swung his hand a little. "After you, Fox."

Olli looked at him and laughed a little. "Thank you." She walked through the door and into the apartment. "Aces! There's even chairs!" She grinned back at him.

Dallas followed her in and closed the door behind him.

It didn't quite close all the way, since the doorjamb was a little splintered, but it was at least most of the way shut.

Olli smiled and set their lunch on the kitchen counter making sure it would stay out of the sweep of the sun. "It's a little dusty. But it should work just fine." She used her right arm to brush most of the dust off the counter before setting their lunch down.

Dallas pulled his fedora off and dropped it on the corner of one of the nearby chairs. "Which one of the buildin's are we watchin'?"

Olli walked over to stand next to him. "That one right there." She pointed at the large, bright red brick building towering over the next two buildings in the row.

"The one with all the glass still in the windows." Dallas looked at her for clarification.

Olli nodded. "That building's always had glass in the windows. As long as I can remember."

Dallas pulled the zipper down on his brown leather jacket and nodded slowly. "Why's that?"

"Used to be Joey Leftfoot's headquarters." Olli pushed her hands into the pockets of her jacket.

"That would be...the mafia don before the family split into three?" Dallas verified.

Olli nodded. "Yeah."

"How did Two-Timer end up with the nice place when they broke the family up?"

Olli shrugged a little. "I'm not really sure, and I certainly haven't cared enough to ask. But if you want my personal theory, it could have been he was with Joey the longest. Not to mention that Razor needed his own place and identity apart from them. And Ace? Too many memories here being under someone else's thumb. I don't think that stifled feeling ever left him."

Dallas made a thoughtful noise. "Well. Shall we settle in?"

Olli nodded and hooked the fingers of her left hand through the rungs on the back of one of the chairs. She picked it up off its feet and walked to where she could see the street running past the front of the building, across the road and down a building. A simple twist and set down, and Olli was able to sit in the chair backwards. She leaned her arms loosely across the top edge of the backrest and looked out the window with a soft sigh. "Time to watch nothing happen for a few hours."

Dallas grabbed the chair with his fedora on it and walked it over to sit near Olli. "You don't think he has a lot of visitors?"

Olli shrugged a little and grunted. "I really don't know. Last I heard, he wasn't running books himself. He has people for that."

Dallas chuckled. "This is going to be fun."

Olli looked at him and scoffed quietly. "I'm glad you think so."

For the most part, Olli wasn't wrong. It seemed like most of the day was spent waiting for any movement at all. When there _was_ movement, it was mostly just men that worked for Two-Timer.

Dallas would ask about each one in turn, listening intently when Olli would explain to him who they were, or who she thought they might be.

By the time it was starting to get dark, not a single car wandered into view.

Olli sighed heavily. She had her jacket half-bunched, half-folded on the back of the chair, one arm draped half across the back of the chair, the other elbow pillowed in the creases and folds, while her fist held up her jaw.

"Anthin'?" Dallas wondered quietly, walking back over from the kitchen, after retrieving a couple of apples from the paper bag Clarence had given them. The bag was now officially empty of any snacks or food. He offered her one of the apples and raised his eyebrows quietly.

Olli dropped her jaw off the fist that was holding it up and took the apple. "Thank you." She shook her head a little and frowned. "No. Not even a little bit."

Dallas didn't even try to look surprised. He dropped into the chair that his jacket was draped over and slouched down far enough his shoulders were resting against the backrest. After taking a large bite out of his apple, he looked over at her while he chewed. "When is Monte comin' back to get us again?"

Olli rubbed the apple on her sleeve and made a thoughtful noise. "Maybe another half hour?"

Dallas nodded and took another bite of his apple. "Did we see anything useful...at _all_?"

Olli looked at him and snapped a bite off her apple. She shook her head and looked at him skeptically. "Nah. Everyone we saw belonged here in one way or another." She took another bite of her apple.

Dallas grunted. "That's what I was afraid you'd say."

Olli scrubbed her hand over the bottom of her face. "Which means we have to come back again tomorrow. And watch again."

Dallas looked at her and took another bite of his apple. "We'll catch a break. We always do."

Olli grunted.

They came back. For the next week they watched the headquarter building taking note of the coming going, trying to find patterns.

There weren't many patterns to find. In the whole week…they only saw four men that appeared more than once. But even then, never at the same time.

Olli did her best to stay patient. Tried not to complain about how long it was taking for anything to happen.

Dallas patiently and consistently continued to ask questions when there was something actually happening outside.

Olli leaned against the wall, a step and a half past where the trim should have been on the left side of the window. She took a long breath and pursed her lips.

Dallas stepped into the room and looked over at her. "I take it nothin' has changed?"

Olli looked at him over her shoulder and smiled a little. She shook her head. "No. I haven't even seen a person in about thirty minutes."

Dallas grunted. "It is pouring today." He swept his fedora off his head with one hand and swung it in a sharp, jerking motion, sending water flying at the floor.

Olli watched him and nodded a little. "I noticed. Not a great day to be out walking around."

Dallas hung his fedora on the back of the chair he usually claimed and shook his head. "Not really. But. I have news."

"More importantly, do you have lunch?" Olli wondered hopefully, walking over to sit in the other chair.

Dallas unzipped his leather jacket about halfway and fished inside. "Here you go. Monte told me to tell you that Clarence is over the moon with excitement that he gets to make us lunch every day. He said that we should go on stakeouts more often so we need lunches."

Olli took the bag that he offered her—a little smushed, but dry—and smirked. "Did he."

Dallas swung out of his jacket, water dripping from every edge. He set it on the back of his chair and stepped around to perch on the very front edge of the chair. "Apparently. He's very excited to provide us lunch."

Olli shook her head a little and smiled softly. "He's very sweet." She opened the bag and offered the first sandwich from the bag to Dallas. "How long have we been here now?"

"Two and a half weeks."

Olli pulled the last sandwich out of the bag and started to unwrap the waxed paper. "Well. At least it's been longer than I thought," She grumbled quietly.

Dallas smiled at her. "We'll find her."

Olli nodded and took a bite. "We will. The good news is…we know she's not going to get hurt."

Dallas shook his head a little. "There's no way. It's bad for business if the entertainment is bloody and bruised."

Olli grunted and funneled another bite into her mouth. She looked out the window and squinted against the rain. "I just hope something shakes loose soon."

Dallas smiled at her and nodded a little. "We'll find somethin'."

Dallas rubbed his eyes and smushed his hands down and around his face while sighing heavily.

They were two days into their third week sitting in the same dusty apartment, watching the front of Two-Timer's headquarters. Now that they had been here for almost a month, they were starting to catch a few routine movements from the people that frequented the building. The problem was, there really weren't many people to begin with.

Olli was convinced that most of the action was hidden away from the front view they could see. She had made a couple trips alone, and with Dallas around the building, trying to find better vantage points and see if there was anything they were missing.

They spend a couple of days in a different building—a terrible old warehouse of some sort—watching from that vantage point, trying to catch something different that might have been of some use to them.

There wasn't from that angle. They had spent hours watching an empty alley.

Olli was irritated, though doing her best to keep it reined in. She hadn't even suggested going into the main building yet.

Dallas was impressed with her stubborn hold to staying where they were and watching. He had expected to tell her it was a terrible plan to go deeper into the target of their investigation days before.

Today had started off the exact same way it had for the last three weeks.

All was quiet on the road below them. Not a single person had stirred the quiet of The District yet.

Olli walked into the room and pivoted her favorite chair around and sat on it backwards. She folded her arms on the backrest of the chair and rested her chin on the top edge of the fold. "Anything happen?"

Dallas scoffed and stretched his hands up over his head, arching his back into the stretch. "No." He sighed and dropped his hands loosely into his lap. "Just like every other morning this week."

Olli grunted a little and adjusted her head on her arms. "Aces. It's been three weeks! Something has to happen soon! I'm starting to wonder if we're wasting time here when we should be out and about trying to find that party boat."

Dallas looked over at her and smiled a little bit. "I know you do. But..." He looked over at her and smirked. "I'd like to remind you that this was your idea."

Olli rolled her head to the side and frowned at him. "I know."

Dallas chuckled and looked out the window again. "Besides. It's not like he's going to dock that boat somewhere close. Everyone would notice a boat on this side of The Harbor. You've said so yourself. And that means Razor would see it, too."

"I know," Olli grumbled.

"And somehow, I get the feelin' we'd already know if Razor found it. Either Miss Birdie or the man himself would have somehow let us know."

CHAPTER 15

THE ONE WITH THE END

O lli pursed her lips and bobbed her head a little. "Lenny didn't find anything on the napkin note."

Dallas glanced at her and bobbed his head a little. He looked out the window again. "We'll find somethin'."

Olli adjusted her head on her arms and sighed a little. "I hope so. It bothers me that the one thing that she didn't want me to do six weeks ago is the one thing that will save her. And if I had ignored her six weeks ago, then I wouldn't be <u>here</u>. Sitting in this chair, watching nothing happen for weeks at a time."

"I know you don't want to hear it." Dallas looked at her and held up a hand. "There's a very good chance she would have been grabbed after you two went home for the night. And we'd be even further behind."

Olli took a long breath and stifled a yawn. Whether from boredom or the sheer exhaustion of the long hours they had spent into the apartment, it was hard to tell. "I know. I do."

Dallas looked over at her and nodded. "I know."

Olli took a breath and blew a breath out between her lips. "Party boat...Aces. What was he thinking? Razor has a death grip on the moonshine and drinking in this town. Everyone knows it, even though I have to real way to prove it so I can arrest him..." An irritated look crossed her face.

"That right there has to be his reason." Dallas shrugged. "From what I hear, they don't get along. And both are greedy." He looked at her and smiled a little. "Way I see it, he's tryin' to up his cash flow."

Olli grunted. "Hard to collect on debts when everyone is broke."

Dallas tapped his nose and nodded. "That's what I'm sayin'."

Olli looked away from the street slowly and focused on him. "People open their purses a lot faster when there's booze involved."

Dallas nodded and smiled at her slightly. "We'll find Miss Birdie."

116

❖

Olli walked into the District Detective office and sighed. It had been a long day. "Hiya, Dee. We're back for the day," she mused to the room at large.

Dee appeared in the middle of the room, a few steps away from Olli's desk. "You're back? You're so early."

Dallas stepped into the room and closed the door. "Just comin' back for a couple of hours before we head back out."

Dee nodded a little and wrung her hands. "Something happened while you were out yesterday."

Olli pulled the zipper down on her jacket and tilted her head. "Yesterday."

Dee looked at her and frowned. "I know. I completely forgot to tell you. I even forgot to set a reminder to tell you." She pursed her lips. "I would have done a reboot, but I was worried I would <u>completely</u> forget if I did." She ran her fingers into her hair a little before pulling them out and folding them tightly in front of her. "And <u>clearly</u> I need it." Her image faded for a moment before coming back visible, though her edges were a little fuzzy.

Dallas stepped forward and lightly touched the collar on Olli's jacket in a silent request. "Miss Dee...it's fine. Just tell us what happened yesterday."

Olli shrugged out of her jacket without comment and looked at Dee quietly, waiting for some sort of information.

Dee paced in a short back-and-forth and almost spun a circle. She almost fizzled out, whitish-grey lines cutting through her before coming back strong again. "There's a letter for you on your desk."

Olli frowned slightly at the way Dee's image was reacting. "Take a beat, Dee. It's all right."

Dee blipped a couple of times and looked at Dallas.

Dallas pushed his hands into his pants pockets and nodded a little. "She's right."

"And reasonable," Dee mused. "You've rubbed off on her."

Dallas smiled softly and nodded once. "Thank you."

"And she can hear you." Olli looked back at them over her shoulder. She picked up the only sealed envelope on her desk and pivoted to sit on the top with a small bounce. A quick scoot to settle herself a bit more on the desk, and Olli reached over to pick up a black and white Bakelite letter opener.

"If the two of you don't mind, and don't need me for a couple of minutes, I'm going to reboot my system?" Dee looked between the two of them.

Olli nodded. "Go ahead, Dee."

"Do whatever you need, Miss Dee." Dallas smiled a little. "We'll take care of ourselves for the time bein'."

Dee's image fizzled for a second and came back to full power. "You've got it." She smiled at them both in a brave way and blipped out of sight.

"That's odd..." Olli mused, not even bothering to watch Dee disappear.

"What's that?" Dallas looked at her and tilted his head slightly.

"This one is sealed." She looked up at Dallas, holding up the envelope and shaking it slightly. "The last one wasn't." Olli glanced at it and then back at him. "I don't think this one came from the front desk like last time."

Dallas frowned a little. "Is there a stamp?"

Olli paused just as she was about to slip the letter opener into the crease. "Oh." She flipped the envelope over and frowned. "No."

Dallas grunted and nodded a little when she held it up to show him. "It looks like it went through the front desk though. It has our stamp on it."

Olli pivoted the envelope to face her again and looked at the blue ink that read:

District Detective Office

Third Floor

"Look at that..." Olli tilted an eyebrow. "If it was stamped..."

"That means someone dropped it in our mailbox," Dallas finished the thought.

Olli looked at him and nodded. Her hand froze just as she was about to thread the letter opener into the crease again. "This is from _her_!" She shoved the letter opener into the crease and ripped it open sharply.

Dallas walked closer and nodded. "That's what I'm thinkin'."

Olli fumbled with the envelope a little, still holding the opener in one hand. She fished out another napkin and looked at Dallas. "It's a cocktail napkin."

Dallas smiled a little and scoffed. "I've really got to hand it to Miss Birdie. She did _not_ seem that smart...any time that I've met her..." He looked thoughtful for a moment and frowned a little. "And now I feel terrible for sayin' that right out loud."

Olli smirked. "Don't feel bad. Gloria perfected the art of looking a _whole_ lot less smart than she actually is. She doubled down on it when she became Birdie and realized that drunk men would do almost _anything_ for her."

Dallas' eyebrows jumped up a fraction of an inch. "Oh. She's one of those."

Olli shrugged and held up the cocktail napkin. "And that's why she's my best C. I."

"Isn't she your _only_ informant?" Dallas tilted his head.

Olli shrugged and bobbed her head. She dropped the envelope on the desktop next to her. "Just because it's the only option doesn't make it automatically the best one." She glanced at him and started to unfold the napkin.

Dallas looked at her for a moment and half-grunted while he nodded once. "That is a _very_ good point."

Olli turned the napkin around and upside down. "Where..." she unfolded another layer of the square. "Aces..._Bird_!" She growled through her teeth. She sent Dallas a dull look when she had the napkin completely unfolded. "Found it. Finally."

Dallas chuckled a little. "What does it say?"

Olli's eyes scanned over the words quickly before she looked up at him. "I have no idea."

Dallas tilted his head.

Olli gnawed on the inside lower left corner of her lip and turned the cocktail napkin around so he could see it.

Olive,

Halfway between here and there.

Bet the farm on it.

Dallas stared at the jet black, slightly shaky lettering. "What did she use this time?"

Olli shrugged. "Maybe her eyeliner? Mascara? I have no idea."

Dallas grunted. "All right. Next question—"

"What are we betting the farm on that's halfway between here and there?" Olli offered in a confused tone.

Dallas tapped his nose and lightly pulled his tie down a couple of inches. "Next question. Are we _here_?" He pointed at the floor in a general gesture.

Olli scooted a little further back on the desk and crossed her legs over each other. She draped the napkin on her right knee and stared at it. Her chin kicked to the right a little and her lips wrinkled a little in a strange way while pursing together. "Maybe?" she wondered, not looking at him.

"Why are we bettin' the farm?" Dallas questioned, stepping forward a couple of steps and dropping into the left of the two black leather chairs that faced Olli's desk. He rested his right elbow on the arm of the chair and set his chin in his hand.

Olli looked up at him. "People only bet the farm in extreme situations." She rested her elbows on her thighs lightly, folded her hands together and set her chin on top of her hands.

Dallas nodded a little and grunted. "I wouldn't do it unless it was a sure bet."

"Me neither. I'd want to make sure I'd get the farm <u>and</u> whatever it was that was after." Olli sucked her teeth and looked thoughtful.

"We <u>have</u> to be the here in that situation." Dallas' hands swung open slightly, and he looked at her with his eyebrows up. "Agreed?"

Olli nodded. "Agreed."

"What are we agreeing on?" Dee wondered, appearing next to them, looking completely refreshed. She was wearing a crisp dress suit in a sweet blush pink. There was a pair of matching silk pumps on her feet. Her hair was up into a perfect French twist, with a fancy hairpin holding it together.

Olli looked over at her and smiled. "Hiya. Reboot went well, I see."

"I feel so refreshed. Sorry about earlier." Dee smoothed her jacket a little with her hands and tugged on it slightly. "So embarrassing."

Dallas shook his head a little. "Don't worry about it."

Dee smiled and walked closer. "You look confused, Boss."

Olli nodded a little. She picked up the cocktail napkin and showed it to Dee without a word.

Dee looked over it and made a thoughtful noise. "I see." She looked between the two of them. "You two want to walk me through this? Like you do when you are stuck?"

"We were discussin' the...obscure words that Miss Birdie thought so kindly to send us." Dallas shrugged.

Dee nodded a little. "All right. Why did she send the note?" She looked at Olli and raised her eyebrows like she expected her to have the answer.

Or at the very least, a theory.

Olli looked put on the spot and pursed her lips. "I think she's trying to tell us where she is."

"Agreed." Dallas nodded, completely sure.

Dee looked between the two of them and loosely folded her fingers together in front of her. "Why the odd sentence then?"

"She's clever. She didn't want to risk anyone but us understanding what she's talking about," Olli piped up right away.

"And using makeup to write it?" Dee asked again.

"I think it's a writin' tool of opportunity." Dallas set the back of his cheek on two of the fingers of his right hand and looked at the girls. "If we're right, and Two-Timer <u>is</u> holdin' her somewhere on a boat of some sort...it strikes me he probably isn't too keen on her havin' somethin' that could stab anyone."

Olli tapped the napkin on her knee again. "Cocktail napkin agrees with that."

Dee nodded and made a thoughtful noise. She looked at Dallas. "What did you say about a boat?"

Olli pivoted herself around on the desktop and reached over the edge of the desk and opened the top drawer. She pulled out the first napkin and held it up. "This made us think that she's on a boat of some sort." She set the other napkin on her left knee and scooted herself back to face them.

Dee disappeared and reappeared, sitting on the desk edge near Olli's left knee. She leaned to look at the first note while primly hooking her right knee over her left. "Mmmm." She nodded slowly. "Where would a boat be between here and there?"

"We think we're at <u>here</u>." Dallas' left hand gestured around them a little.

Dee nodded. "Where would there be?"

Olli looked at her. "Could I see a map of the area?"

Dee raised an eyebrow. "What area?"

"Twenty miles from here." Olli shrugged.

Dee looked at the wall behind Dallas expectantly.

The wall split apart slowly and rolled back on itself, revealing the computer wall behind it.

"Would you like the water as well?" Dee looked over at Olli.

Dallas nodded. "Yes, please."

Dee looked at him and back at Olli. "All right. Twenty-mile radius. Anything else?"

Olli watched the map appear on the screen and gnawed on the inside lower left corner of her bottom lip.

Dallas used his legs and pushed the chair around to the side and back slightly. He looked at the map and whistled softly. "That's a...lot of water."

Olli stared at the screen for a moment and ran her hands up her face, across her temples, and folded them across the back of her head. "So. If I was Birdie...where is there?"

Dallas brushed the office door aside and walked into the room, holding a coffee mug in each hand. "Hey. Any progress?" He walked over to the desk and offered Olli the mug in his left hand.

Olli took the mug without looking away from the computer wall across from her desk. Her legs were hooked over the edge of the desk, swinging slightly. She folded her hands around the mug and set it in her lap loosely. "I have been staring at this map for..." she blinked a couple of times and looked at Dallas, tearing her eyes away from the screen as the absolute last second.

Dallas checked the watch on his left wrist. "It's been three hours, Fox."

Olli groaned and let go of the coffee mug with one hand and rubbed her eyes with her thumb and forefinger. She sighed and yawned at nearly the same time. "I still have absolutely no idea where there is."

Dallas grunted quietly. "How long has it been since you actually slept?"

Olli held the mug up close to her chin and blew on the liquid for a breath. "I don't know... what day is it?"

Dallas started to take a breath and paused to think. "Thursday. No!" He thought a bit. "It's Saturday."

Olli looked over at him and took another breath to blow on her coffee and froze. "Saturday." She looked completely lost and off balance for a moment. "What happened to Friday?"

Dallas frowned a little. "We spent most of it outside of Two-Timer's."

Olli looked thoughtful for a moment. "Oh, yeah...that's right." She sighed quietly and shook her head. "I haven't been sleeping well for weeks. I want to find her so badly."

Dallas nodded a little. "I think we both need a nap, Fox."

Olli looked frustrated and shook her head a little. "I'll sleep when we find her."

Dallas shook his head. He walked forward and pulled the coffee mug away from her and set it on the desktop nearer to him than her. "I shouldn't have brought you this. You need to sleep. You're not goin' to find her if you're exhausted."

Olli watched him and sighed. "Fine. I'll sleep for a few minutes." She scooted off the desk and pivot-fell into the chair that he had been sitting in a few hours before. She shimmed a little so she was even lower in the chair and rested her head on the top of the back rest. Her eyes closed and her hands folded loosely in her lap. "Wake me up in twenty minutes."

Dallas watched her for a moment, not sure what to do. "I don't...think that's a good idea. I was more thinkin'...at home. In bed for a few hours."

Olli opened one eye and looked at him. "Or I could sleep here."

"But why?"

"I'm comfortable and I don't want to get up?" Olli closed her eye again.

Dallas looked at her for a moment and folded his arms across his chest. "I'm going home too, Fox. We've been goin' at blisterin' pace for a long time. A few weeks, basically non-stop. I don't know about you, but my brain is mush. I think we need to take a beat. Have a proper night's sleep."

Olli sighed heavily through her nose. "That makes sense."

Dallas' shoulders dropped a little. He had been anticipating having to argue with her for a bit more. "Really?" he wondered, tilting his head, his tone registering just how much shock at her acceptance of what he had said. He cleared his throat. "I mean...So let's go home. The sooner we get home, take a good sleep...the more likely it is that we'll be able to attack this better tomorrow mornin'."

Olli smirked at the way the pitch of his voice changed. "I just have one question." She opened her eyes and looked up at him.

Dallas unfolded his arms and looked at her expectantly. "What is it?"

"How often did you sleep a whole night when I was missing?"

Dallas started to take a breath and pursed his lips together.

"And before you try and tell me some well-meaning lie...I'll ask Dee. And she tends to blurt the truth without any thought to how it'll affect the world around her." Olli tilted her head.

Dee appeared in the room and looked between them. "You said my name, Boss?" She smiled brightly.

Dallas looked at Dee and then back at her for a moment. "I'm aware of her ability to tell the truth, no matter what."

"Are you talking about me?" Dee looked between them again in confusion.

Olli smirked at him, looking completely proud of herself. "Well?"

Dallas fumed for a minute. "You know, this is bordering on blackmail."

Olli smirked at him. "That's what I thought." She sunk a little further into the chair, resting her head against the backrest of the chair a few inches below the top edge. One foot dropped on the top of the main cushion of the second chair, the second following it loosely. "I'm going to nap here. You may go if you want."

Dallas stared at her for a moment and looked over at Dee.

Dee shrugged a bit. "You know how she gets."

"She can hear you. She's sitting right here."

Dallas clicked his tongue a little and chuckled. "Come on, Fox. Hop to. We'll <u>both</u> get a good night's sleep and come back at this tomorrow mornin'."

Olli opened both of her eyes and looked at him with a small frown. "It's practically morning right now. If I sleep here, I can think about this a bit more before we go back across The Line and watch nothing happen all day again."

Dallas frowned. He looked at Dee.

Dee shrugged a little. "Don't look at <u>me</u>. I can't help you."

Dallas pivoted and walked to the hall tree. He pulled the brown leather jacket off the hook and swung his arms into the sleeves. After plucking the fedora off the top hook, Dallas dropped it on his head.

Olli closed her eyes, content that she had won the battle.

Dallas picked up the black leather jacket and walked back over to where Olli was sitting on the chair. "Come on. Up you get." He dropped the jacket on her lap in a crumpled heap.

Olli started a little and opened her eyes halfway. "You just brought me a mug of coffee!"

"And I changed my mind." Dallas' eyebrows jumped a little, and he smirked a little. "Come on. Sleep is important."

Olli sunk a little lower and hooked the collar of her jacket with one hand. But instead of standing up to put it on, she pulled it up and draped it around her torso and shoulders. She shimmied her shoulders a bit to work it lower around her and took a breath, closing her eyes deliberately.

Dallas looked at her for a minute, unsure what he had just witnessed. "Olli."

"Shhhh. She's sleeping."

"What do you have against sleepin' in your own bed?" Dallas wondered, looked at her and raising his eyebrows, even though she couldn't see it.

"I like sleeping here better." Olli opened one eye for a second before closing her eye again.

"Olli—"

"No. Dallas." Olli opened her eyes and looked at him. "I'll sleep at home when <u>she</u> is."

Dallas sighed and processed for a moment before shaking his head. He walked over to the pair of chairs that faced his desk. After arranging them a bit like how Olli had hers, he dropped into the nearest one, a soft sigh escaping him. He pulled the fedora off his head and dropped it over his face. "All right. Just wake me up before you run off and do somethin' stupid."

Olli snorted and shifted her head and shoulders against the chair a bit. "Sure."

Dee stood in the middle of the room in the same spot she had appeared in. She watched Dallas for a minute and frowned a bit. "So, we're just...sleeping here?"

Dallas grunted. "Apparently."

Olli didn't answer, she just let her head roll to the left and took a long breath.

Dee stood there for a moment longer and nodded slowly. "All right then, sleep well." She blipped out of sight.

The lights turned off a moment later, soon followed by the light from the computer screen. The soft scraping noise of the wall moving back into place broke up the silence of the office for a few seconds.

Only a bit of muted light came filtering through the windows from the street below.

All was quiet in the District Detective Office. Only the sound of two different breathing patterns broke up the quiet.

Tomorrow was a new day.

To Be Continued...

THE ONE WITH THE NEXT BOOK

The door opened to a moderately spacious room that had been set up to be a dressing and state room.

Birdie walked through the door and looked over her shoulder. "You don't have to babysit me, you know. I'm not going to do something <u>idiotic</u> and dive over the side and <u>swim</u> to shore." She put her hands on her hips. Her white upper arm satin gloves were in stark contrast to the blue and gold tea length dress she was wearing. "Do you <u>see</u> this dress?!" She gestured to her general appearance.

"Boss' orders." A gruff voice informed on the other side of the door just before it was pulled closed and a locked snicked shut.

Birdie's shoulders dropped a bit and frowned a little. She fumed for a moment and stamped one of her gold dancing shoes.

It had been almost two months. <u>Two months</u>. She hated this boat. And it seemed like the big man that hovered outside her door wasn't the least bit susceptible to her charms. No amount of flirting, eyelash batting, or arm squeezing had broken through the tough exterior.

Birdie looked around the room for a time without number. This is where she had woken up two months before. She got ready in this room every night for the show she performed in the main part of this floating casino bar.

Birdie hated every second of her new life. She wanted so desperately to go home. She missed her bed and her pillows.

The constant rocking of the waves was nice, as far as getting to sleep...but her apartment was so beautiful. And most importantly.

She could leave.

Whenever she wanted.

Birdie missed that freedom. She missed the stage at The Phoenix, the dresses she had there, even the man who tended bar and always made sure her glass was full. The more she thought about it, the more she missed Olli too.

Birdie sat in the simple, wooden chair that sat just in front of her large mirror. She looked at herself in the mirror. She was going to have to apologize to Olli as soon as she saw her. She had been wrong to demand Olli not do her job. Birdie scoffed to herself a little as she started to take the pins out of her bobbed, platinum hair.

Maybe if she had let Olli do what she did best, then she would be in her cozy, warm, bright dressing room. With her plus chair and her favorite dresses.

Razor was a much better boss too.

It had been so long since Birdie worked with—for—Two-Timer...she had completely forgotten how he ran his family. Birdie didn't know for <u>sure</u> it was Two-Timer's family. But it sure seemed like it was.

No one seemed to have a sense of humor and it was nearly <u>impossible</u> for her to get anything for her performances. Every time she asked for the simplest things they acted like she had practically asked them to bring her back to shore.

Birdie set her hands on the desk in front of her and frowned at her reflection. She looked tired. And frustrated. Sad too. There was only just so much she could do about the bags under her eyes. They were so obvious. There was something in her eyes that hadn't faded over the last couple of weeks.

The small spark of hope.

She had been able to smuggle out two notes, sending them both to Olli. The fact she was able to even get them out in the first place gave her hope she could make an escape. And if <u>she</u> couldn't get herself off this boat...

"Olive will find you," she whispered to herself with a small smile. "She's going to find you. And soon."

***

Birdie dropped into her chair and looked at herself in the mirror. She sighed and picked up the tub of bright red lipstick. After a quick glance at the door, she pulled the cap off the tube and carefully smeared the color on her lower lip. Next came her top lip.

Birdie smeared her lips together and worked them around for a moment. She popped her lips and looked at her reflection for a moment before using the lipstick to make a small, straight line in the top right corner of her makeup mirror.

She had been doing it since the first time she had woken up in the single bed across the stateroom from her. It was a way to keep herself from going crazy, and a way to keep track of the days.

Birdie looked over the marks and pursed her lips. There was a lot more than she thought there was going to be when she first woke up.

She fully believed in Olli's ability to find her. There wasn't a doubt in her mind that Olli was smart enough to find out what was going on and get her out of this place.

Birdie sat into the backrest of the chair. She folded her arms over her chest and looked at herself in the mirror, her reflection pouting back at her.

Maybe the notes she had sent were too cryptic.

Maybe they weren't, but Olli couldn't make the connection to where she was.

Birdie looked around her room again and frowned a little. She had to come up with something else. Something that would give Olli and Dallas some sort of hint where she was.

There was one problem with the whole thing. She didn't fully know where she was. Usually she was kept locked in her stateroom until they were well out to sea.

He had told her it was because that way she wouldn't try to dive over the railing and swim for shore.

Birdie thought it was utterly ridiculous. Of course she wouldn't do that! She quaffed her platinum blonde hair.

How could he think that she would be willing to get it wet in sea water?!

Birdie picked up a little brass compact and clicked it open. She swirled the pad of her middle finger in it and started to pat the blue color on the top of her eyelids. Once she was satisfied with the amount of pigment on each lid, she picked up a soft bristle brush and smoothed it out to an even texture.

There had to be something she could do to help Olli find her. She would just have to think about it a bit more.

Preorder Now!

THE ONE WITH THE REVIEW REMINDER

Thanks so much for spending time with me in Big Town!
I really hope you enjoyed your stay.
Would you consider sharing your experience?
(Even just a couple of sentences!)
Your opinion will help new readers decide to buy!
Which means **more** people will visit Big Town!
Your words mean *so* much to me!
(And the new visitors of Big Town)
It's as easy as clicking right here!
Just choose your favorite store (the more stores, the better!)
And let everyone know what you think!

THE ONE WITH THE OTHER BOOKS

Unofficial Business Mini Series
Olli before she was The District Detective
Unofficial Business
The One With The Leather Jacket
***

The District Detective Series
Main Series
The Silence Broken
Baysnatch
Prussian Blue
Smuggler's Blues
Absconded
***

Razor's Edge Series
A standalone series about what makes Razor, Razor.
Told by the man himself.
Fiddle Game
Pig In A Poke
***

Links to the books

JOIN THE BIG TOWN MAFIA

THE ONE WITH THE AUTHOR BIO

J. Arens grew up on the Western Shore of Southern Michigan. Her days filled with horses, dogs, day dreams of fast cars and a love for great literary detectives. Nancy Drew, The Hardy Boys, Philip Marlowe, Sam Spade, Sherlock Holmes, and the brilliant but dangerous men who inhabit the pages of History during the time of the Volstead Act.

The District Detective series was born out of the need to read books that blended together the best things of all of J. Arens' favorites. All while set in Prohibition Era Middle-America.

When not working on the latest District Detective novel, or coming up with ideas for the next novel, J. Arens can be found attending local car shows, riding horses with friends, cuddling with police dog training drop-out, Dutch Shepherd mix, Dutchess and daydreaming about fast cars.